D1051372

Books by Audrey Peterson

The Nocturne Murder
Death in Wessex
Murder in Burgundy
Elegy in a Country Graveyard
Lament for Christabel
Dartmoor Burial
Death Too Soon
Shroud for a Scholar

Published by POCKET BOOKS

A CLAIRE CAMDEN MYSTERY

SHROUD
FOR A
SCHOLAR

AUDREY PETERSON

POCKET BOOKS

New York   London   Toronto   Sydney   Tokyo   Singapore

This book is a work of fiction. Names, characters, places and incidents are products of the author's imagination or are used fictitiously. Any resemblance to actual events or locales or persons, living or dead, is entirely coincidental.

An *Original* Publication of POCKET BOOKS

POCKET BOOKS, a division of Simon & Schuster Inc.
1230 Avenue of the Americas, New York, NY 10020

ISBN: 0-671-79510-4

First Pocket Books printing December 1995

10 9 8 7 6 5 4 3 2 1

POCKET and colophon are registered trademarks of Simon & Schuster Inc.

Cover art by Kye Carbone

Printed in the U.S.A.

To Shana

Come into the garden, Maud,
  For the black bat, night, has flown,
Come into the garden, Maud,
  I am here at the gate alone;
And the woodbine spices are wafted abroad,
  And the musk of the rose is blown.

—Alfred Tennyson, *Maud* (1855)

On the role of art, on woman's emancipation and the factors that promote civilized progress, on science and its relatedness to religion . . . [Tennyson] offers much that is relevant to modern times. Nor will the variety and vividness of his presentations, and his rare and sustained mastery of melodic language, lose their appeal.

—F. B. Pinion, *A Tennyson Companion: Life and Works*

SHROUD
FOR A
SCHOLAR

Prologue

A<small>T SIX O'CLOCK ON AN EVENING OF MISTY RAIN,</small> a man climbed unsteadily up the stairs of a shabby block of London flats. At his own door, he sagged against the frame and banged with his fist until the door was opened by a young woman who took one look and cried softly, "Oh, Kurt, you promised—"

The man glared at her, red-eyed. "Bloody hell. I stopped at the pub for a pint, that's all."

A small girl, sitting in the corner of a sofa with a doll in her lap, looked up at the man, then lowered her eyes.

The man kicked the door closed behind him. "I'm hungry."

The woman hurried to the tiny kitchen, the man following her. As she reached for a saucepan, he pulled her clumsily toward him. "Give us a kiss, then."

She drew back. "Not when you're like this. I've told you."

He studied her face. "Has the bitch been here again? You were never like this till *she* started coming round."

1

"She came in for a cup of tea. She only wants to help me."

"Help you, is it?"

"Yes."

Blood filled the puffy skin of the man's face, and his eyes bulged forward like a pair of marbles. "You tell her you don't want her help, do you hear? I don't want her anywhere near you—ever."

"But, Kurt, you promised. You said you were sorry and you understood—"

"Never you mind what bloody shit I said. I'm not having some la-di-da woman running my life, and that's flat."

The woman stared back at him. "And I can't go on living like this. I'm going out tomorrow to look for work."

With no warning, the man swung the back of his hand across her face, knocking her against the wall.

"No!" she screamed. "You promised—"

Ducking under his arm, she ran into the little sitting room, standing behind the table. With one leap, the man threw himself across the table, crockery flying, and struck a vicious blow on the side of her head.

Now there were no more words, only grunts of rage, while blows fell on the woman's face, on her arms, on her body.

In the corner, the child shrank back, clutching her doll, looking at the man with a scalding hatred. Then, as she had been told to do in the past, she crept to the door, closed it behind her, and fled down the stairs.

1

I HAD COME BACK TO LONDON FOR THE SUMMER to get my book through its final stages. Expecting a quiet time, I walked instead into a tragedy.

I'd gone down to Devon to attend my daughter Sally's graduation from Exeter University, stayed on a few days, and had just come up to London on Tuesday afternoon. I was about to phone my friend Iris Franklin, when she called me. "Claire, may I use your guest room for the night? That is, unless Neil is there?"

"No, he isn't. Love to have you. Are you coming to the Grainger and Jones affair this evening? Angus MacFinn insists I must come and be presented to some important people."

"I've already told Angus I'd rather not. Actually, I have some reading to do."

She sounded pretty depressed, and when she arrived at the flat just as I was ready to leave, she looked pale and troubled, but I didn't ask. She'd tell me whatever it was when she was ready.

She said, "Be as late as you like. I shall probably turn in early."

I told her I had to leave at nine the next morning for

an appointment and laid out a spare set of keys, in case she decided to go out after all, but when I got back about half past eleven, the keys were still on the table, her door was closed, and her light was out.

The next morning a little before nine o'clock, she wandered into the kitchen in her dressing gown for a cup of coffee and a roll, but we had no time to talk, as I had to dash off to Ealing, a forty-five minute tube ride away.

I urged her to stay as many nights as she liked, and she said only that her plans were uncertain.

"I'll be back for lunch," I said, "and then we'll talk. I want to know what's going on. Okay?"

At that, she smiled—a nice, warm one. "I've missed you, Claire."

I'd missed her too. I'd been back in California for the academic year, making a quick trip to England at Christmas to see Sally and to spend some time with Neil Padgett, the erstwhile man in my life. Iris and I had managed some good chats during that time. I wondered if her current crisis had something to do with her husband, Owen, who was not exactly Mr. Reliable. But who knows about other people's relationships? My own was in major crisis at the moment, to say the least.

My appointment took longer than I expected. The garrulous old gentleman I was interviewing wandered off the subject and I gently brought him back, only to have more digressions. At last I got away, but it was shortly before one o'clock when I unlocked the door at the street entrance to my flat in Bedford Square.

Getting the use of the flat was one of the major perquisites in the divorce settlement with my English husband four years ago. It was a wildly valuable piece of property that had been in the Camden family for eons. Most buildings in the elegant old square were occupied by upscale professionals: solicitors, architects, and other brass-plate types, with only a few sitting tenants left here and there.

When I walked up one flight of stairs and put the first key in my door, I noticed the dead bolt wasn't turned. Wondering if Iris had gone out, I opened the door and walked in, putting down my briefcase and hanging my coat in the entry.

"Hello!" I called out.

No answer.

Looking into the sitting room, I could see the back of her head, the soft, dark hair visible above the corner of the sofa.

"Iris?"

I went around to face her and stopped short.

Dressed in jeans and a sweater, she was sprawled across the corner of the sofa, her head tilted to one side. If I thought at first glance she was asleep, it didn't take long to see there was no chance of that. Her body was twisted, her legs flung out at odd angles, her mouth horrifyingly open, revealing her swollen and protruding tongue.

Stiff with shock, I bent over and put my hand on her wrist, where it lay on the cushion of the sofa. The flesh was cold.

I headed for the telephone in my study, my body sluggish, the way you feel when you try to walk through water. I rang 999 and reported finding my friend dead, adding that she may have been strangled.

Drawn like a magnet, I went back and stood looking down at Iris. Then I began to shake, and tears I didn't notice dripped off my chin until my blouse was wet.

Who could have done this? And why? It seemed indecent to leave her lying there so awkwardly, but my association with Neil Padgett, who was a detective superintendent in the CID, had taught me never to touch anything at a crime scene, as if we didn't all know that from the television anyway.

5

I turned away, grief choking at my throat, and wandered back to my study. Knowing I ought to call Owen, I picked up the phone and pressed out the number. No answer, only Owen's voice asking for a message, so I told him there was an emergency and asked him to call me pronto.

The sound of the doorbell brought me to the intercom, where a police officer said he had come in response to my call.

I knew the routine. First, the uniformed officer examined the body and called back to the station to confirm that there was indeed a dead person and that it appeared to be a homicide. Then, in various order, came the plainclothes officer, usually a detective chief inspector, and a whole phalanx of others, including the forensic pathologist and the scene-of-crime technicians, known as SOCs, who would scour the site for physical evidence.

The detective chief inspector who arrived in due course was a thirtyish, sandy-haired man with a mustache named Dietrich. When he had examined the body, he made a tour of the flat, peering into each room with a questioning look at me.

"This is my daughter Sally's room."

"She lives here?"

"No. Only when she's in London. She's in France now, on holiday."

"And this?"

"The guest room. Ms. Franklin spent last night here."

I noticed that Iris had made up the bed, leaving her personal items still out on the dressing table. She must have planned to stay another night, at least.

The officer picked up a small prescription bottle from the dresser. "Sleeping pills," he said, writing something in his notebook. "Did she use these often?"

"I don't know, but I doubt it."

We went on to the master bedroom, now mine, once shared with my husband Miles during the years of our long-distance commuting marriage, divided between California and London.

Back in my study, the chief inspector, accompanied by a constable, took out his notebook and asked for information about Iris. I gestured to chairs and swiveled my desk chair around to face them. Deitrich wrote down her name and address, then asked for the nearest relation.

"Her husband, Owen Babcock."

"His name is not Franklin?"

"No. Iris was already on the faculty at University College when she remarried. She kept her own name."

"Have you spoken to Mr. Babcock since you found the body?"

I said I had left a message for Owen on his home phone.

"Do you know where he is employed, Mrs. Camden?"

I bristled at the "Mrs." I could be "Dr." or "Ms." but no longer "Mrs. Camden," but I decided it wasn't worth it.

I answered his question. "No, I don't. Owen is a computer consultant. I believe he takes short-term assignments and often has breaks in between."

"I see. Now, Mrs. Camden, from your speech I believe you are from the States. Is that correct?"

"Yes, from South Coast, California."

"You are employed there?"

"Yes. I'm professor of English at the university."

"And who is the proprietor of this flat?"

I explained that it was mine, and why.

"Thank you. Now, if you please, how did it come about that Mrs. Franklin was here?"

"She rang up last evening and asked if she might come."

"Had she done so before?"

"No. I just returned from the States a few days ago."

"How long have you been acquainted with the victim?"

"For three or four years. We met soon after my divorce."

"Can you tell me, please, why Mrs. Franklin elected to spend the night here?"

"I have no idea. We had no time for conversation." I explained the times of my leaving and returning, both in the evening and in the morning.

The chief inspector looked skeptical. "Surely she gave you some reason for coming here?"

"I've told you, there was no opportunity. We intended to talk when I returned at lunch time today." With heavy irony, I added, "As you see, that wasn't possible."

Unperturbed, he went on. "Are there family members other than the husband?"

"Yes, Iris's son David, by her former marriage. He attends Sussex University." My heart contracted as I thought of David. I knew he'd been extremely fond of his mother. Someone would have to break the news to him. Probably Owen, whom David disliked, according to Iris.

"Now, have you any idea who might have committed this crime? Anyone who may have wished Mrs. Franklin dead?"

I shook my head. "No. It seems utterly incredible that it has happened."

At this point, the forensic pathologist arrived, made his examination, and came to the study to tell the chief inspector that it was obvious the victim had been strangled from behind.

Dietrich said, "Time?"

"Best guess, four to five hours. Postmortem this evening at seven." And he was gone.

I looked at my watch. Half past one. That would place the time of death between 8:30 and 9:30. I was here till almost nine o'clock. However, the postmortem would give a more accurate estimate.

Back to me, the inspector went on. "Now, Mrs. Camden, you left the flat this morning at approximately nine o'clock. Is that correct?"

"Yes."

"And you did not return until a few minutes before one o'clock?"

"Yes."

"Will you please describe your movements during that time?"

"Of course. I took the underground to Ealing Broadway, where I had an appointment to interview a gentleman in connection with my book."

"Book?"

"A biography of Mary Louise Talbot, the Victorian novelist. My publisher here in London is Grainger and Jones."

"And at what time did you return here?"

"At shortly before one o'clock." I'd already said that several times, but I knew it was no use protesting. I'd no doubt have to go over it again and again.

He wrote the name and phone number of the old gentleman in Ealing, then looked up. "I see that the flat here has security arrangements for entry. I have sent a constable to question the solicitors and their staff who occupy the ground floor. It appeared to me as I came in that when their offices are open, their receptionist would be in a position to see any visitors who come through to your flat or to the one above."

"Yes. We each have a separate entry phone, as you saw, and there's a divider that screens our part of the entry hall from the offices. But certainly, she might see our visitors if she happens to be looking through her window."

"Since persons cannot gain entry without permission, it would seem that Mrs. Franklin must have admitted someone who was known to her. Do you know if she was expecting to meet someone here?"

Patiently, I said, "I know nothing beyond what I have already told you. If she expected someone, I don't know about it."

"Would she have answered your telephone, had it rung while you were away?"

I hadn't thought of that. What would I do in someone else's flat?

I said, "I'm not sure. She might let the machine take the message, and if it happened to be someone she knew or wished to speak to, she would pick up the phone. As it happens, the machine showed no messages when I returned."

He then asked me about the door locks, and I told him the dead bolt was not turned when I came home, only the lock that snaps automatically when the door closes. I said, "It looks as if whoever did this simply walked out the door, closing it behind him."

He nodded. "What can you tell me about other tenants in the building?"

"Not much, I'm afraid. The solicitors have the basement as well as the ground floor. There's only the lady on the floor above. We meet on the stairs occasionally, but I don't know her well. I'm not here for much of the year, you see."

Now my phone rang and I heard Owen's voice. "Claire, I got your message. What on earth is it?"

"I'm afraid it's very bad news, Owen. It's Iris."

"An accident?"

"Not exactly. It's—that is, she's dead."

"Dead? Where is she?"

"She's here at my flat. The police are here."

"Police?"

The inspector held out his hand for the phone, but before I could hand it to him, I heard Owen say, "I'll be there straightaway," and the line disconnected.

I said, "He's coming here."

"Right, then. We'll wait."

2

AFTER OWEN'S CALL, I LEFT DETECTIVE CHIEF Inspector Dietrich in my study, making phone calls, and wandered out to the kitchen. Remembering I'd had no lunch, I made a pot of tea and nibbled some biscuits, sitting in the breakfast room trying not to hear the voices and activity around Iris's body.

Owen arrived sooner than I expected. I met him in the entry, with Dietrich behind me.

Glaring at me, wild-eyed, Owen cried out hoarsely, "What happened?"

The chief inspector stepped forward. "Mr. Owen Babcock?"

Without answering, Owen brushed past us and strode into the sitting room, staring down at Iris's body.

Then he turned to the chief inspector, who had followed him. "My God, it looks as if someone strangled her! Is this true?"

"It would appear so, yes, sir."

"The bloody bastard! Have you caught him?"

The officer's sandy eyebrows rose. "Do you know of someone who may have wished your wife dead, sir?"

Owen glared. "No, of course not. Why would anyone want to kill Iris? It must be one of those madmen—a Jack the Ripper sort of creature."

Ignoring this, the chief inspector asked Owen to step into the study.

Looking dazed, Owen put out his hand toward Iris, then looked back at the officer and gestured for him to lead the way.

I started toward the kitchen when Owen stopped me. "You come too, Claire."

Surprised, I looked at Dietrich, and he nodded assent. Owen evidently wanted a familiar presence for moral support, so I followed the two men into my study and sat down.

Owen had flopped onto the small sofa, heavy brows drawn in a scowl, his lean body in trendy jeans and a dark blazer with striped shirt and tie. Not handsome feature by feature, Owen was the kind of man who comes over as attractive by the sheer force of believing that he is.

The chief inspector began by asking Owen if he had been at his home when he received my message.

"No, I was at Bertorelli's in Floral Street, having lunch with a friend. I rang my number and punched in the code for messages. I got the one from Claire here. Thought it must have been an accident."

No wonder he got here so soon, I thought. Bertorelli's was in Covent Garden, not far away. The restaurant catered to the in crowd from the nearby opera house, and Owen, a skilled place-dropper, never missed a chance to display his familiarity with the good spots in town.

Unimpressed, the chief inspector went on. "When did you last see your wife, Mr. Babcock?"

"It was last evening, about half past six or so."

"Did she appear much as usual at that time?"

Owen paused, then looked up with the expression

of a boy who's been naughty but is confident of being forgiven. "The fact is, Chief Inspector, we had the devil of a row."

Dietrich wrote slowly in his notebook without looking up. "And what was the nature of the disagreement, please?"

"Oh, what do married people row about? Money. How we spend our time. You know the sort of thing. Nothing that couldn't be mended."

The inspector's next question seemed to startle Owen. "Did your wife carry insurance on her life?"

"What? Oh, yes, now you mention it, I believe she did."

"And who is the beneficiary?"

"Well, actually, there are two policies, one dating from many years back for her son, David. Then, when Iris and I married eight years ago, we each took out a policy for the other."

"What is the amount of the benefit on these, sir?"

"Mmm. I can't say I remember precisely. One expects that death will occur in old age, don't you see?"

The inspector turned a page. "Will you please describe your movements from the time you parted from your wife last evening until you arrived here today?"

Looking more comfortable, Owen said, "Yes, certainly. I told Iris I'd be out late. She was fairly steamed and said, 'Do as you like.' My pal Josh and I made a round of a few pubs. I was still pissed off and didn't fancy another row with Iris, so Josh put me up for the night."

I thought, Iris must have felt the same and had come to my place to avoid seeing Owen again.

Owen went on with his story. "This morning I went back to the house to shower and change. Iris wasn't there. She must have gone out early—"

14

The chief inspector said mildly, "At what time was this, please?"

"Time? About eight o'clock. I had an appointment at nine."

"You live in St. John's Wood?"

"Yes."

"You came in by car?"

"No, by taxi."

"And where was your appointment, please?"

"In the Tottenham Court Road." Suddenly, a look of shock crossed Owen's face. "My God, what time did this—that is, what time was—?"

"Do you mean, at what time was your wife murdered?"

"Yes."

"We do not have that information as yet, Mr. Babcock."

I noticed he said nothing about the pathologist's "four to five hours."

Owen looked at me with tears glistening. "I can't believe it, Claire. I might have been only a few streets away when it happened!"

The chief inspector's impassive voice went on. "What was the nature of your appointment, sir?"

"It was at Morgan Associates. I was meeting with my headhunter."

The inspector raised an inquiring brow.

"The agent who secures engagements for me in computer programming."

"Thank you. Please go on."

"I arrived at just on nine o'clock and Morgan kept me waiting, as he usually does, the bastard. It was twenty minutes before ten when he finally saw me. I read every shitty magazine in the waiting room."

"At what time did you leave?"

"About an hour later. He took half a dozen phone calls while I sat there tapping my foot."

"You left the office at approximately a quarter of eleven?"

"Yes. I went straight on to the two interviews he had arranged for me. They were in the City, and each lasted about an hour. Then I met my friend at Bertorelli's."

The inspector wrote carefully, reviewing names, places, and times. "Now, sir, going back to the office in the Tottenham Court Road, is there anyone who can confirm that you were there during the times you have stated?"

"Certainly. The receptionist was at her desk behind the glass. We exchanged looks of disgust from time to time. She knows only too well that Morgan's always running late."

"And you never left the office during that time?"

With a grimace, Owen said, "I did make a couple of trips to the loo. Had the trots."

After more repetition, the chief inspector told Owen he was free to go but must not leave greater London without informing the police.

As I walked with Owen to the door of my flat, two men came in, wheeling a trolley, and the chief inspector gave the word that Iris's body could now be taken away.

We stood aside as the trolley passed us, the body looking as slight as a child's under its shroud of white sheeting.

I saw Owen shudder, and again there were tears in his eyes. Awkwardly, he gave me a one-armed hug, muttering, "I did love her, Claire. You know that, don't you?"

I wasn't so sure, but I patted his shoulder anyway and opened the door.

When I returned to the study, Dietrich said, "What can you tell me about Mr. Babcock? Was theirs a good marriage despite the row?"

16

I paused. "I'm afraid I'm not much of an authority on Owen. I saw them last when I was here at the Christmas holidays. I can tell you that he's not a model of marital fidelity, but they appeared to have intervals of felicity, if I may call it that."

For the first time, I saw a twitch of amusement on his otherwise impassive face. "You do not like Mr. Babcock?"

"Not much, no, but I'm afraid that doesn't mean he killed Iris. According to his statement, he didn't even know she was here in my flat, and his time seems well accounted for this morning."

"Yes. If you indeed left here at nine o'clock and returned at one, it would appear to place him in the clear."

I didn't like the sound of that "If you indeed," but they could check out the times of my interview with the old gentleman in Ealing. No problem.

I said, "What about the time after Owen left Morgan's office and went to his interviews? He could nip over here in two or three minutes from the Tottenham Court Road, then dash on to the City."

Again that quiver of a smile. "But as you have pointed out, he appears not to have known his wife was here. Furthermore, that would place the time of death at shortly before eleven o'clock."

Remembering the pathologist's estimate, I glumly acknowledged defeat.

Soon afterward, the chief inspector took a phone call and left. Eventually, the technicians finished whatever they were doing and went away, too.

I stood for a while staring out of the sitting room window at the massed green of the trees in the square. As I turned and my glance fell on the sofa where Iris had sat, the shaking and the tears came on again.

Enough of this. Somebody needed to tell Iris's friend Meredith Evans what had happened, and it had better be me. I doubted if Owen would bother. He and Meredith were not *simpatico,* to say the least. I changed into sweats and picked up my keys and shoulder bag. I'd seen a lot of Meredith with Iris, one way or another, and liked her. Instead of phoning with news like this, I'd go and tell her in person.

I walked down Gower Street, which forms the east border of Bedford Square, turned left on Great Russell Street, past the pillared front of the British Museum, and went along Museum Street to the little bookshop where Meredith was what she laughingly called chief of staff. The owner, an elderly Scotsman, had retired and left her in charge, dropping in occasionally to putter among the old books but rarely interfering with the running of the shop.

It was a fascinating place, specializing in scholarly works of all kinds, as one might expect from its proximity to the museum. I asked the assistant at the counter for Meredith, and at his gesture toward the back, I squeezed my way between towering stacks of tomes that looked chaotic but were in fact carefully organized. In a tiny office behind a glass partition, I found her bent over account books.

"Claire!" She looked up with a huge smile. "It's good to see you. Iris said you were coming for the summer."

I said simply, "Very bad news, Meredith," and I told her.

In her forties, with gray-dusted hair and brown eyes that flashed fire when stirred, Meredith was no shrinking violet. Opinionated, intolerant of laziness or apathy, she was nevertheless good fun to be around.

"Damn!" Her eyes bored into mine. "In your flat, Claire? This morning?"

"Yes. She rang up last evening and asked to spend the night. I was surprised she didn't ask you—"

"Decorators have the room torn apart."

"That explains it."

"What about Owen? He'd be my choice for prime suspect."

"She evidently didn't tell him where she was going." I gave her a summary of Owen's interview with the chief inspector.

"Blast! Then who else knew she was there?"

"That's what's puzzling. She may have told someone else, or someone we both knew might have phoned or come to the door."

Meredith frowned. "What about the solicitor people? I've noticed the receptionist can see who comes in if she happens to be looking."

"The police are certainly checking on that." Then I added, "You'll no doubt be having a visit from the chief inspector yourself. They'll be talking with her friends, I'm sure."

She nodded and stood up. "It was good of you to come, Claire. I'd have hated hearing this on the telephone. I'm finding it hard to believe it's true."

I saw the sagging lines of her usually lively face and knew the blow was beginning to reach its mark.

I left quickly, promising to see her soon.

Much worse for her, I thought. She and Iris had been friends since childhood, gone to school together. A big part of Meredith's life would be gone.

I went back along Museum Street to the point where it ended at the museum gates. My feet took me by long habit up the steps and through the entrance, along the foyer thick with tourists, and behind a high wall. Showing my reader's card, I went into the renowned Reading Room of the British Library, where scholars had sat under the great domed ceiling for generations. Instead of card catalogs or computers, one still found listings in the monstrous, leather-bound books that circled the central desk, a quaint but surprisingly workable system that was soon destined to be swallowed up by progress when the library moved to its new quarters in the Euston Road.

I found a seat in one of the long rows of desks that ray out from the center like spokes of a wheel, then went to the appropriate window in the center and presented the slips for the books I had ordered the day before. Back at my seat, I sat in a sort of stupor until the page came with my books. Mechanically, I copied the publication data in one and checked out a reference in the other, glad that no concentration was required.

My biography of Mary Louise Talbot, a feisty Victorian novelist, was lurching toward final completion. I had elected to go with a British publisher because I liked the editor, Angus MacFinn, who had first shown interest in the project. Angus, a troll of a man, was witty, waspish, and deliciously gossipy, and I was captivated from the start. As an editor, he had proved to be both helpful and perceptive. I had some new material to add, then some final checking, and we'd be in the home stretch.

Now I leaned back in my chair and looked up, where the sunlight shot bolts of blue radiance from the dome overhead. This was the place where I had first met Iris. I had noticed this trim person with chic dark hair as I passed along the row, and one day we found ourselves sharing a table in the crowded downstairs café of the museum.

A few tentative remarks revealed that we were both professors of literature, and we fell quite naturally into shoptalk, aware of that spark of interest that fosters acquaintance. Meeting again one day at the London University library, we chatted, and when her friend Meredith Evans came along for a tea break, Iris asked me to join them.

Gradually we advanced to a drink at her place or

mine, and when Neil Padgett came into my life, there was an occasional evening foursome with Iris and her husband, Owen.

It was during my sabbatical, the academic year before this one, that Iris and I became close friends. I had spent some time in the autumn at my ex-mother-in-law's house in Devon, but the rest of that year I'd been in London, seeing a lot of Iris. At that time, Owen was involved in his second affair since their marriage, having won her back after the first one with his contrition and his assurance of undying affection. Iris was cynical but unwilling to admit publicly to failure.

"One divorce was enough, Claire," she would say. Her first husband, David's father, had simply wandered off into an alcoholic haze from which she had made a judicious escape. "When I met Owen, I thought the gates of heaven had opened to let me in."

One day she had said, with a wry smile, "Meredith's a passionate fan of Nancy Mitford and advises me to take a lover of my own, after the French fashion. The problem is, I don't see anyone I fancy who's available. One can't shop for a lover at Harrods, worse luck. Besides, I don't believe it would solve anything at the moment."

I knew that part of her reluctance to divorce Owen was the fear that it would affect her career. The professor who was her department head was an absolute twit who gave lip service to fair play but who deeply disliked academic women. Promotion was looming, and a second divorce, which theoretically ought to be irrelevant, would give him unspoken ammunition against her.

For my part, I had shared with Iris the troubling uncertainties in my relationship with Neil. Her glinting humor and her quiet good sense had served me well in the past, and I'd looked forward to her slant on our latest crisis. Chief Inspector Dietrich would never understand that Iris and I hadn't talked much when she spent the night because we were waiting for a span of free time. A few minutes in passing was not going to do it.

Forcing my thoughts back to the present, I got up from the desk, took a last look up at the cerulean glow of the dome, and made my way out of the museum's front entrance into Great Russell Street. I stopped to pick up some Chinese take-away and walked slowly back to Bedford Square.

When I opened the tall front door, the day had seemed to stretch for such endless hours that I was surprised to find it was only four o'clock, and the solicitors were still there. Years ago a divider had been placed in the entry to preserve some privacy for the residents, but it extended only a part of the way, leaving the receptionist behind her window at the right a clear view of whoever came in and turned left to go up the stairs—only, of course, if she happened to be looking.

Now, as I came in, I glanced over and caught her eye.

"Hello," I said, approaching the window. "Linda, is it?"

"Yes It's good to see you back, Mrs. Camden."

"I expect everyone knows what happened this morning. Did the police talk with you?"

"Yes, for quite some time, but no one here saw anything, so far as we are aware. I left my desk many times throughout the day, and the others would see visitors only if they happened to pass in the entry."

"Can you hear the buzzer if someone in my flat or the one above is releasing the lock to let a visitor come in?"

"Oh, yes, if I am here at my desk, but not otherwise."

"I see. Thank you, Linda."

As I turned to go, she said, "We are very sorry about your friend, Mrs. Camden."

I thanked her again and wearily climbed the stairs to my flat. I put the Chinese food in the fridge and poured myself a generous glass of verdicchio. I answered a couple of messages from the machine and made some phone calls to people who would want to know about Iris before it hit the news.

Then I remembered Deirdre Kemp, the flame-haired lady on the floor above. I wondered if the police had talked to her, but when I looked up her number in my book and rang, I got no answer and, surprisingly, no machine. I didn't know her well, but her appearance of trendy glamour gave the impression of a lady with an active social life who would surely want a record of her calls.

After a while, I warmed up my meal in the microwave and switched on the telly to watch the news. A brief mention of "University Lecturer found dead," but no details.

I'd just finished the last bite of almond chicken when the phone rang. I answered English fashion, with the last four digits of the number, and heard a woman's voice, shrill with hysteria.

"Miss Franklin, he's back—"

I was saying, "This is not Miss Franklin—" but the woman talked over me. "I must tell you—he knows where you are. I believe he knew yesterday—"

The voice broke off, and I heard a terrified scream and the snarl of a man's voice.

Then the line disconnected.

3

MY FIRST REACTION TO THE MYSTERIOUS phone call was that it must have been meant for somebody else, but this thought didn't last long. The woman definitely said "Miss Franklin," and she was terrified.

Meredith Evans might know something about it. I looked up her home number and found the phone engaged. Not surprising, as she was likely sharing her grief with other friends of Iris.

I saw Detective Chief Inspector Dietrich's card lying on the table. From association with Neil, I knew that in a homicide case the officer in charge remained available until the case was solved, or at least during the initial phase of the investigation. If he was not at the station, the call would be forwarded to wherever he might be.

When I phoned the number on his card and explained who I was, I heard the inspector's voice within minutes.

"Yes, Mrs. Camden?"

I told him about the odd phone call. "It may mean

nothing, Chief Inspector, but I thought I ought to report it to you."

"Quite right. Can you suggest any of the victim's friends who might have some knowledge of this?"

I gave him Meredith's name and number, adding that her line had been engaged and that I planned to go to her flat now to ask her that question.

After a pause, Dietrich said, "Will you ring me back at once if the lady has any information about this?"

I agreed and tried Meredith's phone again. Still busy. It was only a quarter of an hour's walk to Meredith's place, and at seven o'clock on a June evening, it would still be daylight for hours. No use taking my car from its spot near my flat. Even with my residence permit, parking was always a pain.

I walked through to Russell Square and along Guilford Street, turning down Grays Inn Road to Meredith's building, where I took the lift up three flights to the attractive flat I'd visited with Iris on several occasions.

Meredith opened the door and went back to the phone to finish the conversation, while I sat, admiring her artful mix of fine old tables and cabinets with the modern luxury of sofas and chairs.

When she had put down the phone, Meredith looked at me with a question. "Something's up?"

"Yes." I told her about the phone call and that DCI Dietrich wanted more information. "Do you have any idea what it could be about, Meredith?"

The brown eyes did their flash and bore. "It's possible. Some weeks ago, Iris was much distressed about a matter of domestic violence she had encountered. One day while walking, she saw a child, a girl of eleven or so, sitting on the steps of a block of flats, weeping. Iris stopped to ask if she could help, and the child sobbed out that her stepfather was beating her mum, and she didn't dare ring up the police because he said he would kill them both if she did.

"Iris tried to put it out of her mind, but she told me that one day she was passing the place again and saw the child playing on the steps. Her name was Penny, and she told Iris she was glad because the man had gone away for a few days. On an impulse, Iris asked Penny to take her to her mother, and they climbed several flights to a cramped flat with a tiny bedroom, where a young woman lay on the bed, her face badly bruised. The arm that lay over the blanket was swollen and discolored, and it was easy enough to guess the condition of the rest of her body.

"She was a timid, soft-spoken woman, distressed in the beginning by Iris's presence, thinking she had come from Social Services. Reassured on that score, she said she was afraid to make any official complaint, repeating the man's threat to kill her and the child if she tried to leave him.

"Iris was haunted by the situation and was half inclined to report the case herself, but I advised her to stay out of it. Now I wonder if she did become involved. I've been on holiday for the past three weeks and have spoken to Iris only briefly since I returned. At that time she said nothing about it."

I asked, "Where do the woman and child live, Meredith?"

She frowned. "I don't know. I have a vague idea Iris said something about a street off Rosebery Avenue, but I can't be sure."

We agreed that Chief Inspector Dietrich should be told, and when Meredith rang him up, he said he would be there in ten minutes.

Accompanied by his constable, he arrived, looking cool and competent. While Meredith told him her story, he stroked his sandy mustache, letting the constable do the writing. Then he asked me to repeat what I had heard on my phone, the woman's voice warning "Miss Franklin" that "he" knew where she was and may have known the day before.

Dietrich said, "The woman sounded in great fear, Mrs. Camden?"

"Absolutely terrified. She screamed when she heard the man's voice. He must have caught her at the telephone and overheard what she'd said."

"It would seem so, indeed." He turned to Meredith. "Can you remember anything further, Mrs. Evans?"

"Afraid not. If I do, I'll let you know at once."

"Very good. Thank you both for your cooperation." And with a nod, he rose, and the two officers left.

Meredith looked at me. "Does he take this seriously or not? He never seems to change expression."

I smiled. "Neil tells me they're trained to look like the Sphinx, but I'd say he's actually pleased to have a lead of any sort. The fact that he dashed over here in person tells us that."

"I suspect they will burrow into all their records for a possible connection. A call to 999 on that date, or perhaps someone in Social Services who was notified."

"A call could have come from a neighbor. In those crowded conditions, neighbors must hear pretty much everything that goes on. Someone there may have taken pity on the woman."

"Yes, but if the man found out, and he knew about Iris, he might assume she had turned him in. If they can trace a connection, at least they'll know who the people are and where they live. Maybe the woman can get some protection."

We talked on for a while, mostly about Iris herself and the appalling tragedy of her death. Meredith had had a phone call from Iris's son, David, who had heard the news from the police.

"Poor lad," she said, "he's devastated."

27

"I wonder if the girlfriend will help him through? I met her only once when they came to the flat with Iris and stopped for a drink. She's gorgeous to look at, but I couldn't form any notion of what she's like."

Meredith shrugged. "Hard to say. Iris had some doubts about her but no worries. Said David was far from ready for permanent alliances. He's only twenty-one."

As I was leaving, Meredith asked after my friend Neil Padgett. "Will he be coming up to London soon?"

I tried to sound casual. "He's in Australia till the end of summer. They wanted a high-ranking CID officer for a special training course."

"What a pity, as you're here in London!"

"Yes, isn't it?"

I didn't add that Neil had actually volunteered for the program, but as I walked back to Bedford Square, the pain of my parting with Neil washed over me like some monstrous breaker at the seashore, suffocating, overpowering.

I might have seen it coming, but I didn't. We'd had some problems now and then, but who doesn't? When we were together in England at the Christmas holidays, it had all seemed good to me. Neil's headquarters were in Devon, where my lovable ex-mother-in-law lived, and where my daughter, Sally, was then at the university. We'd spent some time there, then had a glorious week in London together, seeing friends, going to the theater, dining out.

At the Easter break, Neil had flown to California to spend the holiday with me, and that's when things started coming unglued. Meeting my friends, he muttered that he felt like someone's pet poodle, trotted out when convenient. I was appalled, both at the implication of triviality in our relationship and at the outdated machismo of his attitude.

Some brisk battles ensued, and finally we had clarified the real problem. Neil wanted me to marry him, live with him, be there. It was perfectly reasonable, once we both understood. He hadn't actually expressed this earlier because he didn't realize it himself. During our first year together, I had been on sabbatical, living in Devon or in London, where we saw each other often. Now, the divorce from his wife, who had left him for greener pastures, was final, and suddenly it dawned on him that I'm in California, and we're looking at snatched holidays as a way of life.

It had worked for years in my marriage to Miles Camden. With his gossamer David Nivenish charm, Miles had enjoyed the evanescent comings and goings, leaving him free, as I afterward realized, to follow other inclinations. Neil Padgett had his own brand of charm, but his character, unlike Miles's, was rooted, solid.

Now we faced the nitty-gritty. If I gave up my career, I'd have no income. What if the marriage didn't survive? There's no going back to a job like mine, nor getting another at my age. It's true, I had some money from the divorce settlement, but I wasn't about to live on that until it was gone. If we waited a few years, I could take an early retirement and have at least a small stipend, but those years were the crucial ones, as Neil saw it.

It was pretty hard to see any easy answers. What I didn't expect was that Neil would make the break so soon. He admitted he'd taken the assignment in Australia to avoid the summer in England.

As we sat in the airport, waiting for his return flight to London, he said in an exasperatingly reasonable tone, "If we have the summer together, Claire, it will only make it more difficult in the end."

I said, "This is final, then?"

At that, he dropped his head and put a hand over

his eyes. "Oh, God, I don't know. Let's wait and see, shall we?"

I didn't exactly see the logic of that, but I was willing to wait.

It was at that moment that he uttered the fatal words. "I expect we should feel free to see other people." With what looked like an afterthought, he added, "It wouldn't be fair to you otherwise."

They were already boarding his flight, and as he moved into the line, he put his arms around me. I kept it to a light kiss, turned quickly, and ran.

Remembering all this didn't improve my mood as I walked from Meredith's place back to my flat, through the dusky evening light. Turning the corner into the square, I saw a well-dressed lady emerge from a taxi in front of my building and recognized Deirdre Kemp, my neighbor on the floor above.

While the driver carried two bags up the steps to the door for her, I did the unlocking, and once inside, I offered to take one of her bags.

She gave me a dazzling smile. "That would be most kind."

At the landing for my floor, she said, "I can manage from here. Unless you'd like to come up for a drink?"

"Thanks, I'd like that." Any distraction was welcome, I decided. Besides, she obviously didn't know about the murder. I may as well clue her in. I thanked her and we trudged up the second double flight to her door.

In the days when Deirdre's mother had been the tenant, I had been in the flat a number of times. A charming old lady, Miles and I had both been fond of her. At her death five years ago, the daughter had taken over the lease, but we had seldom met. She traveled a good deal, and I was in London only from time to time. Now I saw that some of her mother's best pieces were still there, but the impression had gone from cozy to elegant. Velvet draperies were looped back to reveal silk sheers, and I was sure I detected the hand of a decorator in the general decor.

Deirdre herself had the kind of glamour that gave a meaning to the word voluptuous. Pushing forty, but with creamy skin and hair softly tinged with red, eyes of bewitching blue, a sexy body, and spectacular legs, she was a guaranteed head-turner. According to her mother, there had been two husbands along the way, neither any longer in evidence, and no number three seemed to have appeared.

"G and T?" she asked me.

I had adapted to a lot of English ways, but I still loathed gin and tonic. "Whiskey, please."

She handed me my drink and sank into a chair, stretching out and kicking off her shoes. "It's good to be home. I've been on the Continent. I love Italy in the spring. So when did you arrive in London, Claire?"

"Only yesterday. There's something I must tell you."

I gave her the story.

"How ghastly for you. A good friend?"

"Yes, I'm afraid so. Iris Franklin, a lecturer at University College."

At her startled look, I said, "Did you know her?"

She shook her head. "No, not at all. I thought the name was familiar."

Within the narrow confines of the academic community, Iris's name might well be recognized, but somehow I didn't expect Deirdre to move in those circles.

Now she explained. "A friend was once a graduate student there. Perhaps that's the connection."

She expressed genuine concern for my loss, then asked after my daughter, Sally. Fortunately, she knew nothing of Neil Padgett, as our acquaintance had never extended that far, so I didn't have to explain his absence.

I told her the police would no doubt be calling her. "I rang you up this afternoon," I added.

She smiled. "And no machine? I turn it off when I'm away."

In a little while, I thanked her and went back down to my flat, where I found messages from one of Iris's friends, and another, more disturbing one.

A woman's low, timid voice. "Whoever you are, please don't tell the police I rang and asked for Miss Franklin! Please!"

4

THE MURDER OF IRIS FRANKLIN OCCURRED ON a Wednesday. During the next few days I tried to force myself back to some desultory work on my manuscript, fogged by painful recollections. I couldn't bear to look at the sofa where I'd found Iris. The horror of her twisted body and distorted face flashed in and out of my sight by day and haunted my dreams at night. Equally agonizing were the unbidden visions of Iris alive. Slim, attractive, self-possessed, dark eyes thoughtful; then the twist at the corner of the mouth, the flash of wit, the wholehearted mirth. A rare and special person, and a promising scholar, at the threshold of what ought to have been a distinguished career.

Iris had received favorable notice from the critics some years ago for her cogent little book on Charles Sackville, one of the wits and rakes in the court of Charles II. Since that time, she had been at work on a more ambitious project, a study of a related group of Restoration court poets. This was the work that our mutual editor, Angus MacFinn, planned to publish, and for which he had high hopes of general as well as academic success.

When I rang Angus to ask if he'd heard about the murder, he had had the decency to express genuine shock and sorrow before shrieking, "My God, Claire, we can't lose *The Court Wits!* There may be enough with what she's done already, if someone can finish it up."

"Don't look at me," I said. "It's not my field. What about one of her colleagues?"

Angus sounded doubtful. "There's Duncan the Dim." He was referring to Duncan Dimchurch, whose field was Restoration literature.

"Good idea."

"But darling, he's frightfully dreary! Still, one could spice him up a bit, and I expect he could do the donkey work."

Angus had ended our conversation with a "till Saturday."

At that moment I was sure I wouldn't want to go anywhere on Saturday, but when the day came, I was ready to get out of the flat and face the world, if one could call a lecture at Kings College in the Strand a part of the real world.

Rupert Mortmain, a senior lecturer in the English department of Kings College, had recently created a stir by revealing his discovery of some potentially scandalous letters concerning the poet Tennyson. On the strength of the letters, he had catapulted to minor celebrity status as a featured participant on a BBC talk show. While Saturday's lecture was intended for students, it was open to the public and would more than likely be covered by the press, hoping for new revelations about Queen Victoria's poet laureate.

No popular worship of a movie or rock star today could begin to match the adulation lavished upon Alfred, Lord Tennyson by his Victorian public. In the years following the 1850 publication of *In Memoriam,* his elegy for his friend Arthur Hallam, Tennyson had become for his contemporaries not merely a poet but a heroic moral leader, like his own version of King Arthur, and a seer who gave them a somewhat muddled but reassuring hope for an afterlife. Every word that dropped from his pen was sacrosanct to thousands, and, with his devoted wife and two sons, he became a symbol of domestic felicity equaled only by the Queen herself.

Whenever a public figure becomes a symbol of moral purity, there is something irresistible in hearing that he may, after all, have shared the fallibility of ordinary men. I was as curious as anyone to know how valid were the rumors that the Great Man might have engaged in an affair with a young woman. Actually, my interest was more academic than prurient, however, since I had already booked a visit the following week to the Isle of Wight, where the poet and his family had lived for many years in a house called Farringford, now a hotel. Mary Louise Talbot, the subject of my biography, had visited the island and met the Tennysons, and I planned to check out some details there. Perhaps I'd mention this to Mr. Mortmain, if I had the chance. I hadn't caught his BBC show in the short time I'd been in London, and I wondered what sort of person he was.

By Saturday morning I'd heard nothing further from Chief Inspector Dietrich, nor had I heard a word from Owen Babcock. As I walked down through Covent Garden toward the Strand, I wondered how Owen was bearing up, if indeed he was as grief-stricken as he'd seemed to be on the day of the murder.

At Kings College I went along a dank, gray corridor and down a couple of staircases to a large lecture room, where little groups stood chatting near a coffee urn. I didn't see anyone I knew, so I took my cup, climbed a few tiers, and slid along to a seat behind the continuous desk that trapped you in, once you sat down. In case of fire, I thought, we'd all be roasted like sausages, as rapid exit was impossible.

In due course, the room filled, and the proceedings began with someone introducing Rupert Mortmain, mentioning his degree from an Oxford college and his publications to date.

When he stepped to the podium, I saw that Mortmain was a tall, thin man, fortyish, with a high forehead, his dark hair shot with gray, sparse on top, but curling on the back of his neck. He had a bony nose in an elongated face, and when he spoke, his arrogant drawl prickled my skin. It didn't take me long to see that this was one of those men you love to hate. When a photographer appeared and knelt at his feet, Mortmain paused with regal condescension until the flash was over, then made a gesture of dismissal with his hand. "Afterward, if you please." No way, I decided, would I approach this creature with my story of a reference in a Talbot novel.

Mortmain began with a reminder that this was by no means a formal presentation. On the contrary, it was a preliminary chat about the early stages of a work in progress. He made a smirking reference to the "quite unmerited notoriety" that had come his way via the BBC, eliciting a few smiles and murmurs, then explained that he could take no credit whatever for the discovery of the letters in question. His sister, Zora Mortmain, had found them in the attic of their home in the village of Freshwater on the Isle of Wight, not far from Farringford, the home of the Tennysons for many years.

"I may say at once," he went on, "that the letters are not dated. They are addressed neither to 'Lord Tennyson,' nor to 'Alfred,' nor to any other name related to the poet. The salutations are all in terms of endearment: 'My dearest,' 'My love,' and the like.

Neither do we know the identity of the writer, who signs herself only with the letter 'M.' It is from internal evidence alone that we deduce that the letters were written by a young woman and that the recipient was indeed the poet laureate.

"Today I shall present some passages in two letters in the series, which will serve to illustrate some elements of identification. The first of these is written in reply to a message received, as the opening makes clear."

In the following rendition, Mortmain raised his tone slightly, to suggest the female voice. "'My dear,'" he read, "'How my heart beat with anticipation as I stood on the chair and reached into the crevice behind the high shelf. With what joy I felt my fingers grasp the folded pages of your dear letter.'"

Mortmain paused, casting his eyes upward in a gesture of deprecation at the sentimental effusions of the writer, then continued to read in that irritating falsetto.

'I confess that I could not wait but sat down at once, there in the summerhouse, and read every word. Can it be true that you think of me as a living Maud? When you recited the beautiful lines to me, your eyes so eloquent, your voice so vibrant, I trembled, knowing how much I longed for your regard.

'It was early this morning when I found your letter. I was sure no one would be about, but I left the summerhouse cautiously, taking the path up to the down, so that it would appear that I was merely out for a walk, then circling back. As I passed D., there was Mrs. C. in her garden with her camera, and we exchanged good mornings. Now it is nearly midnight. I am in my room, with my mending basket at hand. If anyone should come, I can slip this letter out of sight. I can scarcely believe that I am writing to you in this fashion. . . .'

At this point, Rupert Mortmain broke off with a dismissive gesture. "The rest is the sort of thing you can imagine. Our interest lies in the points of identification suggested in the letter. For the benefit of those who have not steeped themselves in Tennyson biography—and that, I daresay, includes the vast majority of Britons today—I shall make these points clear.

"First, the summerhouse. Tennyson had had a small stone structure erected in the grounds of Farringford, where, in good weather, he retreated to write in seclusion. However, this item alone would have little significance, as summerhouses abound in the English countryside.

"More specific is the reference to the poem *Maud*, which Tennyson loved to read aloud to his guests or to anyone willing to listen. Nevertheless, one may say that many men might read passages to their lady loves from a poem so widely known at the time.

"The references to a house, 'D', occupied by a 'Mrs. C.' with her camera, bring us closer to Farringford. The eccentric Mrs. Julia Cameron, obsessed with the then early art of photography, lived in a house named Dimbola, which stood halfway between Farringford and Freshwater Bay.

"When we see that 'Thornbury,' the home of my sister and myself, where the letters were found, stands at what might roughly be described as a third point of a triangle whose other points are Farringford and Dimbola, I believe there is a strong presumption that the location is identified.

"If the summerhouse where our lovers evidently met and where the letters were hidden is indeed

Tennyson's own, we are inclined to believe that the poet himself is the gentleman who has found his 'living Maud.'

"When we turn to the identification of our lady, the mysterious 'M,' I regret that I have not as yet found her, and my search for her continues, as time permits."

Mortmain now read a passage from the second letter suggesting that the gentleman was considerably older than the writer, as she assures him that the difference in their ages gives her no concern. He is far more alluring, she tells him, than the insipid young men of her own generation.

"We have no dates for the letters," Mortmain continued, "but we can suggest parameters. While *Maud* was published in 1855, it is safe to say that the first letter could not have been written before 1863, when Julia Cameron received her first camera, and no later than 1875, when she and her husband departed for Ceylon. After 1870, the Tennysons were less often at Farringford, having settled in Sussex for most of each year. Thus, the decade of the 1860s is the most likely period for the letters. Born in 1809, Tennyson was fifty-one years of age at the beginning of that decade. His wife, Emily, had already, by that date, become something of an invalid, suffering from a spinal ailment that kept her increasingly confined to her couch."

In the rest of his talk, Mortmain described in more detail the location of the three houses, the walks frequented by the poet, and the general terrain of the Freshwater neighborhood on the island. When he then turned to the audience for questions, he fielded the inquiries with an elegantly raised eyebrow that made me grind my teeth.

It was getting on for one o'clock when Mortmain concluded to a round of applause. Angus MacFinn, across the room, gave me a little wave, eyes twinkling. Now, as people began drifting away, others gathered about Mortmain or stood in small groups of their own to chat.

Angus worked his way toward me. "I've booked a table at the Waldorf, darling. I've asked Duncan the D. Will you give him your most dazzling smile and bring him along? We may need him, you know." I promised to do my best.

I now found myself the center of a little group of Iris's friends and acquaintances, including Duncan Dimchurch, who understandably wanted to hear what I could tell them about her death. "One can't rely on the news to be accurate," said a young man who had been one of her graduate students. I told them what I could, consoled by the genuine affection expressed for my friend.

A gray-haired gentleman with a self-satisfied expression oozed into the group and addressed me. "We are very sorry indeed to lose a lovely lady and a distinguished scholar."

I recognized Professor Griswold, Iris's department head. He didn't look very sorry to me as he gave me a vague murmur and turned away.

At a touch on my elbow, I saw Rupert Mortmain beside me. "You're Iris Franklin's friend, are you not?"

"Yes."

"Rather a quiet little mouse, wasn't she?"

I gave him my best drop-dead look. "She was quiet, yes, but not in any sense mouselike."

His mouth twitched ever so slightly, and his eyes, before veiled and inexpressive, now shot bolts of lightning, as if he had been switched on by some massive transformer. He had managed to turn me away from the group, so that we stood apart from the others and very close together, his eyes boring into mine with a kind of naked intimacy.

"Claire," he said. "Claire Camden. Are you married?"

Mesmerized, I said, "No."

"Not that it would matter." He put his hand on my arm, not pressing, just letting it lie there for a long moment. Then he murmured, "Yes," and turned away. I watched as he sauntered toward the door.

The spell broken, I repressed a laugh. Not bad, I had to admit. I'd been hit on in a lot of ways, but Rupert's approach had a certain panache. Nevertheless, at that moment I'd have given very high odds against his ever having a place in my life.

I turned back to the group from which Mortmain had detached me and saw Duncan Dimchurch staring moodily at me. He had evidently been the only one to catch Mortmain's move. As the group began to break up, I smiled at Duncan, as instructed by Angus, and we went along together, up from the subterranean depths to the Strand and across the Aldwych to the Waldorf, where we joined Angus and his party at the lunch table.

5

HALF AN HOUR OF SITTING NEXT TO DUNCAN Dimchurch at the Waldorf luncheon and I'd decided he wasn't so bad after all. I'd seen him from time to time at academic parties where, as a bachelor with no known personal attachments, he was an unobtrusive guest. Poor Duncan, as I'd always thought of him, was not, it is true, exceedingly swift at repartee, but he earned good marks with me now for his kind words about Iris.

"I'd always admired her enormously, Claire," he said, his round eyes blinking at me earnestly. "She was so clever, so witty, yet such a fine person. Her students adored her, and with good reason."

Duncan went on in this vein for some time, while I worked on my prawn cocktail and felt my Duncan-gauge shoot up ten points Celsius. I was seized with guilt for having suspected him of resenting Iris as a more successful rival in their field. Duncan had published a few articles and was said to be working on a longer project of some sort, but like Mr. Casaubon in *Middlemarch,* he had reportedly accumulated masses of notes without any concrete result.

Engrossed in lapping up Duncan's praise of Iris, I vaguely heard voices at the table chatting merrily. It was when I heard Rupert Mortmain's name that I turned toward the others, Duncan following my lead as I listened to a young woman at the end of the table.

"I agree that Rupert is immensely clever, but what has he actually revealed of his letters? Why doesn't he produce the lot straightaway and let the world see them?"

Angus MacFinn's cherubic face crinkled. "If one has tumbled across a little pot of gold coins, my dear, why not spend them one or two at a time and keep the hoard to oneself? Isn't that what Mortmain intends to do?"

"Do you mean he'll sell them?"

A fiftyish man in tweeds gave a malicious snort. "They'll be worth a packet in the end, won't they? Meanwhile, he's got the BBC hanging on his every word, to say nothing of the prospect of a lucrative book. One can see the title—*The Living Maud: Tennyson and the Mystery Maiden.*"

The young woman laughed. "Instead of the immortal line, 'Come into the garden, Maud,' we'd have 'Come into the summerhouse, Maud.'"

The conversation moved on, and Duncan seized my attention again. "Poor Iris!" His eyes were shiny. "I've been thinking about her work on the court wits, Claire. What will happen to the manuscript now?"

For one traitorous moment, I wondered if all this had been a buildup to worming his way into the job of finishing Iris's book, but a look at his transparently naive countenance reassured me.

"I don't know, Duncan," I said. "Angus may be looking for someone to see what can be done with it."

"Ah, very good. I'd offer to help, but I haven't a moment to spare from my own work."

"Of course," I said, "I understand."

43

We joined the general conversation again, and when the lunch party broke up, we sauntered out into the Aldwych, Duncan attaching himself to me like a faithful dog.

"How long will you be in London, Claire?"

"Only for the summer."

"I'm having a few people in soon. Would you and—er—your friend like to come?"

I remembered then that whenever I'd seen Duncan at a party, I'd had Neil Padgett with me.

"Neil's abroad for the summer," I said, "but do give me a ring, if you like."

Duncan beamed. "Perhaps we can dine one evening."

Oh, dear. A party was one thing. An entire evening with Duncan alone would be pretty uphill. Still, I'd asked for it, hanging on his every word like Desdemona listening to Othello's tales of war.

I murmured assent, and as the party broke up, I saw Angus closing in on Dimchurch with a predatory gleam in his eye.

Back at the flat, I checked my messages, stifling the unbidden hope that I'd hear Neil's voice. I didn't. There was, however, a message from David, Iris's son, leaving a number where I could reach him. It was not, I noted, the number of his stepfather's flat.

When I pressed out the number, a Jeeves-like voice said, "The Ward-Jones residence here." The home of the girlfriend's parents, if I remembered correctly.

I gave my name and asked for David Franklin, and presently David came on the line. "Claire, thanks so much for ringing. May I come to see you?"

"Of course. This afternoon?"

"Yes, please."

I knew why he wanted to come. He needed to *see* where his mother had died, to *hear* from me how I'd found her. He needed to face the reality of what must otherwise seem like a dream from which he would surely awaken.

When he arrived an hour later, he was not alone. The tall, slim young woman with him stood aside while David put his arms around me and we stood for a moment in silent pain.

Then he said, "I believe you've met Fiona Ward-Jones?"

We both murmured greetings, and I led the way to the sitting room, where I gestured toward a pair of chairs, brought brandy, and sat on the far end of the sofa, avoiding the place where I'd found Iris.

As I had guessed, David wanted to hear everything, and I held nothing back. At last, he said, "It must have been someone she knew. She'd not have admitted a stranger."

Fiona spoke for the first time. "What about Owen? Meredith Evans told us he seems to be in the clear."

I reported in detail the police interview with Owen. "I'm sure they are checking out his story. The spouse is always a prime suspect."

Fiona said, "I'd believe it of Owen," but David shook his head. "I've never liked him much, but I can't believe he would do something like this."

I looked at his open countenance and the dark eyes so like his mother's and thought what a dear he was.

"Besides," David added, "what reason would Owen have? If they weren't getting on, they could divorce."

Fiona pushed at the mass of long brown hair that hung to her shoulders. "There's the insurance, darling. He gets the same as you."

David blinked. "Yes, I expect he does." He looked at me. "Do you know, Claire, they each had these rather large policies for the other—three hundred thousand pounds, I'm told. The same as mine, except that mine was taken out when I was very young, when the charge was less."

I didn't say so, but I agreed with Fiona. That amount, half a million when translated into dollars, constituted a real motive. Murder had been committed for far less than that. Could Owen have bribed the receptionist to say he was in the waiting room? Surely the police had thought of that. I wished I'd hear from Chief Inspector Dietrich, but would he tell me anything if I asked him? Probably not.

"We've been to see Mother's friend Meredith," David said. "She has a theory that someone might have gained entrance by asking to speak with a solicitor. Then the person remained in the building and came up here to your flat."

"Not a bad idea," I said, "but this door is double-locked. It's still likely to be someone known to your mother."

At last, our conversation moved away from the murder. I asked David if he still enjoyed his studies at the University of Sussex. I knew that Fiona, a year older than David, had just taken her degree, while he had another year to go in history honors.

David smiled. "Yes, it's a good place, and we both like living in Brighton."

Fiona frowned. "Daddy's being tiresome. He wants me to go into his office as a sort of assistant, but I intend to stay with David in Brighton." Daddy, it seemed, was a solicitor in a prominent firm in the City.

"You'll not be reading law?" I asked.

"Lord, no. It's ghastly dull."

David smiled at her fondly. "Fiona's a lazy little beast, aren't you, darling? A born lily of the field."

Fiona reached across and took his hand where it lay on the arm of his chair. "I've never fancied grubbing about in an office, if that's what you mean."

David turned her hand in his, then brought it up to his lips. They exchanged a long look, evidently continuing an unspoken dialogue between them, but David said nothing.

Fiona stood up. "Shall we make a move?"

I had gathered up the things Iris had left in my flat and handed the carryall to David. With tears in his eyes, he hugged me again, and Fiona gave me a languid hand. I wished them well, and they went out, arms twined around one another.

It was only afterward that I remembered. Fiona had expressed not a word of grief over Iris's death.

As I closed the door, I heard the double ring of the phone in my study. It was Meredith Evans, asking how the lecture had gone. She got my unedited blast on the character of Rupert Mortmain. Sounding amused, she said she'd caught his last show on the BBC and agreed that he was an arrogant twit, but nonetheless rather attractive.

I didn't mention his coming on to me. I'd have told Iris, but I wasn't sure I knew Meredith well enough for that kind of confidence. I did, however, report his snide remark about Iris.

Meredith snorted. "Mouselike, indeed. He must not have known Iris well to say that."

"I agree. Did she ever mention him to you, Meredith?"

"Can't say she did. They were not at the same college, of course, only under the larger umbrella of the London U. Obviously they've met, but I doubt if it went much beyond that."

At her question about the Tennyson letters, I reported the essence of Mortmain's talk.

She said, "I wouldn't mind having those letters for the bookshop, but I've no idea what he'll want for them."

"Angus thinks he'll sell them to the highest bidder."

"Very likely. Wouldn't most of us do the same, I expect, if we had the chance?"

I told her about my plans to check out the Tennyson references in one of Mary Louise Talbot's novels, and she said, "Tennyson will be a hot topic now, after Mortmain and his letters."

I laughed. "Yes, no doubt. I've booked a few days on the Isle of Wight, staying at Farringford. It's now a hotel, you know."

"Yes. I grew up near Portsmouth, and my parents had a small place on the island at Yarmouth, where we went every summer. In recent years, since Mother and I were both widowed, we've gone less often. But look, Claire, the Farringford's a bit pricey. You're welcome to use the cottage if Mother isn't there."

I thanked her warmly and said maybe another time.

"By the way," I added, "I've just had a visit from David and his lady friend."

"What do you make of her?" she asked.

"A spoiled little rich girl, I'd think, but I may be quite wrong. They seem to be a devoted couple."

"Yes. I believe they've lived together for more than a year. Iris said recently she rather thought the girl would eventually go off with someone in her own set, leaving David heartbroken for a time but ultimately better off. One can't see Fiona enjoying the academic life, which is where David is headed."

We talked a bit longer, wondering if the police had located the battered woman who had tried to warn Iris that "he" knew where she was.

Meredith said, "I expect a man who's violent with one woman would be a candidate to be violent with another."

"Yes, especially if he suspects her of interfering in his life. But how could he possibly know she was here?

And even if he had come here to my flat looking for her, Iris surely would not have let him in?"

"Certainly not. There may be no connection whatsoever."

As if our conversation had conjured up the woman, we'd no sooner rung off than my phone rang again.

"Are you Miss Franklin's friend?" The timid voice I'd heard before, calm this time.

"Yes," I said.

"I'm so sorry to disturb you. I rang you before and asked you not to tell anyone of my call."

"Yes, I remember."

"I wanted to say that it's quite all right now. Please forgive me for being a bother."

"Not at all. I'd like to speak with you about Ms. Franklin—"

But I heard a click, and the line went dead.

6

O N MONDAY MORNING I SET OFF FOR THE ISLE
of Wight, driving south through heavy rain that
obscured the signposts on the motorway and kept me
in the slower lane, allowing the maniacs to sizzle past
on my right. After a couple of hours of this, when I
had taken the turnoff toward Portsmouth, the sky
suddenly cleared, sending puffs of white cloud gam-
boling innocently across the horizon as if they knew
perfectly well it was summer.

On advice, I'd booked my ferry crossing well ahead
of the day, and I saw why, as I showed my ticket and
was directed into a lane to wait my turn to drive
aboard among the hordes of summer visitors flocking
to the island. A pleasant half hour or so across the
Solent brought us to Fishbourne, from where I followed the signposts along to Freshwater, at the western tip of the island. The gently rolling terrain of the
green countryside was dotted with farms and villages,
and everywhere was the special spruceness of tourist
country.

During my journey, I'd had time to get my mind
back to Mary Louise Talbot, planning what I hoped to

accomplish here. I'd like to find the house where Talbot had stayed when she visited the island. While there, she had heard a tale of a young woman who had fallen to her death from the attic of that very house, with rumors of a love affair and a possible suicide. Some years later Talbot had set her novel *Matilda* on the Isle of Wight, and I hoped to find out more about the real-life source for the character of her heroine.

My book was what is known in the trade as a "critical biography," meaning it focused as much on an analysis of the works of the author as upon the events of her life, indicating the influence of the one upon the other. Talbot's attacks on the plight of women under the pressures of Victorian society were especially significant for today's readers. She deplored the custom that rendered genteel women dependent upon a "suitable" marriage, without recourse to other sources of livelihood or social acceptance.

Talbot herself had found the courage to flout convention in her own personal life. She had lived out of wedlock for some years with her future husband until he was free to marry, and the women in her novels, unlike the simpering nonentities churned out by many of her contemporaries, were often persons of spirit and intelligence who didn't buy the myth of male superiority but usually had to live with it. In one novel a widow must ask her wayward son's permission before she could pay the servants their wages. "Had she been permitted to manage affairs," the lady thought, "how efficiently it would all be done. She would know precisely how to arrange matters, with none of the haphazard carelessness that now prevailed." That women held no control over their own money was another source of Talbot's oblique attack. "Lady Millicent," she wrote, "knew quite well that her husband had made unwise investments that had eaten up most of the money from her dowry, yet she sat quietly, her eyes downcast, while he explained to her the vagaries of stocks and bonds, making it clear that he was in no way at fault."

Through the success of her writing, Talbot herself had managed to escape from the webs that enmeshed so many women of "good family." Ignoring the shocked disapproval of some of her relations, she had enough financial independence to go her own way. An incredibly energetic woman, she wrote a three-volume novel at least once a year while raising a large family, maintaining an active social life, writing copious letters, and keeping a daily journal of her activities.

It was from Talbot's journal and letters, fortunately preserved by her heirs, that I had drawn the most rewarding information about her life. In a letter to her husband, dated June 12, 1874, she described the visit she and her eldest daughter had paid to her friend Mrs. James on the Isle of Wight.

"Lovely weather for the crossing," Talbot had written, "although raining as we came into Freshwater. What Mrs. J. calls her 'cottage' is in fact a comfortable house, built half a century ago, nestled among fine old beeches, with a cupola adorning the central gable. Along the lane is the home of the remarkable Mrs. Cameron, a lady of immense energy and enthusiasms, a great friend of the Tennysons. Indeed, we had scarcely arrived and were seated at the tea table when the lady herself burst into the room, exclaiming at her delight in meeting me at last, the author who had given her so many hours of pleasure. You know, my dear, how uncomfortable I find such gushing tribute. Yet, Mrs. Cameron's transparent countenance glowed with such good humor that I was at once captivated. She asked me if I would sit for my photographic portrait, amidst groans from those round the table and droll descriptions of how one must sit in absolute stillness for many minutes during this procedure. Nevertheless, I gave my consent."

For the purposes of my own biography of Talbot, I was glad that the photograph had been taken, for the portrait, showing Talbot's strongly handsome face and forthright expression, was to be the frontispiece of my book.

Now I brought my mind back to the present as I drove into Freshwater and followed the hotel map to Farringford. I'd recently reviewed some works on Tennyson before coming down to the island, and consequently, the house looked familiar to me when I arrived, since every biography of the poet featured a picture of the house. Built in the late eighteenth century, during the heyday of the Gothic revival, its pleasant Georgian proportions had been ornamented with imitations in wood of Gothic stone traceries and crowned with inappropriate battlements, but these seemed unobtrusive to me, adding a quaint charm to the attractive exterior.

I was shown to a comfortable room overlooking the green lawns and dark, brooding trees of the grounds. After a quick sandwich and a cup of tea, I obtained a map of the local area from the desk and set off for a stroll down the road toward Freshwater Bay.

It was easy enough to find Dimbola, where Julia Cameron had lived. Originally two cottages, Mrs. Cameron had bought them both and had a tower constructed to connect them, resulting in an odd-looking structure that suited the eccentric lady and her complacent husband. I turned into the lane where the house still stood, with a sign offering bed and breakfast, and walked on past various dwellings, most of which were not there more than a century ago, when the Tennysons had chosen this end of the island for its seclusion.

A large house, standing back among towering trees,

looked promisingly like that described by Talbot in her letter, and when I saw the cupola adorning the central gable, I was sure this was where she had visited her friend Mrs. James. Whether the present occupant would have any knowledge of the past was another question, but I had to start somewhere.

I rang the bell, waited, and was hesitating about a second ring when the door opened to an elderly lady who looked at me curiously as I explained that I hoped to learn something of a Mrs. James who had occupied the house in the 1870s.

The lady thought for a moment, her eyes alert. "That would be my great-grandmother."

Evidently deciding that I was suitable, she asked me to come in, leading the way through dark, high-ceilinged rooms toward a garden at the back, and murmuring that on such a fine day we might venture outdoors.

"May I offer you a glass of lemonade? I'll only be a moment."

Scarcely able to believe my good luck, I sat on a wicker chair beside a low table, reveling in the lush green lawn, the splash of colors in the flower beds, and the grand old trees that stood like stately sentinels overhead.

Carrying a tray, my hostess returned, setting it between us, smiling. "I'm Leila Ward."

"Claire Camden," I said. I gave her my card with the London address.

"You are an American, I believe?"

"Yes. My husband was English." I'd found this went over well with the older generation. The younger ones couldn't care less.

Mrs. Ward filled our glasses, and I accepted a slice of wonderful cake. I quite sincerely admired the garden, and after other bits of small talk, we came to the purpose of my visit.

At my mention of Mary Louise Talbot, I got a vigorous nod. "My grandmother was nine or ten years of age when Mrs. Talbot visited here, and she remembered her well. We have many of Mrs. Talbot's delightful novels here in the library, including the one she brought with her, inscribed to my great-grandmother."

Better and better, I thought. I told her how Talbot had recorded in her journal the pleasure of her visit.

"I shall have my eightieth birthday soon," Mrs. Ward said, eyes bright with the pride of the elderly for whom advancing age is a badge of achievement. "My grandmother lived to eighty-six, and well I remember her stories of life here on the island. Our most illustrious residents were, of course, the Tennysons. She often saw the great poet striding down toward the bay, wearing his wide-brimmed hat, with his cape flapping in the wind."

I listened with pleasure to her tales of people and events, including the redoubtable Mrs. Cameron, whom they all admired despite her eccentricities.

I told her how Mary Louise Talbot had been persuaded to sit for her photograph, and got amusing accounts of how the indomitable lady would seize upon any person who interested her and persist until they agreed to sit for her.

At last I asked about the story of the young woman who had fallen to her death from the roof, as told to Talbot by her hostess, Mrs. James.

Her face clouded. "Oh, dear, yes, what a dreadful thing. She had come as governess to the elder children and had been with the family for more than a year. My grandmother, the youngest, was an infant at the time and heard of it only long afterward. Her eldest sister, however, remembered it well, as she had been extremely fond of the young woman. It was rumored that the governess had fallen in love and was rejected, but nothing was ever proved. She had burnt some papers—the ashes were found later in the grate in her bedroom—and had gone up through the attic to the round room, as we call the cupola, where she stepped out onto the leads and either fell or cast herself off into the grounds below."

"Were the children in the house at the time?"

"No, the family was away on holiday. It seems that she had declined to accompany them to the seashore, asking to remain in the house with only the gardener and one maidservant."

I asked Mrs. Ward if she was aware that Talbot might have used some part of the story in her novel *Matilda.*

Her gentle face looked puzzled. "That's odd. I've read *Matilda,* although many years ago. It was set here in the island, to be sure, and the young woman was a governess, but I don't believe I thought of the connection with my family."

I smiled. "Yes. I believe Mrs. Talbot was careful to avoid direct parallels. The novel was not written until some years after her visit here and was not published until 1886."

Now I asked the question so crucial to literary researchers, my heart doing a little flip-flop. "Do you know if any letters or papers exist dating from the time of the tragedy? If so, I should be most interested to have a look at them, with your permission."

Mrs. Ward sighed. "There are all sorts of old letters and photographs in the box room. I haven't seen them for years. When my helper comes tomorrow morning, I shall ask her to bring them down and have a look, shall I?"

"I'd be most grateful. I'm at the Farringford for several days. Would it be convenient for me to come back tomorrow?"

She smiled. "Yes, of course, my dear. This is all

rather exciting. Everyone who comes to this part of the island wants to know about the Tennysons and even about Mrs. Cameron, but our family has not as yet been the object of research!"

I thanked her warmly and walked back up the road toward the hotel, feeling I'd hit the jackpot in finding this wonderfully alert and charming old lady still living in the house visited by Talbot. Now, surely, all those delicious items in the attic box room would produce some clues that would tie the tragedy of the governess more closely to Talbot's novel.

As I climbed the stairs to my room at the hotel, I detoured at a sign that pointed to the Tennyson Library, a large room containing the usual memorabilia found in homes of famous persons. I browsed among the framed photographs of friends and family, the kneehole bureau where Tennyson had worked, the cases of books, and other items preserved for posterity. The great poems of his youth—"Ulysses," "Tithonus," "The Lotos-Eaters"—had all been written long before he came to live at Farringford in the turbulent days before fame had come to him, but the imaginative *Maud,* with its hero whose passionate love drove him to madness, had been written here and, of course, the grand epics of King Arthur and Camelot.

Back in my room I looked at a small map of the hotel and grounds and decided to go exploring. I knew that the summerhouse, now perhaps to be made infamous by Rupert Mortmain, no longer existed, but the brochure indicated its former location. I went downstairs, following a walk past a collection of cottages—part of the hotel accommodations—along a path in the woods, and across a small bridge to what Tennyson had called the Wilderness, where the summerhouse had stood, providing the seclusion he sought. It had always struck me as odd that, according to contemporary descriptions, the poet himself had decorated its walls with weird dragons and kingfishers flying through reeds. Was such exuberance an expression of a middle-aged man suddenly caught up in a love affair?

As I stood looking at the small clearing, I heard the crackle of footsteps in the woods and turned to see a man stop abruptly, then step forward with a mocking smile.

It was Rupert Mortmain.

He walked past me for several yards, then pointed downward. "It was just here. You can see the foundations through the undergrowth."

I gave him a stony look and said nothing.

His eyes charged up for a fleeting moment, then went blank again. "I expect my letters will set off a spate of pilgrims looking for the dear old summerhouse."

I felt anger surging up to my throat. He thinks I've come here because of his talk on the letters—maybe even hoping to see him again.

I kept my cool. "Actually, I'd booked this visit before I left the States."

I had turned away when I heard him say, "Did you, now? I see I was mistaken."

He stepped toward me and stood very close, exactly as he had done on the day of his lecture, his eyes intense. "I've been reading Mary Louise Talbot. She's rather good."

That stopped me. Talbot may have been a bestseller in her day, but today she was not on everybody's current list by a long shot, and I would have thought Mr. Arrogant would curl his lip at her.

"I understand you're doing her life," he went on. "Is that why you're here?"

Just as no mother can resist admiration of her child, no scholar can fail to respond to interest in her topic. I felt myself thawing. "Yes, she visited Freshwater in the 1870s."

"I see." With a swift movement, he touched my arm lightly. "Come and see the view from the Down."

He started off toward the path beyond the clearing.

Why not? I thought. Anyone who reads Talbot can't be all bad.

He glanced back only once to see that I was following, then led the way in silence as the path rose sharply through the woods, presently becoming so steep that steps had been cut in the nearly vertical hillside.

I stopped for breath, and he looked down at me, his eyes intense. "It's easier from here," he said, and indeed, the steps soon gave way to a gentle incline. Emerging from the density of the trees, we came out onto a broad, grassy meadow that crowned the hill.

Below lay the blue sea, winking in the afternoon sun, the white cliffs of the bay cutting like crescents into the green pillows of the distant downs.

I said softly, "It's lovely."

We stood in silence for a time. Then he said, "Come," and he strode off to the far side of the meadow, where a path led down toward the bay.

Again I thought, Why not? And pulled by an invisible cord, I followed him down the hill.

7

At the bottom of the hill, Rupert Mortmain turned away from the bay and went along a few streets into the village of Freshwater, while I walked meekly at his side, half amused, half fascinated.

Outside a tea shop, he stopped. "Shall we?"

I smiled. "Yes, please."

Suddenly, a childlike delight transformed his face, as if I had given him an unexpected but wholly welcome gift.

He found us a table in a corner, ordered tea and cake without asking me what I wanted, and turned his radiant face to me.

"Claire! You don't remember that we met before, do you?"

Surprised, I said, "No, I'm afraid not."

"It was at a large party during the Christmas holiday, in St. John's Wood."

Now I remembered the party, given by one of Iris's colleagues, but I had no recollection of Rupert.

He went on. "You were with a good-looking chap. Is he a serious attachment?"

I shrugged. "Yes and no."

He nodded, as if that settled the question.

"Now, tell me about your research on Talbot and why you are here."

I did. I was still talking when our tea came, and after three cups and two slices of cake—this seemed to be my day for cake—Rupert was still listening intently, interjecting questions about how Talbot had handled the young woman's story in her novel and how much we knew of the real-life incident.

Eyes gleaming, he said at last, "You do see that your governess with the mysterious love affair could be my letter-writer?"

I stared at him with what Keats would have called a wild surmise. "The lady in the summerhouse?"

"Why not? The letters are obviously written by an educated lady. If her lover was our friend Tennyson himself, she would most certainly have kept it secret. And nothing could be more hopeless than such an affair. Divorce was unthinkable."

Bemused, I said, "The dates are right. Talbot came to the island in 1874, and Mrs. James told her that the tragedy had happened some years earlier. In your lecture you placed the most likely dates for the letters in the 1860s."

"Exactly! When you consider how scantily populated it was here at that time, surely there can't have been all that many candidates."

"Yes. And the two families were on friendly terms. Talbot mentions in her journal that the highlight of her visit here was dining with the Tennysons. After the meal, Alfred read *Maud* with great gusto to the assembled guests."

"And the Tennyson boys would undoubtedly have known the James children and hence the governess."

I poured another round of tea and told him about Mrs. Ward and her promise to look through the letters in the attic. "They might prove to be quite useless. On the other hand, there might be something to confirm what we're looking for."

Suddenly, Rupert's brow lifted in the old supercilious manner. "Are 'we' in this together, then?"

I backed off hastily. "Sorry. It's your project, not mine. I'll stick to Mary Louise Talbot."

Testily, he said, "That's not what I meant."

But his eyes had gone blank again, dampening the brief flicker of our mutual enthusiasm.

I looked at my watch, exclaimed that I must be off, thanked him for the tea with a gracious smile, and walked quickly away.

Back at the hotel, I had a long bath, watched the news on the little telly, read for a while, put on a proper dress, and went down to the lounge for a drink. The tall windows gave onto the view of the downs and a glimpse of the sea beyond, which was said to have enchanted Alfred and Emily and confirmed their desire to buy the house.

After an excellent dinner, I strolled through the grounds, the weather having held so that I needed only a light cardigan over my shoulders. I tried to push away the longing for Neil, but the plain truth was that I desperately missed him.

Reason said to be fair, to understand his dilemma, but reason didn't compete very well with anger and pain.

I wondered about poor Emily Tennyson. Did she know what went on in the summerhouse, if indeed it did? The Victorians didn't talk much about sex, even in their private diaries, but the circumstance of an invalid wife who had two children and then no more probably told its own story. What made the Mortmain letters so sensational was that not even

Tennyson's most unflattering biographers had suggested infidelities on his part.

My thoughts wandered to Rupert himself. What an odd creature he was, all flattering admiration one moment, and eyes of reptilian cold the next. What if my governess turned out to be the young woman of the Tennyson letters? Would I want to collaborate with Rupert on the research? Not on your life. His moods were too unpredictable for my taste.

The next morning, after breakfast, I took my car for a long drive around the area, following the south coastal road for a time as it wound along the downs, skirting high cliffs that dropped dramatically to the sea. Eventually, I turned back and drove through the village of Freshwater, where I'd had tea with Rupert the afternoon before, then on to Yarmouth, on the north, where another set of ferries crossed to Lymington.

The island narrows almost to a point at its western tip, so that Freshwater Bay faces the English Channel on the south, while Yarmouth, only a few miles to the north, stands on the Solent, the strait that lies between the Isle of Wight and the mainland.

I found a car park not far from the ferry terminal and strolled into the village of Yarmouth, wandering through shops, buying a silk scarf for my daughter Sally, and treating myself to a gorgeous hand-woven tote bag I couldn't resist. At a pharmacy I studied the rows of hair tints. The mirror told me that while blond hair doesn't show much gray at first, it does start looking drab. Sally had said it was time to lighten it up, but I felt too lazy to cope. Maybe I'd see a hairdresser when I got back to London.

By eleven o'clock a warm sun had burst out of the morning clouds, luring summer visitors to outdoor tables for their morning coffee. I'd brought my copy of

Talbot's *Matilda* and settled in one corner of a café garden with a cappuccino and a roll, reviewing some passages in the light of what I'd learned from Mrs. Ward about the governess. Now and then I looked up, half expecting to see Rupert Mortmain materialize, as he had done the day before. He didn't, but I fancied I could see his face floating in the air like the Cheshire cat.

Talbot had certainly gone to some length to avoid parallels with the story confided to her by her hostess, Mrs. James. To be sure, the novel was set on the Isle of Wight, but the town of Freshwater was given a fictional name, and the only direct connection to Tennyson was a passing reference to a famous poet, also unnamed. Talbot wrote in her journal that the governess had had an unhappy experience in her previous post with a family on the mainland, and Talbot took this as the kernel of her story, developing it into her own creation.

In the novel, Matilda goes first to a family who treats her as little more than a servant, leaving her to deal with undisciplined children who make her life a torture. Only in novels like Anne Brontë's *Agnes Grey* had readers found such a realistic treatment of one of the social ills of the period. Matilda is then subjected to the overtures of the grown son of the house, who becomes so abusive when she rejects him that she is forced to run away in terror.

When she obtains the post on the island, the kindness of the family there fills her with gratitude. In the course of time, Matilda meets a local man, married, older than she. They find pleasure in a shared love of poetry, and gradually they fall in love. They begin to meet at a little clearing in the woods, where he speaks of the hopelessness of his love for her.

Needless to say, they don't "have sex," as they would do in any self-respecting twentieth-century novel, but the relationship becomes, in my view, more suspenseful, for Matilda is a passionate young woman who, through all the Victorian double-talk, is clearly tempted to give herself to him. It is the man who breaks off the relationship because he truly loves her and will not be the cause of her downfall.

In the climactic scene of the novel, Matilda, in despair from what she feels is her lover's rejection, climbs to the attic of the house, sees an open window, and contemplates throwing herself to her death. In the end, her courage prevails and she opts for facing life.

Talbot then gives Matilda the conventional happy ending, when she marries her first love, a young man she has known from childhood.

The bare outline of this plot might, with endless variations, be found in the dozens of popular Victorian novels that appeared each year. What set Talbot apart was not only the superior quality of her fiction but the adroit ways in which she undercut the social conventions of the day. Talbot went as far as she dared without losing the custom of the powerful lending libraries, whose policy was to reject anything which might bring a blush to the proverbial maiden's cheek. Needing the money for her growing family, Talbot was careful to prick with her subversive needle wherever she could, but within practical limits.

I sat stirring the dregs of foam in my cappuccino and wondering about the real governess. It was an intriguing possibility that she might be the writer of the Tennyson letters. From the standpoint of literary research, there was little doubt that Rupert Mortmain and I would both benefit from a confirmed identification of the young woman in question. For me, however, it would mean merely an interesting note on the source for the character of Matilda, while for Rupert, it would add substantially to his discovery of the

Tennyson connection, with its broad interest for the general public.

Eventually, I went back to the hotel for a light lunch; and at two o'clock, the time appointed, I walked down the road, turned onto the lane, passed Dimbola, and rang the bell at the house with the cupola.

Mrs. Ward greeted me with a delighted smile. "Oh, my dear! Do come see what we've found!"

She led the way to a sitting room, its french doors open to the garden, the floor a mass of boxes overflowing with letters, photographs, old dance programs, and albums of all sorts.

"I'd no idea there was so much, and my helper tells me there are yet more in the box room! I've been totally absorbed all the morning."

She gestured me to a chair and, looking pleased as a child, handed me a photograph brown with age, the edges curling. "I believe this is your governess."

I saw a full-figured young woman, her dark hair loose and flowing over her shoulders, her eyes alert in an appealing face. On the back someone had written. "Our dear May as 'Cordelia,' by Mrs. Cameron, Summer 1863."

Mrs. Ward said, "My grandmother remembered hearing her elders speak in sorrowful whispers of the governess as 'poor May.' From the date, it must surely be she."

I expressed my gratitude and asked if she had found any letters referring to the young woman.

"It's all such a muddle," she sighed. "Much of it obviously dates from recent decades, but there seems to be no order at all. Of course, some letters are tied in packets, and those would form coherent groups, but some of the ties have slipped away and the contents scattered among all sorts of odds and ends."

I had spent enough time grubbing through similar collections in the course of my research to assure her that this was more the rule than the exception. It was now time to approach the delicate matter of what access I might have to all this material. In the past I had encountered every variation, from those who urged me to take it all away before they tossed it out to those who frankly wanted a price for their treasures. More often they were pleased, as Mrs. Ward appeared to be, to be able to contribute to a bit of history, and this was indeed her response to my question.

"You may photocopy whatever you like, my dear, and if the originals are helpful, I shall ask my son if he has no objection, and you may have those as well."

Now, we settled down, with much laughing and exclaiming over various items, to organize whatever could be clearly identified into chronological order and to set aside for further examination the things that refused to fall into obvious categories.

By four o'clock her suggestion of tea sounded marvelous. We had been sitting on the floor for the last hour, and when I stood up, she gave me a rueful little smile and held out her hand. "One of the inconveniences of age is that once down, one can scarcely get up again."

I gave her my hand, and we went off together to the kitchen like old friends. I carried the tray to a shady corner of the garden, where we chatted amiably, agreeing that we had done enough for the day and that I would return in the morning for another sorting session.

Back at the hotel, I asked for my key and was given a message.

"My sister asks you to dine with us. I'll call for you at half past seven." Signed, "R.M."

That was Rupert, all right. No phone number to

ring if I'd been otherwise engaged. Half tempted to refuse, I thought, why not go? Besides, I was curious to meet the sister.

And I had a treasure to show him, for Mrs. Ward had insisted that I take the photograph of the governess with me to be copied.

8

P ROMPTLY AT HALF PAST SEVEN, RUPERT DREW up in front of the hotel, where I was waiting. Silently he drove the short distance to his house, passing through a residential area and turning up a long, narrow drive, through a dark tunnel of interlaced branches, to the top of the hill. Thornbury stood in a small clearing, so surrounded by trees that nothing could be seen in any direction. A lonely spot, I thought. No neighbors in sight.

As we walked to the entrance, I saw scaffolding along one side of the house, and the bay windows across the front were only partially painted. Bare ground, with builder's equipment standing about, filled the area where a garden would be.

Presented to Zora Mortmain, I saw that Rupert's sister managed to look like her brother and still be attractive. The long, bony facial structure was the same, but the hand of the sculptor had smoothed here and stroked there, producing a striking effect. The dark hair, gray-streaked like his, swept back in waves close to her well-shaped head.

Standing side by side, their height the same, they might have been twins. Perhaps they were, for Zora's eyes shot electric flashes toward me as she held out a long, slender hand.

"Thank you for coming on such short notice." Her voice was brisk, the apparent courtesy of her remark negated by the negligent tone that seemed to suggest that, of course I'd have come.

Rupert stood watching the two of us with an amused twist of his mouth, as if he expected we might entertain him by launching into armed combat.

Then he said, "Sherry?" and turned to a trolley, where he poured three glasses without waiting for my answer.

We sat in chairs, like the three points of a triangle, while I waited for the customary remarks upon the weather or the usual small talk: "Is this your first visit to the island?" None came.

I looked with some curiosity at the odd furnishings of the room: the shabby sofa—on which we did not sit—and the tables untidily laden with books, papers, and skeins of wool. Rugs lay here and there, unrelated to one another in color or design.

Perhaps any changes awaited the remodeling, I thought, remembering the scaffolding outside.

Zora at last broke the silence. "Rupert tells me you may have discovered the identity of the lady who wrote the letters to Tennyson."

I said, "It's possible. Of course, I have no proof."

Her eyes did a Rupert-like charge. "I'm the one who discovered the letters. Come, I'll show you."

Startled, I glanced at Rupert, who looked amused but detached.

I followed Zora up two pairs of stairs to a narrow passage, where she led me into a low-ceilinged room whose sides sloped under the eaves. Bits of abandoned furniture stood about: a bed with a worn mattress, chairs with arms or legs askew, a battered desk. Against the inner wall a brick chimney ran through to the roof, on one side of which an open door revealed a storeroom filled with odds and ends of discarded household items.

With the air of a guide revealing a sacred shrine, Zora stepped into the room, reached above her head, and carefully removed a loose brick from the wall.

Her voice vibrated. "They were here, locked in a metal box. No one had found them before. For more than a century, they had waited here—for me."

I did my best to sound reverent. "It was a marvelous discovery, indeed."

She looked at me with approval. Emerging from the cupboard, she came toward me, standing very close, exactly as her brother was wont to do. Then she reached out and lifted a handful of my hair, looking at it closely.

"You've made your hair lighter."

I smiled. "Actually, I haven't done it yet, but I think it's time to start."

She seemed not to hear me. Certainly, she made no response. Dropping my hair, she started down the stairs, and I dutifully followed. On the first floor, she opened a door to a room containing a loom and assorted materials for handweaving. "My workroom," she announced.

I'd noticed her handsome woven skirt and was grateful for a topic of conversation when we presently gathered at the dining table. The meal, when it came, consisted of pot pies from the microwave, a plate of sliced cucumbers and tomatoes, a good French bread, and plenty of wine. It was the sort of meal I quite enjoy, and I felt relieved that neither of them was revealed as a gourmet cook. Nevertheless, I expected the usual disclaimers, the apologetic murmurs about the simplicity of the menu. In fact, neither of them seemed to take any notice of what they ate nor to care for my opinion.

Asking about the weaving, I learned that Zora sold her woven products to shops on the island, and Rupert showed none of the arrogance toward his sister's occupation that I half expected. When I mentioned having bought my little carryall in Yarmouth that day, Zora said, "Yes, it's one of mine. I noticed it when you came in." She named the shop, adding that they did very well for her there. "They take everything I offer them."

Abruptly, without transition, Zora gave me one of her piercing looks. "You saw Mrs. Ward this afternoon. Did you learn more about the governess?"

I looked at Rupert, who said without inflection, "My sister takes a proprietary interest in everything to do with the letters."

I described the quantities of material from Mrs. Ward's attic and our efforts that afternoon to sort them out. I'd wondered why Rupert hadn't asked me about this on our drive to the house, and now I saw that he had evidently waited for his sister to have the pleasure of making the inquiry.

I added, "Mrs. Ward tells me there's yet more material in the box room."

Zora said, "What about the young woman?"

"I have a photograph, but we can't be sure—"

"Where? Did you bring it with you?"

I looked toward the sitting room. "Yes, it's in my bag."

Zora pushed back her chair and strode swiftly from the room, returning to thrust the woven bag into my hands. She stood over me until I came up with the photograph, then took it from me and studied it eagerly, turning it over and reading aloud the inscription, "Our dear May, as 'Cordelia,' by Mrs. Cameron,' Summer 1863."

Taking it to Rupert, she leaned over his chair while he examined it.

Now, at last, Rupert stopped looking detached and shot a galvanized flash at me. "Tell us about this."

I repeated Mrs. Ward's recollection that the name of the governess had been May and that the family had regarded her with great affection. I told them about the rumors of suicide, that papers had been burned by the young woman, that they had suspected a love affair but had no clue to the identity of her lover.

Brother and sister exchanged a long look.

I saw the problem. "If the governess is your letter writer, I can understand she would burn the letters from Tennyson to save his reputation, but why would *her* letters be here in this house?"

Zora answered quickly. "We *have* assumed that the letter writer lived here at Thornbury. We thought perhaps she asked for her letters to be returned to her, and hid them away here."

Rupert said, "If it *was* the governess, perhaps she knew someone who lived here and asked that person to keep the locked box for her. But why?"

I said, "Why not burn her own letters along with his?"

"Exactly."

I broke the ensuing gloomy silence. "Isn't it Tennyson who would want to keep her letters, not she? *He* may have known someone who lived here—"

Zora nodded. "It would have to be someone he trusted. No biography mentions any close friend living in this location, but we are scarcely half a mile from Farringford. He talked freely to people of all classes, if they interested him. It could be a person not important enough to be mentioned."

Rupert said softly, "After her death, he wanted to

keep her letters but could not risk hiding them in the summerhouse any longer. So he brought them here."

I said, "I haven't seen all of the letters. Is there anything to indicate the possibility of suicide in what she wrote?"

Dead silence. Then Rupert said, "No, nothing of that sort."

Going back to our earlier discussion, I asked if he knew who were the occupants of Thornbury at the date in question.

The old supercilious eyebrow went up. "My dear Claire, I've been working on that from the beginning. The records show that a couple named Wilson bought the house in 1847. The husband died in 1860, and his widow lived here until her death in 1872, when the eldest son took over. If we accept the 1860s as the date of the love affair and the writing of the letters, it would mean that Tennyson may have known the widow and entrusted the letters to her."

Zora interposed. "My theory is that the widow probably took lodgers, as the house is fairly large, and that it may be one of these who was the poet's friend."

We continued to speculate about the whole puzzle for a while. Then Zora announced she would bring the coffee and took off for the kitchen.

The summer sun had gone down at last, and in the dusk I saw the shadowy trees outside the windows, while the lighted room was dimly reflected in the glass. When Rupert rose and walked behind me, I could see his figure as he stopped and bent slightly over me.

Then I felt his hands on my shoulders, and I sat very still. His hands moved, his thumbs gently pressing at the back of my neck, his fingers circling my throat. Mesmerized, I felt idiotically that if he tried to strangle me, I would be unable to move.

Slowly, his hands slid back and I felt him gather my

hair and lift it. Then he bent and kissed my neck, letting my hair fall gently back into place.

In the glass I saw him move toward the kitchen, and presently he emerged with a tray of cups, which he carefully set at each place.

While we had our coffee—no sweet had been offered—Rupert behaved so precisely as he had before that I began to doubt my own senses. Had I imagined the whole thing? I looked at the window, where I'd seen his reflection as he bent over me. I put a hand to my neck, where his kiss had touched me, and the shiver that ruffled my skin convinced me it was no phantom.

When at last I rose to go, expressing my thanks to Zora, she looked at me oddly, as though she was not quite sure who I was. Then her face cleared and she said, "The photograph, of course. You'll see that Rupert has a copy."

She turned and left the room.

Startled, I looked at Rupert, but he made no explanation or apology, simply leading the way to his car. With a glance at the scaffolding, I asked, "Have you lived here long?"

"Eight years."

"Eight *years?*"

I couldn't see his face in the dark, but I recognized the tone of mocking amusement in his voice. "Yes. My sister often begins upon a project but rarely sees it to completion."

I suppressed the desire to ask why *he* didn't see it to completion. Not my problem.

Down through the narrow black tunnel of the drive and out along streets that skirted the village, Rupert drove in silence the short distance to the hotel.

He walked me to the door. No move. No embrace.

"Claire," he said, "you are going to Mrs. Ward in the morning?"

"Yes."

"Will you give me an introduction to her?"

I can't say I was surprised. He could have gone to her on his own, but knowing that I had established friendly relations with her would give him a better entree.

"I can ask her in the morning," I said, without much enthusiasm.

"Splendid! Here's the number at Thornbury. Give me a ring, if you will."

He handed me a card, said good night, and walked swiftly to his car.

Thoughts of Iris pushed me away from sleep for a long time that night. I'd tried for days to keep my grief under the surface, but it wasn't easy. I longed for someone to share my feelings, but the last thing I wanted was to talk to Rupert about Iris.

I wondered if the police had any leads. Probably not. Meredith Evans had promised to phone me if she heard anything new.

After a restless night, I woke to summer rain beating on my window. Fortified with a substantial breakfast, I decided to take my car down to the Beeches, short as the distance was. No point in getting any wetter than I had to.

Mrs. Ward greeted me with a smile, and we set to work on our sorting. I read through many letters from sisters and cousins to "Dear Letitia," the name of Mrs. Ward's great-grandmother, and at last found a reference to the governess.

"What was your grandmother's name, Mrs. Ward?"

She looked up. "It was Alicia."

"And in what year was she born?"

"I believe it was 1864."

"Then look at this!"

I gave her the letter. Signed "Your loving cousin,"

the writer congratulated Letitia on the birth of her "little Alicia," and remarked at how fortunate she was to have "May" for the elder children, especially as the former governess was "not all that you wished for."

Mrs. Ward looked gleeful. "How exciting! It does seem to confirm that 'our dear May' of the photograph was indeed the governess."

Eagerly, I read through the remaining letters in the box and found only one other reference to the governess, a comment upon the "lovely red tones of her hair."

I said, "In the photograph her hair seems quite dark, doesn't it?"

Mrs. Ward smiled. "You young people are accustomed to color photography. I remember the days of black-and-white, when red hair always appeared to be dark."

As she handed the letter back to me, I noticed that her hand was trembling, and her face had lost its color.

"Are you all right?" I asked.

"I do feel rather odd. Perhaps a glass of water?"

Sitting on the floor, as we had done the day before, she leaned back against the sofa behind her.

I hurried to the kitchen for the water, and when I returned, I found her lying on the floor. She didn't respond to my voice when I knelt down beside her, my heart pounding. I could see that she was breathing, but one side of her face was pulled downward.

Where was the phone? None in this room. Frantically, I searched the adjoining room, then ran to the entry hall, where a phone stood on a small table. A woman answered the emergency number, and I reported what had happened. When I started to describe the location of the house, she said, "Mrs. Leila Ward? We know the house. Someone will be there straightaway."

Of course, I thought, in a village, everyone knows everyone else.

I left the front door open and hurried back to where Mrs. Ward lay. I saw an afghan on the back of a sofa and spread it over her, holding her hand and making consoling murmurs, although I didn't know if she could hear me.

Within minutes, a brisk, fiftyish lady arrived. "I'm Beth Carter from the house next door. I was called from the station." She knelt beside her friend. "Leila?"

No response.

"Oh, dear. A stroke, I should say. Quite sudden, was it?"

I described what had happened, repeating it for the doctor when he came.

In the end, Mrs. Ward was taken to the hospital at Newport, the only large town on the island, and I took the neighbor's phone number so that I might speak with her later on.

It was still raining when I drove back to the hotel, heartsick and depressed. I sat in my room, staring out at the rain. I had a light lunch, did some reading, took a walk in the drizzling rain, and fell asleep on my bed, assailed with disturbing dreams.

When I awoke, I rang for a pot of tea, turning on the telly for the sound of voices. An hour later I noticed, lying on the table, the phone number Rupert had given me. I'd have to tell him I hadn't had a chance to speak of him to Mrs. Ward. He'd probably be annoyed, but I didn't care. I rang his number for the simple reason that I knew no one else on the island, and I wanted to hear a familiar voice, even if it was Rupert's.

When he answered, I found myself on the edge of tears. "She was such a dear lady. I can't believe it."

"Where are you now?"

"In my room."

"I'll meet you in the Tennyson Library in the hotel in five minutes!"

What on earth? In a daze, I picked up my room key and wandered along the corridors, up steps and down steps, to the room where the poet had worked.

I was standing by a tall window when Rupert arrived. Without a word, he turned me to face him, looked at my woebegone face, and gathered me in his arms, rocking me gently, pressing my head against his shoulder, his hand caressing my hair exactly as I had done with Sally when she was a child.

Tears for Mrs. Ward oozed from my eyes, mingled with all the repressed tears for Iris and for Neil. In the comfort of being held, I scarcely thought of Rupert himself, only of a presence that brought me consolation.

Finally, I found a tissue and blew my nose. "I hadn't yet spoken to Mrs. Ward about you."

"It doesn't matter."

"I did find something of interest, though. Do we know if your letter writer had dark red hair? The governess did."

He gave me an approving pat on the shoulder. "Good work! Yes, she mentions that our poet admired her lovely red tresses."

I managed a watery smile.

"Feeling better?"

"Yes, thank you."

"Good!"

He gave me a light kiss on the cheek and disappeared down the stairs.

9

By THE NEXT AFTERNOON, I WAS BACK IN MY
flat in London. The word on Mrs. Ward was that her
chances for survival were good, but recovery would be
a very slow process. Her son, who was abroad on
business, had been summoned to her bedside. Without his permission, nothing further could be done
with the masses of material we had been examining.
The neighbor, Beth Carter, had arranged for the
boxes to be safely stored.

There wasn't much more I needed to do, in any
case. It was Rupert who would benefit from further
research, and he had been remarkably patient about
the delay.

I checked out the messages on my machine. Sally
was enjoying France; there were requests to ring
assorted friends; and a woman's timid voice, which
sounded familiar, gave me her number and asked me
to ring.

Nothing from Neil.

Why did I keep hoping?

Pushing back the pain, I listened again to the soft-
voiced woman. Of course, the one who tried to warn

Iris that "he" knew where she was, then begged me not to tell the police about her call.

I looked at my watch. Three o'clock. The wife beater would no doubt be at work. I pressed the number and heard the woman's voice. When I told her who I was, she thanked me for ringing and asked in quavering tones if I had told the police about her call.

I said I had, and she sighed, then said it was quite all right, as she had learned there was no reason for concern.

Obviously, she meant the man had an alibi for the time of Iris's murder, but I decided to play it as unsuspecting.

"Since my friend died," I said, "it has meant a great deal to me to talk with people who knew her. May I come to see you?"

A pause. "I don't believe that would be possible."

"Will you come here to my place?"

Another pause. "I'm not sure—"

"Shall we meet somewhere? A coffee bar?"

"Yes, I could do that. Do you know the Sainsbury's in Islington?"

"Yes."

"There's a coffee bar across the road. I'll be there in an hour with my little girl. Can you come then?"

"Yes, very good."

And we rang off.

I answered some of my other messages. Angus MacFinn reported that he was working on Duncan the Dim to take up Iris's manuscript.

"He seems to be quite smitten with you, darling," Angus said with a giggle. "I trust you will make whatever sacrifice is needed in the cause of scholarship."

I laughed. "Up to a point, Angus."

I told him about the governess as a source for

Matilda but said nothing about the connection with Rupert and the Tennyson letters. The story would have been all over London by nightfall, if I knew Angus.

I rang Meredith at the bookshop and told her the news that I was meeting Iris's mystery woman at last and would report whatever I found out.

Deciding the other calls could wait, I set out for Islington, taking the bus to avoid the bother of trying to find a parking place. As the Number 38 lumbered up the hill along Rosebery Avenue, I remembered that this was the area where Iris had told Meredith she had first encountered the weeping child.

I got off the bus at the top of the hill, walked along the crowded high street, and turned along toward the Sainsbury's, where shoppers emerged, pushing loaded baskets. I passed assorted small shops, and at a few minutes before four o'clock, I came to a coffee bar and stepped inside, scanning the crowded tables.

A dark-haired woman, sitting at a table with a little girl, stared at me, then lifted her arm in a tentative greeting. I nodded, took my place in the queue for coffee, bought a plate of sweet buns, and joined them at their table.

She was a slender woman, pretty, and more poised than I expected. "I'm Joyce Hansen, and this is my daughter, Penny." The girl's uniform reminded me that school terms were not over yet.

I smiled at them both, giving my name and offering the buns to be shared.

When we'd covered the weather and a few words about Penny's school—she was eleven and in the top form of her primary school—we edged around to Iris. I explained that I'd been in the States since Christmas, and asked Joyce how long she had known my friend.

She said, "Penny met her first, two months or so ago."

The child nodded. "Miss Franklin came along one day and we talked a bit. Then another day, when Mum was not feeling well, she came upstairs."

Fine, I thought. If that was the version they wanted, I'd bide my time.

Many exclamations followed about Iris as such a lovely lady and expressions of shock and sorrow at her death. We seemed to be running dry when a school friend of Penny's came along to collect her for their afterschool club meeting.

Seizing my chance, I said, "I understand we couldn't talk freely with Penny here, but I do know from a friend of Miss Franklin about your trouble. May I ask if your circumstances are better now?"

Her soft eyes filled with tears. "Oh, yes. My husband suffers from a bad temper, you see, but often I am to blame. He doesn't like me to go out to work, and if I bring up the subject, he quite naturally becomes angry."

Clamping my teeth, I murmured, "Why does he object?"

"He believes it makes it look as if he's not a good provider. Also, he is inclined to be jealous and to suspect that other men may make advances toward me."

"I see. Is he Penny's father?"

"Oh, no. Her father died when she was five. I worked as a clerk in a solicitor's office until Kurt and I were married three years ago. I quit because he asked me to."

"When he is angry, does he strike Penny as well as yourself?"

Finally, a spark of defiance shot from her eyes. "No. He knows I will leave him if he ever touches her!"

I kept my voice low. "Joyce, you do understand that your husband's violence is beyond the ordinary? I believe my friend Miss Franklin urged you to get help, did she not?"

"Yes, she was most kind. But you see, Kurt knows that he is wrong to hurt me, and afterward he tells me he is sorry and is very tender with me."

Her deep flush told me that passion played a big part in these reconciliations.

"When he has been drinking," she went on, "he sometimes loses control. His father was an alcoholic, and Kurt has tried not to follow the same pattern. He has promised me never to have more than a pint when he goes to the pub."

Sure, and may pigs fly, I thought.

"Have you any family who can help you if—that is, if things go badly again?"

"No, I'm afraid not. My parents are in Canada, and I have no brothers or sisters."

"What about neighbors? Surely, there is someone you could call upon?"

Now she flushed again. "I've not made friends with anyone in the building. I'd rather they didn't know."

I could guess that one. With her genteel speech and manner, she was probably cut off to some extent from her fellow tenants. The women would think she gave herself airs, and she was too shy to forge common ground with them.

Moving closer to what I needed to know, I said as a statement not a question, "Your husband knew of your acquaintance with Miss Franklin. I expect he would resent any sort of interference, would he not?"

"Yes. He asked me not to see her again."

"When was this?"

She gave me a forlorn look. "Just before she—that is, before she died."

"That's why you phoned my flat to warn her that he knew where she was that day?"

"Yes."

"You were afraid he might harm her?"

"Oh, no! Not then. But I thought he might speak roughly to her."

"Then why were you concerned that I might have told the police about your phone call?"

"Don't you see? If the police came to question him, he would be furious with me for speaking to Miss Franklin after I had promised not to."

"But it's more than that, isn't it? When you heard she had been murdered, you were afraid he might have killed her in a fit of anger?"

She gave me a clear-eyed look. "I *did* think of it, yes, but I soon learned that it was impossible. Kurt is a driver for a haulage firm, and I spoke with one of the men who worked with him that day. Then I knew that he was at work and couldn't have been involved."

We sat in silence for a time while I swallowed my disappointment that I couldn't pin the murder on the revolting Kurt.

Keeping my tone casual, I said, "I'm wondering how you knew that Miss Franklin was at my place?"

"Actually, I rang her up at her home on the Tuesday evening to tell her that we must not speak again in the future. She was just going out the door of her flat, and she gave me a number and said to ring her there in an hour."

"At what time was this?"

"At about half past six."

That would be right. Iris arrived at my place as I was leaving, around seven o'clock.

"And you spoke to her later that evening?"

"Yes. At first, there was no answer. Then your machine message came on, and when I gave my name, Miss Franklin picked up the phone and we talked. She said she understood about Kurt, and she hoped I would get some sort of counseling if he became violent again."

"How did you know where I live?"

A pale smile lit her face. "One day I'd told her how much I had liked working for the solicitors in Bedford Square, and she said her friend Miss Camden lived there above a solicitors' firm. We thought at first it might be the same, but it wasn't. Mine was farther round the corner on the west side of the square."

"How did Kurt know Miss Franklin was at my place?"

Now the smile faded.

"He came in while I was on the phone, and he insisted on knowing who it was and hearing every detail of our conversation. He always suspects it's another man phoning me."

I could well imagine Kurt's method of getting her to tell him whatever he wanted to hear. Joyce was obviously an intelligent and attractive young woman. Did she have to tie herself to this clod?

I looked up to see a good-looking, fair-haired young man coming toward us. As he bent over Joyce, saying "Hello, luv" and giving her a kiss, I saw the logo on his uniform, a circle enclosing the letters GLH, which I recognized from seeing huge lorries labeled "Greater London Haulage."

I tried not to show my amazement at Kurt's appearance. This Adonis was the wife beater? Oh, dear.

Joyce made the introductions, and Kurt gave me an engaging smile. We did the weather for a couple of minutes, and I took off as gracefully as I could, hoping Kurt would make no connection between Claire Camden and Iris Franklin.

Dreamer, I thought. He'll work it out, all right, but if he really is a reformed character, I needn't worry.

10

On the high street in Islington I saw two of my buses lumber by before I reached the stop, and when a taxi appeared with its light on, I leaped in and sank back while the driver battled through the peak-hour traffic.

I'd read enough over the years about spousal abuse to know that wives often call the police at the time of a severe beating but rarely press charges afterward. Prosecutors cannot persuade them to come into court to testify, often because the man provides the only source of livelihood for themselves and their children, and sometimes because they love the man and believe, against all past experience, that his promises of reform will be kept. That was the trap in which Joyce Hansen was caught, and after meeting Kurt, I understood a good deal more than I had before. Who would believe that this attractive, apparently sweet-natured Dr. Jekyll was a closet Hyde?

Easy enough to blame the woman for allowing herself to get sucked into a destructive relationship. Here was Joyce, an intelligent and attractive young woman, raising a child on her own. How thrilled she must have been when handsome Kurt came along and wanted to marry her. A father for Penny, a lover for herself, and a man who wanted to support them financially as well. Of course she would quit her job if he wanted her to.

I could only guess at how things developed, but the big clue seemed to me to be her assumption that she herself was to blame for her husband's violence. I'd often thought men must be amazed at how easily they could convince their female partners that whatever happened was their own fault. How many generations of women grew up being told by their mothers that father was not to be contradicted, that his word was law, that it was their job to avoid making him angry. There were plenty of authority figures like policemen and judges to back up this attitude. Women like Joyce, by nature gentle and affectionate, were easy victims; but even strong-willed women were not always exempt from such deep-seated convictions.

Easy enough, also, to say to someone like Joyce, "Just leave him." But what of his threats to kill her if she tried to break away? I wouldn't be willing to bet on taking that risk. Such men did kill.

Back at the flat, I poured myself a glass of wine and sat in the window seat in my study, looking out at the trees in the square. The familiar ache of not hearing from Neil was there in all its irrational persistence. Wasn't I, in a different way, allowing myself to be a victim of my own passion?

I was startled to find that I'd half expected a message from Rupert Mortmain. I felt again his kiss on my neck as I sat at the dining table at Thornbury. And only last night we had stood in Tennyson's library, and he had held me and rocked me like a child.

Come on, Claire, you're hoping to hear from *Rupert?*

Well, why not? He could be wonderfully kind when he dropped the arrogant pose.

The phone interrupted this colloquy with myself. It was Meredith, wanting to know about my meeting with the Mystery Woman of Islington. I told her all. In the end, I said reluctantly, "I suppose we must tell Chief Inspector Dietrich about this."

Meredith groaned. "We certainly promised to let him know."

"Yes, but Joyce says her husband was at work that day. He must be in the clear."

"We can't be sure of that, can we?"

"No, I suppose not. What if he finds out who reported him?"

"He won't find out if the police don't tell him."

"Then, what about Joyce? If Kurt is questioned, he'll know she told someone something."

Meredith hesitated. "I do see the danger. This is a man who brooks no interference in his life."

We tossed it back and forth awhile longer, both of us knowing that, in the end, I'd have to report it.

I rang up the police station, left a message and my number, and in a quarter of an hour, the chief inspector was on the phone. "Mrs. Camden? You have the name and address of the party in question?"

"Name, not address. But I'm concerned that if you investigate, we might set off some problems."

Half expecting a stern insistence, I heard instead a mild "Mmm, I see. I'd be happy to listen to your reasons. When are you free?"

"I'll be at home this evening. Can you come here to the flat?"

"Yes. In an hour?"

"Fine."

I'd popped a pasta dish into the microwave, finished off my meal, and set out a tray with coffee and biscuits when the street buzzer sounded.

I recognized the chief inspector's voice, buzzed him in, and when my doorbell rang, I scrutinized him carefully through the peephole before turning the double locks on the door.

"I applaud your caution," he said.

I hung his coat on a hook in the entry. "I've always been pretty careful, but I confess to being rather paranoid since the murder."

"Very good. I'm constantly amazed at the people in London who open their doors to anyone who knocks."

I poured the coffee, and he sipped and nibbled while I ran through the meeting with Joyce Hansen and the astonishing Kurt.

Dietrich brushed a crumb off his fair mustache. "You expected him to look like Beelzebub?"

"No. I pictured a tough guy with bulging biceps and a swagger, not Mr. Mild-and-Charming."

He laughed. "They come in all shapes and sizes, Mrs. Camden. In my days on the force I've seen 'em all, as you Yanks would say."

Now, notebook in hand, he began to write. "Finding a Kurt Hansen who is employed by Greater London Haulage should present no problem. We can confirm his work hours for last Wednesday, and Bob's your uncle."

"You do see the problem there? Anyone who's asked about Kurt's activities that day will tell him the police are asking. No use pretending they won't. He'll put that together with his wife's warning on my phone to Miss Franklin and quite possibly with my meeting with her this afternoon."

"Yes, I do see. We can work with some finesse in cases like this one. An officer can request worksheets for several employees over a period of perhaps a week or two so that Kurt will not be singled out."

I nodded. "That would help."

He gave me an approving look. "It's very decent of you, under the circumstances, to let us know about this."

I shrugged. "I have a good friend in the CID, and I suppose I realize how important it is not to withhold information."

"Is your friend here in London?"

"No, in Devon."

Dietrich looked mildly interested. "My former chief went down there some time ago. They made him a DS—that is, a detective superintendent. Padgett, his name is. You might know him?"

Oh, Claire, you idiot. You might have known better. Neil used to say the service was worse than a village for gossip.

"Yes, we're acquainted," I said, trying to sound casual.

"Greet him for me, if you will."

"He's in Australia for some months."

"I see. In any case, I'm grateful for your help. We have no leads whatever in the Franklin case. We've talked with her son, with people who knew her at the university, with other friends, including of course your friend Mrs. Evans. Nothing. This Hansen chap is at least a blip of hope."

Knowing that I knew Neil had certainly opened him up, I thought. Maybe even made him more aware of keeping an eye on my safety.

Seizing my chance, I asked, "What about her husband? Has Owen's story held up?"

"Sorry to say, it has done. As you know, the spouse is usually a prime suspect, but the time element in this case seems pretty clear. You left the flat here at approximately nine o'clock that morning?"

"Yes."

"Right. Babcock arrived at the office in the Tottenham Court Road at precisely nine o'clock. The receptionist confirms the time, because she had just opened the office when he appeared. She remembers chaffing him about being early, as he's usually late himself. They all agree that he left there at about a quarter of eleven."

"What about his visits to the loo that he mentioned?"

"The young woman remembers his complaining about eating spicy food the night before and 'having the trots,' as he put it. However, she is certain he could not have been out of the office for more than five minutes at a time."

Holding my breath, afraid he would suddenly clam up, I asked, "What did the postmortem show as to the time of death?"

He seemed to have no problem answering me. "That's the crux. The victim had consumed coffee and some sort of bread or a roll only a short time before her death. Perhaps half an hour at most. According to your statement, Mrs. Camden, that was shortly before nine o'clock."

"Yes. Iris came out to the kitchen only a few minutes before I left. She poured herself a cup of coffee. I had set out some cheese Danish on a plate, and she was eating one as I said good-bye."

Dietrich gave me a mildly speculative look. "Exactly. The official estimate of the time of death is between nine and ten o'clock, but more likely the earlier part of the hour."

I frowned. "That does seem to let Owen off the hook, doesn't it?"

"I'm afraid so."

I poured more coffee, and he took up his notebook again, saying briskly, "Now, as to your identification of Kurt Hansen, even if he was not at work at the stated time—and remember, his wife presumably does not know the time of the murder, only the day—we have the problem of why Miss Franklin would admit him to the flat, knowing he would at the very least be angry with her."

"That's what I'd have thought, Chief Inspector, until I met the man this afternoon. I now see that he could have fed her a line about his remorse, perhaps even said he'd come to ask for her help or advice. He could charm the birds from the trees, if he tried. I believe Iris would have been willing to talk with him if he presented himself in that light."

"Mmm. Good point. We'll check him out. If he's in the clear, he should never know the check has been made. If he is not, however, you realize he will be questioned?"

"Yes, of course."

"Rest assured that we shall make every effort to keep your name out of it."

"Thank you. Will you let me know, if that happens?"

"Yes."

Now, with no change in his bland expression, Dietrich dropped his little bombshell. "I'm glad of this opportunity to speak with you, Mrs. Camden. It has been suggested by some of my colleagues that you yourself have the best opportunity to have perpetrated the crime. I have refuted this, since you appear to have no motive. However, we are having some difficulty with your alibi."

"My *alibi!* Then I *am* a suspect?"

"The old gentleman whom you visited in Ealing cannot confirm the time you arrived nor the length of time you were there."

I breathed with relief. "Oh, I see. Yes, the poor old dear was fairly dotty. He remembered the past clearly enough and was able to give me anecdotes about a collateral descendant of my subject, but I noticed that when it came to the present, his mind was not clear. That was why the interview took longer than I'd expected. I had to keep him from wandering off the subject."

"Can anyone else verify the times in question?"

"Oh, dear, I'm afraid not. He evidently lives alone. I believe a daughter looks in on him, but she was not present when I was there. I took the tube, and I saw no one I know, either going or returning."

"I have spoken with the daughter and she confirms her father's mental instability. Unfortunately, it leaves us with your word alone."

I shook my head. "I can't quite believe this. I suppose I ought to be frightened, but it seems too utterly bizarre to me that anyone would imagine I could have killed Iris."

He gave me a solemn look. "I agree. Without more specific evidence, I have declined to have you formally questioned."

I thanked him, and he went on. "Another odd thing has turned up in the case. In looking over Miss Franklin's bank statements, we have learned that approximately two years ago, she withdrew an amount of a thousand pounds *in cash.* Then, approximately one year ago, there was another withdrawal of the same amount, again in cash. Have you any idea what might have been the purpose of these withdrawals?"

Surprised, I said, "I have no idea. Iris had a comfortable income and very likely the usual savings account somewhere. I know that she and her husband had separate accounts, but why the cash? I don't believe she has done much traveling in the last two years, and even so, she would have used travelers' checks."

When he had gone, I paced around the flat, feeling caged and restless. Plenty of daylight left. I needed to get out and walk. I rang up Meredith, who said by all means come along, and twenty minutes later I was sitting in her flat, a cup of tea in my hand.

"So," I said, "now we have the theory that *I* murdered Iris."

Meredith frowned. "The CID prides itself on solving cases, and when they have a murder investigation that's going nowhere, they no doubt want to pin it on someone."

I nodded. "Yes, Neil certainly has had to rein in overeager officers who are sure they have the solution to a crime. I suppose police everywhere want to bolster their statistics and get personal recognition for successful cases."

"From the police point of view, they have only your word for what happened that day. That leaves them an opening to create their own scenario."

We agreed that I was fortunate to have an officer like Dietrich leading the case. At least, he seemed to want real evidence before he let fantasy take over.

I added, "Another odd thing came up." I told her about the cash withdrawals from Iris's account. "Do you know anything about this?"

"No idea."

When at last I got up to leave, I saw the lines of grief in Meredith's face. I said, "I know you miss Iris."

Tears blurred her eyes. "She was so charming, so bright, like a little star. At school she was never one of the bold ones, but everybody loved her."

Later as I walked back to Bedford Square in the soft dusk of the summer evening, I was haunted by the image of those two schoolgirls—delicate, dark-haired Iris and sturdy, downright Meredith. Both had been fine students, I knew, from their occasional reminiscences of their school days, Meredith also good at games, Iris admiring from the sidelines as Meredith captained the hockey team.

As I neared the flat, my mind swung back to my habitual thoughts of Neil, and I discovered they were interlaced with little images of a reformed Rupert Mortmain, shaping up, at the very least, as an entertaining companion.

A little variety would do me no harm, I thought.

11

FOR THE NEXT TWO DAYS, I GOT BACK TO WORK on my book project, going down the checklist of things yet to be done. I spent several hours on the *Matilda* material, drafting an account of what I had learned on the Isle of Wight about the governess as the source for the title character of the novel. The eternal problem was the balance of space. Mary Louise Talbot had published more than thirty novels, each of which received some attention in the biography. How much information on this book could I include in my text? Should some of the details be relegated to an endnote?

I tried out several versions, saved them all on the hard disk, and deferred the decision for the moment. Sooner or later, I'd have to go back to the island to get copies of the letters Mrs. Ward and I had located so far and to look for more material. A phone call to the hospital at Newport told me only that Mrs. Ward was "resting comfortably." By Saturday evening, the neighbor, Beth Carter, reported that the lady's son had arrived and that there was no change in the patient's condition.

"We've put all of the old letters back into the boxes," she told me, "and set them to one side."

Glad that my sweet lady was still alive, I thanked Mrs. Carter and rang off. It was much too soon to ask the son for permission to go through the boxes. After a decent interval, maybe.

In those two days, I did a lot of productive work on the book, spending hours in various libraries checking out references. For recreation on Saturday evening, I had a long phone chat with Sally in Normandy—forget the phone bill—and went early to bed, where I tossed around for a while.

Why hadn't I heard from Rupert Mortmain? And why did it matter? Did I really want to see him again? Well, yes, if only to see what he would do next.

On Sunday morning I decided to give myself a day off, with nothing on the agenda until late evening, when Duncan Dimchurch was hosting a party.

I spent a leisurely morning, dawdling over a late breakfast and reading the paper. There was nothing in the news on Iris's death. Since the first couple of days, the case had dropped out of sight. It would no doubt be news again only when the police found someone to "help with their enquiries," double-talk for having a hot suspect. I was glad my address hadn't been given out. Except for a few phone calls from journalists in the beginning, I'd heard nothing further from the press.

Reveling in my lazy day, I stretched out on the sofa with a book. An hour later I had dozed off, when the door buzzer jarred me awake.

Staggering to the intercom, I heard a familiar voice. "Claire! It's Rupert. Are you alone?"

My heart gave a flip. "Yes."

"Good! I'll come up."

"I'm not dressed."

"Never mind."

When I opened the door, he tossed his wet coat to me, strode into the sitting room, picked up the remote for the television, and tuned to BBC 1.

"It's about to begin. Come!"

I watched as he pushed the newspapers onto the floor and leaned back on the sofa, muttering irritably, "Come along."

Bemused, I asked, "What are we watching?"

"My program, of course. It was taped last week."

I couldn't help laughing. He was behaving exactly as if we had been married for years.

Running a hand through my disheveled hair, I gathered my robe around me and sat down beside him. "What if I hadn't been here? You'd have missed it."

"No, no, I've set the tape at my place. I was out and decided to watch it with you."

"You might have phoned first."

He gave me a curious glance, as if such a course of action had not occurred to him, and stared back at the telly.

I said, "Come to think of it, how did you know where I live?"

He blinked, then actually turned and looked at me for the first time. "My dear girl, you hand out your cards to anyone who asks. You gave me one the first time we met—at the party last Christmas."

"Did I? I don't remember."

"You did."

I stood up. "Look, Rupert, I'll just pop into some clothes—"

He snatched my hand and pulled me down. "Shhh! It's starting."

Arts Chat had been a Sunday staple on the BBC for ages. The genial host, a well-known columnist, collected a few spirits with controversial opinions and generally let them rip. On today's show the announced topic was Alfred, Lord Tennyson, and the proceedings got off to a good start when a heavily bearded poet, appropriately grungy, declared that Tennyson's work was absolute rubbish. "No one ought to be forced to read such claptrap today. It ought to be dropped from textbooks, for a start."

With an urbane smile, the author of a major critical study of Tennyson's work began to quote:

> The woods decay; the woods decay and fall.
> The vapors weep their burden to the ground.
> Man comes and tills the field and lies beneath,
> And after many a summer dies the swan.

The poet grunted. "I'll grant you a few good lines here and there, but when the hero of 'Locksley Hall' toys with the idea of taking a native woman as wife and then rejects it with horror because he is 'the heir of all the ages, in the foremost files of time,' I simply puke."

They went on trading quotations. When the poet offered the tortured convolutions of "The Higher Pantheism"—"Is not the Vision He, tho' He be not that which He seems?"—Rupert broke in. "I agree that bad Tennyson does not aid my digestion after a heavy meal, but we cannot forget the exquisite simplicity of 'The Lady of Shalott':

> On either side of the river lie
> Long fields of barley and of rye,
> That clothe the wold and meet the sky;
> And through the field the road runs by
> To many-towered Camelot;

I was startled to see how Rupert came over on the tube. His tone was arrogant, to be sure, but his lean body looked positively sexy, and the slightly mocking smile was engaging. I stole a look at the real Rupert beside me. It was like looking into a kaleidoscope and seeing all the same pieces take on a new form. With a mental shrug, I turned back to the program.

Now the host chuckled. "Gentlemen, you have amply demonstrated for us the battle that has raged in our century over Tennyson's verse. Would it be fair to say that what the Victorians adored the twentieth century abhors?"

The poet growled. "Absolutely. It's the incessant moralizing that turns one's stomach."

The critic smiled. "Poor chap wasn't priggish himself, according to all reports, but he was caught up in the spirit of the age. He says repeatedly that he saw it as his duty to 'teach' morality, a mission which today we regard with some distaste. Now we understand that Mortmain here may cast some doubt on Alfred's own conduct."

Rupert gave a few words of explanation about the letters from the young woman for the benefit of the viewers unfamiliar with their existence. Then he took a photocopied sheet from his pocket. "Here is a letter that leaves us little doubt, I believe."

"'My love,'" he began in a gentle tone, with none of the mockery he had used on the day of his lecture. "'My whole universe is alight with joy. Lying in your arms, feeling your kisses, so gentle, then so pressing, I felt that no other persons in the world had ever shared such ecstasy. I fear that you will suffer from remorse for what has happened. Please, please, my dearest, *never* feel anything but the joy of sharing our love. I was a girl. Now I am a woman, and a woman proud to know that I have been honored by your affection. I shall always hear your voice as you murmured the words from the exquisite lyric:

> Now folds the lily all her sweetness up,
> And slips into the bosom of the lake:
> So fold thyself, my dearest, thou, and slip
> Into my bosom and be lost in me.

I shall love you to all eternity.' "

Rupert carefully folded the paper and restored it to his pocket.

The silence that followed the reading of the letter was broken by the poet. "I for one am glad he was gutsy enough to do it."

The critic looked slightly dazed. "I confess it surprises me, though why it should do so, I cannot say."

The discussion moved to the sort of artists' colony that had developed around Farringford, including G. F. Watts, the painter, and Julia Cameron, the artist photographer.

The critic chuckled. "Virginia Woolf wrote a wickedly witty little play called 'Freshwater' for the private amusement of her Bloomsbury friends, in which Watts spouts high-flown pronouncements about art while his beautiful young wife, the actress Ellen Terry, drifts off with a lover; Tennyson pops up, reading passages from *Maud;* and Mrs. Cameron shampoos her husband's hair on stage."

With smiles and quips, the discussion went on for some time, when the host turned to Rupert. "Have you identified the young lady who wrote the letters?"

Rupert, the master of the enigmatic look, replied, "Not as yet. I have, however, a prime suspect. More on that when my suspicions are confirmed."

When the program came to an end, Rupert switched off the telly. "Thank God it went well. One always fears making an absolute ass of oneself."

"You were marvelous!" I said, and he looked at me in genuine surprise. "Do you think so?"

"Yes, of course."

He stretched out and put his feet up on the table. "Now, my pet, ravishing as you look in your dressing gown, it's time to dress. I'm ready for luncheon, and I know a wonderful little place in Richmond."

"But I had a late breakfast."

"No matter. You can eat again."

I stepped into the bath, half expecting to find him lurking about as I emerged. I wasn't ready for that, and I was glad to see he had stayed put.

The morning rain had given way to dazzling sunshine as we set off in Rupert's Escort. By the time we reached our destination, I had no problem eating again. The restaurant, overlooking the river, was excellent, and afterward we joined the Sunday strollers along the promenade.

When we stopped to look out at the boaters, the water shimmering in the sunlight, Rupert asked after my "Lady of the Letters," making consoling murmurs about her recovery.

"You'll be speaking to her son about the letters, will you?"

"Yes, but not immediately."

"Of course."

Having expected him to urge me to get on with it, I felt a return of the warmth I had felt that night in Tennyson's library. "I'll ask him for both of us, shall I?"

He turned, his eyes charged with intimacy. "Thank you."

On the drive back, I was drowsy from the wine and the warm sun and must have dozed, for when I awoke, we were in the square. Rupert had found a parking spot and walked me to the door, where he held me in a kiss that started out lightly and warmed up as I joined in.

I was thinking, Okay, Claire, make up your mind, and was about to ask him to come in, when he pulled back, kissed me lightly on the nose, and said, "Good-bye, darling. Lovely day!" And he was gone.

Back in the flat, I made myself a cup of coffee and sat, musing about Rupert and his oddities. Had I really wanted him to come upstairs? I found myself reliving the day, smiling, frowning, puzzled, amused.

An hour had gone by before I thought about Neil.

The invitation from Duncan Dimchurch had said, "After eight," which meant no one would come much before nine. Meredith, who was a well-liked figure among the local academics, had also had a card from Duncan. I met her at half past eight at the Russell Square tube station, as neither of us wanted to risk driving after an evening of even mild drinking, and Duncan lived conveniently close to the West Hampstead station. We'd share a taxi home.

When we emerged into West End Lane, still in the daylight of high summer, Meredith led the way down the hill and two streets over, having been there before with Iris. We followed other guests down the area steps to a basement flat, where Duncan was receiving with a cordial smile. As we approached, the smile faded, and his round eyes gave us a tragic look. "Darlings, I'm so glad you've come. We must talk, but later."

Meredith said, "What on earth's the matter, Duncan?"

"I'm not sure. I'm afraid there's something dreadfully wrong. Wait until Angus MacFinn comes, and we'll confer. Do go through to the garden—"

And he turned to greet new arrivals.

I said, "What can he mean?"

Meredith shrugged. "Duncan is such a fusspot. It's probably merely a trifle."

We collected glasses of champagne and went through to a small but enchanting garden, so exquisitely arranged that I had new respect for Duncan's aesthetic sensibilities.

Needless to say, Meredith knew more people than I did, and when I was introduced, the first questions were always about Iris. A lot of the guests were her former colleagues, some from her own department, some from other disciplines.

At one point we found ourselves in a group that included Professor Griswold, her department head. Someone was speaking enthusiastically about Iris's work on the court wits when Griswold pasted a look of regret on his complacent face. "A great pity the work was not finished. It would no doubt have been a splendid contribution."

Someone said, "I believe she had done a substantial amount of the work. Perhaps someone can complete it."

Griswold's smug expression didn't waver. "Yes, perhaps so. We shall see."

Sometime around ten o'clock, Angus MacFinn arrived, burbling with bonhomie, as usual. Duncan had long since given up his vigil at the door and was mingling with his guests. Meredith and I had loaded our plates from the food table, and I was on my third glass of champagne, when Angus oozed up, giving us each a ritual kiss. I was giving him the latest on my Isle of Wight visit, omitting any mention of Rupert Mortmain, when Duncan joined us, back to the face of gloom.

With a conspiratorial gesture, he said, "Come in here, you three, if you please." He led the way to what was obviously his study and closed the door.

Angus gave us a merry look and murmured, "I feel like the Third Murderer. Are we planning a crime, Duncan?"

The round eyes were solemn. "I'm afraid something dreadful has happened to Iris's manuscript."

Now Angus shrieked. "Whatever do you mean?"

We all sat down, and Duncan began his story. "As you know, I'd promised to have a look at the material to see if I might help. It was not until today that I got around to it. By yesterday I had everything ready for this evening. I needed to pick up some items from my office in college, and while there, I went into Iris's office. The staff secretary had already given me a key."

I remembered that Iris had done all of her research work in her office, as Owen often brought people home at all hours. "Impossible to concentrate," she had said. During the good times she had enjoyed the partying, and at other times she had an escape route.

Duncan went on, "I turned on her computer, found her files, and saw only half a dozen chapters listed. When I brought them up, they looked like early drafts rather than completed work. Then I tried to find the rest, and there was nothing!"

Meredith said, "She must have used a password."

Duncan shook his head. "We were chatting about that one day, and Iris said she never used one. She joked that she might forget the word herself, and besides, who would want to steal the stuff?"

I said, "She must have had backups."

"Certainly. The box, clearly labeled 'Backups,' is on her desk. There were three floppies in the box. I inserted each one and found only material for lectures and tutorials. There must have been others for the court wits manuscript, but I could not find them. I even searched her desk, feeling rather rotten, but it seemed important."

Angus assured him it *was* important.

Duncan looked at each of us hopefully. "I thought one of you might have a clue?"

We all looked back at him dismally, having nothing to offer.

Now Angus took charge. "It's possible she had

some material at home. Will one of you check with her husband on this? And, of course, query any friends who might know something. Duncan, you must make a thorough search of Iris's office. If you feel you need authorization, ring up her son and ask his permission. I myself will scour my own office. I've talked with Iris many times about portions of the manuscript, but I never keep drafts of that kind. Nevertheless, I'm confident we can solve this problem."

Duncan cheered up at once. "Thank you, all of you! I've been in such a state of shock. If I may have her son's telephone number, I'll have a look first thing tomorrow."

We all agreed not to despair, and went back to the party.

On the way home in the taxi, Meredith and I admitted to being less sanguine. I offered to see Owen to spare her the bother.

As we said good night at her door, she shook her head. "It must be a deliberate act. Someone actually wanted to destroy her work. But why?"

12

THE NEXT MORNING, AROUND TEN O'CLOCK, Iris's son, David, phoned me to say he had heard the news about the missing manuscript from Duncan Dimchurch. "I'm with Duncan now at Mother's office, Claire. Any chance you could lend us a hand?"

"Of course." If David needed a little moral support, I'd certainly be there.

It was no more than a ten-minute walk for me to University College. The morning clouds were lifting as I reached the campus, looking deserted now that term had ended. I found my way to the English department, where I had occasionally met Iris in her office. If painful memories tightened my throat, what must it be for David?

At the department office, I said hello to Mrs. Hester, the staff secretary, a plump lady of uncertain age, and got another testimonial to Iris. "She was a dear. Always patient and courteous, not like some I could name." And her eyes rolled toward the door of Professor Griswold, the department head.

David was sitting in front of Iris's word processor as I came in. I planted a motherly kiss on his head, and he gave me an affectionate smile. "Thanks for coming, Claire."

Duncan Dimchurch stood by a file cabinet, a folder in his hand. "We thought you might do her desk, that is, if you don't mind? I only glanced through it yesterday, as I mentioned, hoping to find computer disks or a manuscript, but the correspondence and the personal things—"

"I understand."

I set to work, noting that a carton had been placed on the top of the desk. Into this I put a marble penholder, a fine pair of Italian bookends, and other items of the kind for David to take away. The top drawer produced the usual paraphernalia of pens and pencils, paper clips, and so on, at which David, after a quick glance, shook his head. "Mrs. Hester will dispose of everything we leave when we've finished," he explained.

The lower drawer of the desk contained file folders of current materials for teaching: lecture notes, syllabi, and a file for each student in her tutorial for the term just ended. I checked that each of these contained only what the label said it did.

Then I lifted out a file marked "Correspondence," dating back a year or so. Among the usual correspondence on academic matters, there was the occasional personal letter. Like most computer users, Iris and I had joked that we no longer wrote by hand unless forced by dire necessity. I found her copy of a letter to myself, dated in April, and sudden tears blurred the page as I remembered receiving it, with its humorous account of two plays in the West End, one she hated and one she loved. Both of us were too busy to write often, and our letters were sparse and never personal. Only in conversation did we talk about husbands and lovers.

In the end, I put to one side all of the letters relating, at least tangentially, to her work on the court wits. Others were probably in files in the cabinet Duncan was working on.

One letter puzzled me. Dated the eighth of June, only a week before Iris's death, and addressed to something called Autographs, Ltd., it asked for an analysis of the age of an enclosed sheet of paper. Attached to Iris's copy of the letter was a blank sheet of pale blue paper, presumably a mate to the one sent with the letter. It looked to me like a good-quality letter paper of some kind.

I showed it to Duncan. "Might this have something to do with her project?"

He read the letter and studied the sheet. "I have no idea what it means, but I know little or nothing about the dating of paper."

When asked, David said he had no idea and didn't remember his mother mentioning anything about it. "Not that I'd expect she would, as we haven't met often during term time." He swallowed hard and turned back to the computer, causing me to exchange a glance of commiseration with Duncan before we returned to our tasks.

Wondering if there had been a reply to the letter, I went through the recent correspondence again but was hardly surprised to find nothing. It looked like the kind of thing that would take some time to answer, although, like Duncan, I certainly knew little enough about the dating of paper.

In the end, I put the letter with the other correspondence to be saved, and having finished the desk, I joined Duncan at the file cabinet, where I offered to help.

Duncan stood up, looking gloomy. "I'm truly baffled."

David turned and gave him an inquiring glance, and Duncan went on. "There *must* be a printout of the text somewhere, but I've made a preliminary search through the entire cabinet and found nothing. Now I'm going through each folder to see if there might be bits and pieces."

I said, "Her printouts ought to be in plain sight. It isn't as if she would expect anyone to make off with her work. All of us, I'm sure, do think of the danger of fire. I sometimes put my backups in my car, but it would never occur to me, nor to Iris, to be afraid of theft."

I sorted through the bottom drawer of the file cabinet but had no more luck than Duncan had, and in the end, we had to report utter failure.

David stood up and stretched. "I'm afraid you're right. On this end, it's hopeless. I thought I knew a few tricks with these machines but found nothing."

At a voice from the doorway, we all looked up to see the bland face of Professor Griswold surveying the scene. Duncan didn't exactly genuflect, but he looked at his department head with the reverence of a young knight in the presence of King Arthur, saying, "Good morning, Professor."

Griswold's voice was sanctimonious. "May I be of assistance?"

David, who knew quite well the history of his mother's treatment by this misogynist, gave him a cool look and remained seated. "I believe not, thank you."

Duncan burbled, "We cannot find any record of her work on the court wits, sir."

Griswold's brows rose to his hairline. "Dear, dear! Surely there are disks or copies?"

Duncan shook his head. "No, nothing. It's most distressing."

"Most distressing, indeed. A dreadful loss. Do keep me informed." Griswold nodded vaguely and oozed off down the passage.

David and I exchanged murderous glances but said nothing. Poor Duncan was at the mercy of this beast, but at least he had the advantage of not being a woman.

David said, "I didn't want to believe this could be a deliberate act, but I've checked all the backups, and there's nothing there either. Mother was a dedicated backer. We've talked about that many times. Either the disks themselves are gone, or the pertinent material on these has been erased. And if there's no printout, it means someone must have systematically destroyed everything."

We all now addressed ourselves to the bookshelves. David filled a carton with those he wanted to keep, and we put aside whatever related to the background of the Restoration period as well as to the poets of the court of Charles II. David told Duncan he may as well take the lot. "It's your line of country," he said, "and you may want them later on if we do find the missing text."

Now I asked David about checking out Iris's flat, in the hope that she had kept some material there.

"Actually, Claire, I'm not keen on seeing Owen. Meredith has offered to sort out Mother's clothing and other belongings on the weekend, but we really need to know now."

"Shall I ask Owen if I may have a look?"

"Oh, yes, please."

As we finished the sorting, Fiona arrived to collect David, saying a languid hello to Duncan and me.

David told her the status of the search for the disks and said, "Look, darling, why don't you have a go?"

Fiona shrugged. "I can't think I'd have any better

luck than you've had." But she dutifully sat down, her long hair falling forward as she turned on the machine, and began systematically searching the files while we packed up the books and other objects.

When we had finished, she shook her head. "Sorry, I've found nothing but some sketchy bits of early chapters."

David said, "Right. That seems to be it."

Fiona expressed neither surprise nor distress at the loss of Iris's work, and I found myself hoping, as Iris evidently had done, that David didn't end up married to this selfish and uncaring young woman.

Duncan said he would arrange for his share of the books to be transferred to his own office. Then together we carried David's cartons to Fiona's car. David thanked Duncan and me for our help, and we watched as he stood for a moment, looking at the building where his mother had spent so many fruitful years of her career. Then he sighed, climbed into the car, and drove away.

It was inevitable that Duncan should ask me to lunch, and he did. Discovering that we shared a passion for tandoori, we headed for Southampton Row, where I introduced him to one of my favorite spots.

Over lunch, I said, "Great party last night, Duncan. I loved your garden. I have a hopelessly brown thumb, but I like to look at other people's achievements."

He talked with enthusiasm about his hobby, but soon came back to Iris and her work, giving me that earnest, round-eyed look. "I suppose I ought to feel a certain sense of relief that I may not have to defer my own work after all, to attempt the completion of her court wits. But actually, Claire, I feel the loss dreadfully. She had talked with me from time to time about the project. She was keen, of course, to make it clear that 'wit' was used in the sense of the exercise of the intellect, not of farcical comedy, and she took the view that her poets were not trivial fops but rather sharp observers of court life and its complexities."

I nodded. "Yes, I remember."

Now, he talked about David with such concern that I felt again that escalating warmth toward him I had experienced that day at the Waldorf. Duncan wasn't really "dim," I thought, in spite of Angus MacFinn's wicked nickname. Not scintillating, perhaps, but a man of intelligence and character.

When Duncan asked me about my own work, I gave him a brief account of the source for Talbot's *Matilda*.

"You went down to the Isle of Wight, then?"

"Yes, last week." Too late, I could see where this was leading, and it did.

"Did you see anything of Rupert Mortmain? He lives down there out of term."

"Yes, actually, we did meet once or twice."

Now Duncan looked so forlorn that I said lightly, "Rupert's an odd creature, isn't he?" I hoped this would sound suitably detached from any interest in Rupert, but Duncan didn't seem to buy it.

"Some women find him fascinating, so I'm told."

I shrugged. "No accounting for tastes, is there?"

When the bill came, Duncan seized it with such a proprietary gesture that I hadn't the heart to offer my share. No older than I, Duncan seemed to belong to an earlier generation, to whom remnants of chivalry still clung like tattered banners hanging in baronial halls.

As we stepped out into a radiant day, I said, "I'll walk from here, Duncan."

Impulsively, I kissed his cheek before walking briskly away. I went along to the bookshop in Museum Street, where I found Meredith and filled her in on the morning's activities. I also mentioned the curious letter asking for an analysis of what looked like letter paper.

Meredith shook her head. "I've no idea. Iris said nothing about it to me, but remember, I'd just returned from holiday and saw her only once, before—before the murder."

"I'll give Owen a ring now about the disks. There may be something at the house."

Meredith nodded. "Thanks, Claire. The less I see of Owen the better. He's leaving a key for me on the weekend and scuttling off somewhere, to avoid me, no doubt. Another friend is coming along to help me with her things."

When I got back, I put in a call for Owen and managed to get a couple of hours' work done. Around half past five, I was having my pot of afternoon tea when he answered my message.

"Claire? How can I help you?"

He didn't sound too pleased to hear from me, but I ignored that and told him what I wanted.

In the tone of the computer expert who assumes the rest of the world is still writing on papyrus, he said irritably, "What do you mean, Iris's manuscript is missing? She has a hard disk, floppies. It must all be there somewhere."

"I'll explain when I see you, Owen. What time will be convenient?"

"I've just come in. Can you come along now?"

"Fine."

I took my car and made my way through the clogged streets to the Prince Albert Road. A few twists and turns brought me to the street where Iris and Owen had found the charming semidetached house, with its walled garden, eight years ago at the time of their marriage. I wondered if Owen would be able to

115

meet the mortgage payments without Iris's income, and then I remembered the insurance. He ought to be on easy street when that came through.

Owen tried to look pleased to see me, but his smile was more like a grimace. "What will you have, Claire? I'm having a brandy and soda."

"Just the soda, please." I didn't feel like drinking with Owen, and I didn't bother to ask how he was bearing up, but he told me anyway.

"It's been a bad time for me, Claire. Iris and I had our tiffs, as you know, but we truly cared for each other."

I gave a noncommittal "Mmm," and sipped my soda.

"How are things with your friend Neil?"

"Fine."

"Splendid."

Having exhausted his obligatory small talk, Owen got down to business. "What's all this about Iris's manuscript?"

I was about to tell him when his phone rang. As he went to answer it, I said, "I'll go on up, shall I?"

He nodded, and I went up the stairs and along the passage to the large room that contained Iris's desk, bookshelves, a lovely mahogany wardrobe, and a daybed.

It didn't take long to see that there was no manuscript printout in the desk, but that didn't rule out disks. The computer on her desk was an older model than the one in her office but obviously compatible, and similar enough to my own that I could bring up the files. I found her address list, a collection of tax-deductible items for the Inland Revenue, and a variety of notes on assorted topics, but nothing whatever on her research project.

In the desk itself a folder for copies of correspondence revealed some letters to friends and family, personal but not intimate, exactly as one would expect. She wouldn't keep copies if there were dark secrets.

The handsome wardrobe was filled with clothing, shoes, and lingerie, not winter things stored away but looking like things she would have been currently wearing. I looked again at the daybed, noting the nightstand with its lamp, telephone extension, and books. It seemed pretty clear that Iris was sleeping here, not in the conjugal bedroom. Not that that proved anything significant. Plenty of people slept in separate bedrooms and still had an active sex life, but put together with Iris's own remarks about Owen, it cast some doubt on his claim of their mutual affection.

In one drawer of the wardrobe I saw assorted items that reminded me of my own gift box, where I put things I'd bought for Sally or others until time for birthdays. In Iris's drawer were a small, leather-bound volume of poems by John Donne, a pair of gold cuff links in a jeweler's box, a pretty little evening purse of black silk with silver threads forming a floral design, and a silk Ascot tie in a Simpson's gift folder. What I didn't find in the wardrobe, to no one's surprise, was a computer disk.

As I gave a last, sorrowful look at the room and started down the stairs, I heard the double ring of the phone again, and Owen's voice, low and urgent. "No, not now. Someone's here." A pause. "I'll ring you back."

He didn't ask me whether or not I'd found anything, and I didn't bother to tell him. I could see that he'd forgotten why I came, and I was sure the voice on the phone was that of his current flame, whoever she might be. I didn't care to linger.

Back at the flat, I rang Angus MacFinn and gave him the final report, getting his wails.

"Darling, it's simply ghastly! We've announced *The Court Wits* as forthcoming next year!"

I was in no mood for Angus. "Surely, death is a valid reason for not finishing a book?"

"Yes, of course," he oozed. "But do take care of yourself, darling. Yours is already in the spring catalog!"

13

Later that evening I phoned Beth Carter, the neighbor of my dear old lady in Freshwater, and heard the good news that Mrs. Ward was showing marked improvement.

Mrs. Carter added, "Her son is still at the house, but I believe he's leaving tomorrow. If you give him a ring, he'll be able to tell you more than I can do."

I found the number in my book and heard a brisk masculine voice. "James Ward here."

When I identified myself, his tone warmed up. "You're the American lady looking at the letters? My mother is regaining her speech, and one of her first questions was about you. She was quite taken with you, I gather."

"I felt it was *my* pleasure to know *her*, Mr. Ward. Please tell her how happy I am that she is recovering."

"I shall. She will be in hospital for some time yet. If you wish to continue examining the letters, it can be arranged. Our household helper has been with us for many years and can give you access to the house, if you wish."

"That would be marvelous. There is another scholar who is also interested in the material." I gave him Rupert Mortmain's credentials, which were considerable, and added that he was also a resident of Freshwater. He said he had no objection to Mr. Mortmain's joining me in the search and gave me the telephone number of the helper, a Mrs. Lathom.

When I put down the phone, my first thought was how pleased Rupert would be to hear the news. My second thought was that I had no idea where he lived in London, no address, no phone number. I didn't even know whether he was still in town or had gone back to the island. Of course, I could ring up his sister, but why chase after him? If he wanted to know what was going on, he could telephone like any normal person.

But who said Rupert was like any normal person? Rupert didn't seem to operate with connections: a conversation, a meal, a kiss—all these seemed to him to be quite disparate events, with no sense of continuity.

When the phone rang half an hour later, I was irritated at my own disappointment when it turned out to be Joyce Hansen, sounding pleasantly excited. "I wanted you to know that I shall be working at my old job starting tomorrow!"

Surprised, I said, "That *is* good news, Joyce."

"When we met at the coffee bar the other day, I told you that Kurt objected to my going out to work. Yet that very evening he told me he understood he had been unfair and said I might look for something to do. Today I went back to my solicitors in Bedford Square, just round the corner from you, and they are taking me on for a partial day, from nine to three."

"And Penny?"

"She's nearly twelve. After the end of term, she can be on her own, and her friend's mother has promised to keep an eye on her, as well."

"Very good."

There was a slight pause, and now came what I took to be the real purpose of her call. "Kurt tells me the police have been asking at his workplace for the time schedules of the men over the past two weeks. Do you know if this had anything to do with—that is, with what happened to your friend?"

So much for the subtlety of the police, I thought. "I believe you said your husband's time was accounted for on that day?"

Her voice quavered. "Yes, it was. It's just that he wouldn't want to be chivvied about to no purpose, would he?"

"No, of course not. Perhaps the police were investigating something else altogether—a robbery, most likely."

She sighed. "Yes, I'm sure it must have been that."

No way was I going to admit to any knowledge of the case. "It's no good asking me, Joyce," I told her. "I have no idea what the police are doing."

She seemed satisfied with that, and when I'd wished her good luck in her job, we said goodnight.

So, I reflected, the revolting Kurt seemed to be sprouting wings. Had he really reformed? Surely, such characters did sometimes shape up, didn't they? I'd have to ask somebody who knew more about it than I did.

Another phone call—this seemed to be my evening for the phone—turned out to be David Franklin, bursting with excitement. "Claire, good news! I've learned that we may very likely retrieve mother's book after all!"

"David, that's marvelous. Tell me."

"A friend who's into computer science says there are disk doctors, as they are called, who have ways of bringing up erased material. I've spoken with a chap who does this. He's coming tomorrow to pick up

Mother's computer and the backups. He tells me that if the system has not been used much since the erasures, it should all be there. We assume she would have known the files were gone if she had used the machine after the deletions."

"Yes, of course. Then, whoever did this must have done it after—"

"After she was killed, or very shortly before. It was the end of term. She may have planned to wait until the holidays began before getting back to her project."

"I'm so glad, David. Now that you mention it, I have heard vaguely of experts who do this sort of thing. Somehow I imagined it to be obscure and impossibly difficult."

"Exactly. It seems that with the new technology, it's relatively simple. I've told Aunt Meredith and she's delighted."

When we'd said good night, I rang up Angus MacFinn to let him know the good news, getting his shrieks of joy. Duncan Dimchurch was less ebullient but equally pleased.

Glad as I was that Iris's work would not be lost after all, I felt haunted, as I had been all day, by the realization that someone had hated Iris enough to try to destroy her work. Was it the same person who had hated her enough to kill her?

The next afternoon, as I was leaving the flat, I saw a fair-haired child with one foot on a skateboard, making a slow circle on the pavement nearby. She gave me a half-expectant look, and I stopped, as recognition dawned.

"Penny! Were you looking for me?"

She flashed me a mischievous smile. "Only if you came out, I'd say hello."

Smiling, I remembered Sally at that age, the blond

ponytail, the winsome face. "It's good to see you, Penny."

"School was dismissed early today, so I came along to wait for Mum."

Of course, the solicitors' office was just along the square. I started walking toward my parked car, and Penny rolled along on her skateboard beside me.

"So," I said, "are you glad your mum will be working again?"

"Yes, it's what she needs—not to sit about the flat all day."

"I see. Will you manage on your own?"

She gave me a look that said what a silly question. "Of course. I'll do the shopping and the housekeeping. She's happy now, you see, as *he* is being kind."

"Your father?"

Sizzling fire from the blue eyes. "Kurt's not my father! Only my *stepfather.*"

"Of course," I said. "Sorry."

"That's okay."

I longed to put my arms around her, but I knew it would be wrong. Penny didn't want sympathy, she wanted respect.

When we got to my car, I held out my hand. "It was good to see you, Penny. Come whenever you like."

As I drove off, I thought that just as the children of alcoholics often become the parental figures, it seemed to me that a victim of abuse, like Joyce, would become abject and dependent out of constant fear and that Penny was similarly taking on the role of caretaker.

By the next evening, I'd still had no word from Rupert, and nothing new had turned up on Iris's missing manuscript. I was getting plenty of useful work done on Talbot. There was no hurry about getting back to the Isle of Wight to fill in the missing bits on *Matilda,* although it would probably be better to go while Mrs. Ward was still in the hospital, so as not to disturb her when she came home.

It was about eight o'clock when the phone rang. "Claire, it's Rupert. Have you asked if I have been approved to look over Mrs. Ward's material with you?"

With suppressed laughter at the understatement, I said, "Yes, I spoke to her son, and he seemed to think that an old Oxonian, now a senior lecturer at Kings College, would pass muster."

"Good. When was this?"

"I spoke to him on Monday."

"Monday? And this is *Wednesday!* Why didn't you let me know?"

Sweetly, I said, "I didn't know how to reach you in London."

"My dear girl, don't be daft. I'm not in London. I'm back on the island. You might have rung here."

"You might have said what your plans were."

A pause. "Oh, I see. You want me to report my comings and goings, do you?"

I giggled. "Not really."

"Well, then, come down tomorrow. You needn't bother with your car, as the car ferries will be booked, so take the 7:40 from Waterloo to Lymington Pier and cross as a foot passenger. I'll meet you in Yarmouth."

Oh, why not? "All right. I'll be there."

Let's face it, I hadn't booked any dates because I was pretty sure this would happen.

I rang up Meredith to ask about the cottage at Yarmouth, saying nothing about Rupert. "I thought I might go down tomorrow. Any chance?"

"Absolutely. The woman next door at number six has the key and looks after the place for us. I'll ring her and tell her you're coming."

My offer to pay was brushed aside. "We let the

place for two months in the spring and again in the autumn, enough to pay the rates. We keep the summer for ourselves and our friends. Iris and David used to come at least once each year."

I wrote down the address, thanked Meredith, and found myself humming cheerily as I packed my bag. A call to Sally to tell her where I'd be, another to Mrs. Ward's housekeeper to say I'd be there in the morning, and I was ready for the morrow.

It was raining in London when I left the next morning, but, exactly as it had done on my first visit to the island, the sun beamed down on the ferry as we crossed the Solent, sustaining the island's reputation for fine weather. Coming into the pier at Yarmouth, I saw how compact was the little village, clustering with its sharp-gabled roofs around the inevitable church tower, while the yacht haven bristled with boats of all description at this high season.

Rupert was there, frowning irritably. "You're a quarter of an hour late."

"I didn't actually pilot the ferry personally."

"No, no. I'm simply no good at waiting."

"Have a book with you; that's what I do."

"I *do* have a book, but the crowds are distracting."

By this time, we had made our way toward the car park, where he unlocked my door and hurried around to his own.

"Did you arrange for us to have access to the house?"

"Yes, but first I must leave my things where I'm staying. I have a friend's cottage here in Yarmouth."

Now he looked at me sharply. "We thought we'd put you up at our place. Zora's expecting you."

"Sorry," I said lightly. "It's very good of you, but this is already arranged."

Grumpily, he drove to the address I'd been given. I

suppose I had expected a picturesque fisherman's cottage on the seashore and found myself instead at the last but one of a row of narrow little houses with peaked gables, standing in the heart of the village, only two streets away from the main square.

The neighbor at number 6 duly let me in and showed me about the hot water and the space heaters while Rupert fidgeted. I took my bag upstairs and saw that between the rooftops there was a delightful view of sea and harbor. Already in love with the little house and its homely furnishings, I came down, smiling at the neighbor as she handed me my keys.

Rupert gave her a brief nod and hurried me out to the car. He drove at temperate speed, I was glad to note, into Freshwater Bay, along the lane past Dimbola and on to the Beeches.

Mrs. Lathom, the housekeeper, a motherly woman of perhaps sixty, was waiting for us. I performed the introductions and asked after Mrs. Ward.

"Coming along very nicely, bless her dear heart."

Rupert gave her a look of warm sympathy. "That is very good news, indeed. I have not had the pleasure of meeting Mrs. Ward, but Mrs. Camden has told me what a delightful person she is."

As we proceeded into the sitting room where the boxes of materials stood along the wall, Rupert continued to beam at Mrs. Lathom, who asked if we would like coffee.

"That would be most welcome," said Rupert the Charmer, without asking me, and Mrs. Lathom went off to the kitchen, smiling to herself.

I didn't rate the same treatment. He began to lift the lids from the cartons, saying, "Look here, Claire, let's organize our search. First, we need to find the letters you've already looked at."

Amused, I said, "Whatever you say, Rupert."

He looked at me oddly but decided to ignore the irony. "Do you recognize any of these?"

I saw with despair that all the piles Mrs. Ward and I had sorted had evidently been lifted at random and placed in the cartons. However, some batches were still together, and these were on the top, so that gradually I was able to reconstruct a good deal of our work. I found both of the letters that referred to the governess, the one remarking that the family was fortunate to have "May" for the elder children, and the other referring to the "lovely red tones" of the governess's hair. We set aside anything dated before 1863, that being the likely year in which the governess came to the island to take up her position with the James family, and sorted the rest according to dates.

We drank our coffee, nibbled biscuits, and became absorbed in our work, reading out passages of letters to each other and attempting to place keepsake items, such as drawings, sketches, and bits of inexpensive jewelry, in possible relation to information in the letters.

The bulk of the letters, as might be expected, dated from recent decades, but even these could not be ignored, for a descendant at any period might hear recollections of the governess and mention it in correspondence.

Mrs. Lathom, dazzled by Rupert, cheerfully brought us various containers to aid in our sorting. At one o'clock, she asked if we would be wanting a meal.

Rupert said, "Thank you so very much, but we have sandwiches."

"Right, then. I'll be going along. You're welcome to make tea, and please do leave everything locked up when you leave. Will you be wanting to come in the morning?"

"Yes, please. At nine o'clock."

When she had gone, Rupert opened his case and produced some wrapped sandwiches and a large bunch of grapes. "I'll make the tea," he said, and went off toward the kitchen.

We took our lunch to the garden, where I had sat under the magnificent trees with Mrs. Ward.

"Delicious," I said, savoring the egg mixture on wonderfully fresh bread. "Did your sister do these?"

"No, no, I did. Zora and I don't live in each other's pockets, you know."

Birds cheeped over our heads, and the sunlight, broken up by the trees, scattered yellow dots over the table.

"Gorgeous day," I remarked, startling Rupert out of some private reverie.

Blinking, he stared as if making an effort to remember who I was. "Oh, yes, yes. Fine weather."

Had I really expected anything else from him? I smiled to myself, thinking that nothing Rupert did, or did not do, should surprise me. When Mrs. Lathom left, I hadn't really thought he would clasp me in his arms and cry, "Alone at last!" On the other hand, after that passionate kiss on Sunday, some small sign of affection wouldn't have been amiss.

Instead, he said, with his familiar tone of irritation, "I'd no idea this sort of thing could be so tedious. All these women seem to write about nothing but the care and feeding of infants."

Now I remembered why I had thought him so detestable. Stiff with anger, I said, "If you became pregnant every year or two and gave birth to eight or ten or more children, you might find little else to think about. The ones who didn't die in childbirth could make it to menopause and die of cancer."

Instantly, his eyes charged up. "Good God, Claire, you're absolutely right. One knows that sort of thing and forgets the reality of it."

Why didn't he leave me comfortably hating him? Mollified but not quite forgiving, I swallowed the last bite of my sandwich, nibbled a few grapes, and stood up. "Time to get on with it. Come along when you've finished."

Meekly, he gathered up the tray and followed me into the house.

We worked through the remainder of the afternoon and found only one item of special interest, but this one put Rupert into a mood of exhilaration.

Addressed to Mrs. James from her sister at Newport, dated 21 August, 1865, the letter expressed the writer's distress on learning of the death of the governess. "Now, Letitia," the letter went on, "there is something perhaps I should tell you. When our Robert came to you this month, he awoke one night rather late, and looking out of his window, he saw the figure of the governess, wrapped in shawls, slipping out of the house. The night was not cold, and on an impulse, he put on his long coat and followed her. She went along the lane and took the path leading up through the woods toward Farringford, turning off toward the place where Mr. Tennyson has built his summerhouse. At first she seemed unaware of Robert's presence. Then, as the leaves crackled under his feet, she turned and looked back. Afraid of being detected, Robert stood very still, then cautiously crept back to the house.

"He is extremely distressed at learning of the young woman's tragic death and has confessed this to me, knowing that he ought not to have done what he did. I do apologize for him. During the two weeks of his stay with you, this occurred only the one time. I shall not tell his father, as I do not want him beaten. He is a good boy, as you know, and I am certain he will never do such a rash thing again. I trust we may keep this between ourselves, dear sister. The young woman may have been distressed about some personal matter and went out for a walk, although it does seem an odd time of night to do so."

Rupert was gleeful. "It was one thing for us to speculate that 'our dear May' might have stolen out at night to meet her Alfie in the summerhouse. This gives us concrete evidence!"

I agreed. "Mrs. Ward told me I might photocopy anything I wished. Let's take it with us when we leave."

By six o'clock we were ready to quit for the day. Rupert drove back to Yarmouth, where we made our copies on the machine at the post office. I declined his invitation to dinner, getting no protest. He left me in the village, where I picked up some basic foodstuffs in the shops before heading back to my little gabled house. I made a simple meal, spent a quiet evening with a book, and, lulled by the sea air, enjoyed a dreamless sleep upstairs in the big old-fashioned bed.

14

THE NEXT MORNING A DIFFERENT RUPERT ARrived at my door at a few minutes before nine o'clock. Fairly bouncing with energy, he greeted me with a cheery "Good morning, my love." A drizzly rain oozed from dark-streaked clouds overhead, so it certainly wasn't the weather that invigorated him.

At the Beeches Mrs. Lathom opened the door for us, then announced that Mr. Ward would be coming to stay at the house on the weekend—today was Friday—and if we wanted to continue our work, we'd best ask him. "He's ever so fond of his mother," she added. "He'll be visiting at hospital a good deal, I expect."

With that, she took her leave, explaining that she came "only the two mornings," and hoping that we might find what we were looking for among the old things.

We set to work at once. Concentrating on the letters dating from the 1860s to the end of the century, by lunchtime we had found several references to the governess, but none that added anything beyond what

131

we already knew. There was a good deal of amusing gossip: the schoolmaster's wife had left him and gone to live on the mainland; the underhousemaid had been seen larking about with the gardener, "and he twice her age"; the clergyman at St. Catherine's in Freshwater was becoming suspiciously High Church—"Incense, my dear, if you can believe it!" and so on.

We also found a number of photographs by Mrs. Cameron, in addition to the one of "our dear May." Many of these were of children, others of adults done up as mythological or literary figures.

Rupert and I had both been reading up on Julia Cameron, and now we compared notes, recalling that her family had given her her first camera in 1863, so that she was still experimenting with the medium in the first year or so. Yet she had felt from the beginning that her photographs should be works of art, not mere reproductions.

I picked up one of a man of perhaps forty, titled "Macbeth" and dated "1864." With his black beard and piercing, dark eyes, he had a look of tragedy that suited the character.

I said, "She loved to do people from Shakespeare, like this one." I held it out to Rupert. "Later on, she went in for photographing the rich and famous, but at this early period, she corralled anyone she could lay hands on and persuaded them to sit for her. She adored children as subjects, but how on earth did she get them to keep still for eight or ten minutes?"

Rupert laughed. "I expect those Victorian children were fairly browbeaten. I'd never have lasted without wriggling about, nor would Zora."

I had brought our sandwiches for the day, and since it was still drizzling, we sat cozily in the kitchen with our pot of tea, exchanging remarks occasionally about the letters.

Out of the blue, Rupert gave me one of his charged-up looks. "You know, my dear, you are quite enchanting."

I nearly choked on my tea and managed only a questioning eyebrow.

"I adore the way you look at me as if you find me amusing."

"I *do* find you amusing, Rupert."

"Splendid!"

When we had finished our meal, he said, "I'll do the washing up."

I left him to it and went back to the cartons.

When Rupert came in, I said, "Listen to this! It's to Letitia from her dear sister again—what a treasure that woman is—and she's referring to the discovery of the burnt papers in the grate of the governess's room. Till now, Letitia, I have assumed that if they were letters, as you believe they were, they came from someone she knew before she came to the island, but now you tell me that poor May rarely received letters in the two years she was with you. Then, surely the burnt letters could have no bearing upon her death. On the contrary, this seems to me to confirm that her fall was an accident and not what has been so wickedly rumored—that she took her own life because of a lover. Surely she would not take such a desperate step unless some recent event had occurred.'"

Rupert shouted with glee. "Yes, indeed! One doesn't expect an exchange of letters between persons living a ten-minute walk apart. But *we* know, don't we, my pet?"

I grinned. "I believe we do."

Putting the letter to one side, we read on, and by midafternoon we had finished the early material. I groaned. "I suppose we'd better tackle the twentieth-century stuff."

"You're forgetting something, love. Your Mrs. Ward

said there was more in the attic. There may be early ones there. Let's have a look first."

"But we haven't asked—"

"Nonsense, She offered to have them brought down, did she not?"

He was already at the foot of the stairs, and I followed him up three flights to the top floor. We passed rooms that had obviously housed the servants and came to a room filled with discarded odds and ends.

Rupert nodded. "Here we are, the box room. And here, my dear, is a trunkful of memorabilia."

But only the upper tray proved to hold letters and papers. When we had lifted it out, we saw that the rest of the space was filled with clothing, all of it in the style of the 1920s and after.

We sorted through the letters and found nothing earlier than 1918, and a quick scan produced nothing of interest to us.

Rupert closed the lid of the trunk and stood up. "Let's have a look at what your lady called the round room."

We found a small staircase leading up to the cupola, where a curved band of windows at the back of the house gave a dramatic view of Freshwater Bay, of chalk cliffs, and of the English Channel. The rain had stopped, and a pale sun was turning the water from gray to patchy blue.

We stood in silence, knowing this was the place from which the governess had plunged to her death. Then Rupert released the catch of the central window, seized the sash, and pulled upward.

No luck.

He pulled again, and the window shot open, bringing in a rush of sea-scented air. Rupert bent his head and stepped through the low sill onto a wide ledge, from which a gable of perhaps a dozen feet sloped downward. I came out after him and stood by his side.

Suddenly, I felt his hand at my back. Startled, I gave a little jump and felt my foot slip. In one sickening moment, I lost my balance and knew that I was falling. My feet went out from under me, and lying on my back, I slid slowly downward on the roof, which was still slick from the rain. Desperately, I reached out with my hands, trying to find something, anything, to hold on to, but the leads gave me nothing to grasp.

I felt absolute terror, as I knew that I would inevitably go over the edge, when quite suddenly my feet came up against a barrier that stopped me.

I lay perfectly still, afraid to move.

I heard Rupert's voice above me. "Keep still, darling. Your feet are on the gutter, but I don't know how strong it may be. I've reached down and I can't get near you. Don't move. I'll go for help."

I called out, "Yes, I'm all right."

I heard his footsteps running across the bare floors of the round room and down the little staircase.

I turned my head to one side and saw the board of the gutter running along the edge of the roof, a space of a few inches beyond the roof itself, just enough to make a precarious barrier. With one foot, I pushed it lightly and was not reassured when I felt it give way a fraction of an inch or so. I could see that it had once been white but had not been painted for a very long time. How much pressure would it take? I didn't want to put it to the test.

Lying as still as I could, I felt my heart give great lurches in my chest. I forced my mind to follow Rupert's movements. Now, he had run down the stairs. Now, he had reached the telephone. Now, he had dialed 999. Now, how long would it be before they arrived?

Remembering the day when I'd summoned help for Mrs. Ward, I tried to think how long it had been before they came. Five minutes? Ten? I breathed deeply, knowing that I mustn't panic.

Sooner than I expected, I heard Rupert's voice again, speaking softly so as not to startle me. "I'm here, love. I've rung up for help, but I've found something we might try. It's a drapery cord, very strong, and with a loop at the end. I'll lower it to you, while I put it round my waist and brace myself inside of the window frame. If you want to try it, I may be able to pull you up, because I'm not sure how long that gutter will hold."

In a moment I felt the soft silk of a woven cord drop near my chest. I put my hands through the loop and gave a tug. "It feels strong," I called out.

"Good. Shall we try a short haul?"

"Yes!"

I held the cord firmly with both hands, with my arms stretched out above my head. I felt the cord tighten, and my body began slowly to slide upward on the leads. The pitch of the roof was not steep. If it had been so, I'd have gone straight over in the first fall.

Rupert called out, "Shall I go on?"

Again I cried, "Oh, yes!" and within another minute or so, I had come up close enough to the ledge that I could turn and hold out my hand to Rupert.

He pulled me up, and I stepped over the low sill of the window and into his arms.

"Oh, my God, Claire. Oh, dear, sweet, lovely Claire."

He held me, crooning endearments, until we heard the sound of the doorbell far below and ran down to the entry to report that we had managed the rescue.

The man from the fire brigade clucked in disapproval. "Much better to have left it to us, sir," he said.

He insisted upon visiting the scene, and when we

stood with him at the window of the round room, he looked at us with understandable curiosity. "Whatever possessed you to step out onto the ledge, may I ask?"

We acknowledged our folly, apologized, and watched while, like a reproving nanny, he firmly latched the window, as if we might repeat our idiotic behavior the moment his back was turned.

Downstairs Rupert saw him to the door while I sank into a deep chair, my body shaking in the aftermath of fear. I heard Rupert rummaging in cupboards, and at last he gave a triumphant cry and emerged, carrying two snifters of brandy.

"I knew it must be somewhere. No British household is without its medicinal bottle."

I didn't bother with sipping but took a couple of large swallows instead, and the effect was soothing. Within minutes the shaking stopped, and a tide of warmth surged under my skin.

Rupert surveyed our cartons, all carefully labeled according to the dates of letters, with other items sorted largely by guesswork. "We mustn't risk having these mingled again. I'll take the lot upstairs."

I nodded, gratefully lying back with closed eyes while he made several journeys to the box room.

It was getting on for five o'clock when he had finished. Bending over me, he planted a kiss on the top of my head, saying, "I've booked us to dine at the Farringford. Would you like that?"

A landmark—the first time Rupert had ever asked my consent. I smiled. "Yes, I'd like that very much."

He left me at my little house, where I waited patiently for the water to heat and at last sank into a luxurious bath.

Later, in the elegant dining room of the hotel, with its tall windows overlooking the grounds, we lingered over the meal, chatting amiably. Why had I disliked

Rupert so much at our first meetings? I could scarcely remember.

Eyes alight, he said, "Our next step, of course, is the newspapers. There must be accounts of the death of the governess. Tomorrow we'll go to the library in Newport, shall we?"

Again, asking me, not announcing. I agreed. "While we are there, I'd like very much to visit Mrs. Ward at the hospital, if that could be arranged."

"Absolutely. Is there a phone at your place?"

"No, the neighbor relays messages, I believe, and there's a call box on the corner. I'll give them a ring in the morning."

Neither of us mentioned the incident on the roof, but our awareness of it was there. All through the evening I could feel his embrace and hear the echoes of his words of affection.

So it was that when we came back to the gabled house, and he held me in his arms, we both knew that he would come upstairs and share the big old-fashioned bed with me.

15

As we set off for Newport the next morning, halfway across the island, the sun shone innocently down as if yesterday's showers had never happened. Looking at Rupert as he drove, I smiled to myself. I didn't want to analyze how I felt about him. Enough that he was a charming and sexy man who was marvelous company when he was in a good mood. And today he was at his best.

"You've not been to Osborne, have you?" he asked, glowing with good spirits.

"Queen Victoria's house? No."

"There'll be time after the hospital visit. We can run up then, shall we?"

I had the feeling he nearly forgot the "shall we?" but remembered in time. He was trying, I thought. I'll give him that.

Newport, the principal town of the island, was the seat of the county council and of its reference library, where we were given copies of the Isle of Wight *Observer* for the dates beginning in the summer of 1864. We divided the issues between us, alternating dates, and Rupert was the first to find a reference.

"Here it is," he said softly. "22 August 1865."

Headlined "Freshwater Tragedy," the account simply stated pretty much what we already knew: that on the preceding day, Miss May Gordon, governess, had fallen to her death from a great height at the Beeches, the Freshwater home of her employers, the James family, who were away on holiday. The gardener had found her body. Only the underhousemaid was in the house at the time.

Then I found an account of a coroner's hearing held two days later on the 24th of August. The newspaper obligingly carried a detailed report of the proceedings, and Rupert pulled his chair close to mine so that we could read together.

First, the gardener described finding the body "all of a heap" on the gravel walk.

The coroner asked, "Did you hear anything prior to this?"

"May be I hear a cry but most like one of the dogs yipping."

The local constable was called and stated that at approximately three o'clock that afternoon he observed the body lying on the walk, directly below the central portion of the house.

"Were you able to determine the place from which the fall occurred?"

"I believe so, sir. I examined the windows on the second and third stories of the house directly above and found them securely fastened. Howsomever, the window of the round tower at the top of the house was open."

"It is your conclusion that the lady fell from there?"

"Yes, sir. We dropped a line from the gable there, and it pointed to the place where she were found."

The local doctor reported that he examined the body at approximately half past three o'clock and estimated the young lady had been dead for an hour or more. He had later performed a postmortem examination of the body.

The coroner asked, "Is it possible, Doctor, that death was owing to any cause other than the fall?"

"Most unlikely. The sprawling position of the body, the broken bones, the absence of any injury not consistent with a fall appear to rule out foul play."

Now the underhousemaid was called and stated that a lady had come to call that afternoon.

"At what time was this, Rosie?"

"I can't say, sir, but 'twere after luncheon. I told her as the family were away on holiday and only Miss Gordon were at home. She said as she would speak with *her*, and just then Miss Gordon comes in and says I may go."

"Now, Rosie, do you know who was the lady who called?"

"It be Mrs. Hendrick, sir, wife of schoolmaster."

"At what time did the lady leave the house?"

"That I don't know, sir. I went out to greengrocer, and she were gone when I come back. Later I hear gardener shout out and that's when we see poor Miss Gordon lying there."

Then the coroner asked if Mrs. Hendrick, the wife of the local schoolmaster at Freshwater, was present to be questioned. The police officer in charge of the case explained. "The lady is away on a visit to her family in Hampshire, sir. She left that very afternoon, accompanied by her children, and probably knows nothing of what has taken place."

The hearing then closed with the verdict of "Death by Misadventure."

When we laid down the newspaper, Rupert put his hand over mine and held it in silence for a moment. We were both keenly aware that *my* body might have been lying "all of a heap" on that gravel walk.

We looked through subsequent issues of the newspaper, finding that the item quickly disappeared. Then as now, a tragedy was no longer news unless something else occurred.

We noticed that nothing had been said about letters being burned. The rumors about a mysterious lover and a possible suicide probably floated about later on and faded away in the end, as such vague suspicions generally do.

When we left the library, we set off to find a place for a meal, sauntering along the streets, going in and out of shops that were open on a Saturday in deference to the tourist trade of high summer.

In one shop I stopped to examine a case of old jewelry while Rupert wandered down another aisle. On the top of the case a basket contained half a dozen evening bags in various styles. One caught my eye—a black silk shot with silver, with a violet woven in the center. Why did it look familiar? Then I remembered a similar bag in Iris's gift box in her wardrobe.

I picked up the bag, and the shop assistant smiled at me. "These are made here on the island by a lady in Freshwater."

"A Miss Mortmain?" I asked.

She looked at my tote. "Yes. I see you have something of hers."

I asked the price, decided to splurge, and bought it as a possible birthday gift for Sally.

At another shop I found an inexpensive paperweight with a picture of Tennyson, as a joke gift for Rupert, and over lunch, I gave it to him, getting a sardonic chuckle. He in turn offered me a blue ceramic brooch, "to match your eyes," he said, giving me one of his charged-up looks.

I showed him the little black bag. "It's one of your sister's creations."

"Yes, she's clever, is she not?"

I started to tell him where I'd seen its companion

and found that I wasn't ready to talk about Iris yet. Rupert and I bantered cheerily, both of us feeling the tingle of intimacy of newly minted lovers, but our relationship was too tenuous, I felt, for talk of death. Later, maybe, but not now.

As we sipped our wine, Rupert mused. "What did we actually learn from the newspaper accounts of the governess's death? There's nothing that actually confirms her as the letter writer, is there?"

"No, but we learned the exact date of her death. That in itself has to be useful."

"Yes. In any case, if we review what we have learned from the material at Mrs. Ward's place, it seems to me we have enough for a solid case, when we put these together with the governess's own letters."

He ticked them off on his fingers. "We have the references to May as the governess. We have the photo by Mrs. Cameron labeled 'May as Cordelia.' We have the reference to the 'lovely red tones of her hair.' We have the story of the nephew who followed her late at night to the summerhouse. And finally, we have the statement that she rarely received letters in the post, suggesting that the burnt letters are most likely those from Tennyson himself."

I grinned. "It seems conclusive to me. You should have enough material for a fascinating little book."

"Yes, I believe I should."

After lunch we went on to the local hospital, where I was pleased to see my dear Mrs. Ward for a few brief minutes. Her son was there, a distinguished-looking man in his fifties who asked after our research and assured us we were welcome to copy whatever we needed. My lady's speech was difficult to understand, but the smile in her eyes was the same. When I presented Rupert, she studied his face, then looked back at me, nodding and patting my hand.

When we were back in the car, Rupert laughed. "I

seem to have obtained your lady's seal of approval."
And he kissed me lightly.

From Newport we drove up the side of the estuary toward East Cowes, where Victoria and her beloved Albert built Osborne House, their holiday home, a century and a half ago. What had begun as a summer place turned into an impressive Palladian mansion, with extensive grounds leading down to the sea.

We paid our admission and joined the next tour, Rupert showing extraordinary patience, I thought, as we went slowly along corridors and through reception rooms filled with pictures, statuary, pedestal vases, and things under glass domes. When we reached the royal apartments above stairs, I was touched by the domesticity of the rooms where nine children had played and and studied and slept, and where devoted parents had obviously interested themselves intimately in their young lives.

Leaving the house, we strolled through the grounds and visited the Swiss Cottage, built as the children's playhouse, where everything was scaled down to their size. I said, "It makes one realize what a powerful effect the Queen had on society. She adored her Albert and regarded it as her primary mission in life to be a good wife and mother."

Rupert smiled. "Exactly. She fostered everything in the British soul that longed for security, for the home as the castle."

I looked at him curiously. "I find all this rather endearing, but it doesn't strike me as your cup of tea."

"No, it isn't, actually, but I like taking people about on the island. We've been here only a few years, and to the natives we are still 'overners,' but I've grown fond of the place. It's the closest I've felt to a real home."

I wondered if this was an opening to some confidences about his past life, but he looked away with the old aloof expression, and I decided it could wait.

Later that night, as I was drifting off to sleep, Rupert slipped quietly away, as he had done the night before, coming back in the morning.

He had proposed a sightseeing jaunt for the day, and I'd happily agreed. It was a Sunday, a perfect summer day, and he was in buoyant spirits, at his most charming and affectionate. We joined the throngs of visitors touring Carisbrooke Castle, then went on to the popular beach at Sandown, where we took off our shoes and picked our way along the coarse sand, through the throngs of holiday-makers, to wade in the cool water, with its shallow waves.

"Now for the Shanklin Chine," Rupert announced.

"What on earth is a 'chine'?"

"It's a gorge, carved out by the water coming down the cliff to the sea. It's really quite lovely."

And so it was. Out of the bright sunshine and wide beaches, we found ourselves in an enchanting grotto of dark trees and ferns, with little streams and waterfalls cascading down the steep slope.

"We'll have our tea at the Old Village," Rupert announced. Amused, I saw that he was giving me a standard tour, and I thoroughly approved. Enough to seek out-of-the-way spots after you'd seen the basics.

Near the top of the Chine, a street of thatched cottages straight out of a tour guide produced an old inn where we had a marvelous tea, and afterward, on the long drive home, he took minor roads through the interior of the island, past farms and villages, coming out at last at Yarmouth.

It had been an altogether lovely day, and I told him so.

I hadn't had much chance to shop for food, but I managed to make us a little supper out of the microwave, with a bottle of table wine I found on Meredith's shelf.

Afterward, we made love in the quiet comfort of

mutual fondness. I had to admit that Rupert was getting to be a habit I liked.

As he was leaving, he said, "Look, my pet, I've promised Zora to take care of some tiresome business affairs tomorrow, but she wants you to come to us for early supper. Will six o'clock suit you?"

Lazily, I murmured assent, and when he had gone, I smiled to myself and stretched like Scarlett O'Hara in the big bed.

16

THE NEXT MORNING IT OCCURRED TO ME THAT so far as my own research was concerned, I had more than enough to suggest that the governess, May Gordon, was the source for Talbot's *Matilda*. There was no reason to stay on the island when I really ought to go back to London and finish up my work. But let's face it, I was hooked on two counts: there was Rupert, and there was the mystery of the governess. Why did her letters turned up at Thornbury? Was her death accident or suicide, and would we ever know?

Over coffee and the last of my rolls, I picked up a book I'd brought with me and hadn't looked at yet: *Julia Margaret Cameron: A Life*. There she was, the ugly duckling among the beautiful Pattle sisters, but brimming with energy and self-confidence. Married happily to a man much older than herself, who had made a fortune in Ceylon, Julia's vitality encompassed her own children and a wide circle of friends. In 1863, when her grown children gave her her first camera, she quickly developed a hobby into a career that brought her unexpected fame.

As I looked through the reproductions of her photographs, I came to one that startled me and set me off on an investigation that took a good part of the day. I visited the local library and, after many inquiries, was directed to a primary school in Freshwater. The central portion of the building, I was told, had housed the first boys' school in the village, dating back to 1860. After much searching, the records of those early years were located, and I pored over them, taking notes.

In the late morning I had walked the three miles or so into Freshwater, having lunch before going to the school, but now I took a taxi back to my little house. By six o'clock I was dressed and ready to greet Rupert with the results of my research.

Twenty minutes later, no Rupert. I was about to look up his number when I heard a beep and looked out to see him at the curb. I picked up my jacket, left a night-light burning, and stepped out. He opened the door of the car from the inside, and I climbed in.

"Sorry I'm late," he said. No kiss, no endearment.

Oh, dear, I thought, we're being moody again.

I asked if his day had gone well and got a snort. "Not so you'd notice. Damn all solicitors. A pettifogging lot."

Silently, we drove through the outskirts of Freshwater and up the narrow drive through the tunnel of trees and foliage to the house. The barren patch of ground, the scaffolding, and the half-finished paint seemed even more forlorn to me than it had on my first visit. There was something slightly disturbing about an English home with no attempt at a garden, so universal was the general fondness for growing things.

Zora greeted me, if you could call it that, with a look so vague that I decided both must be upset over whatever had not gone well with the business matters that day.

She handed me a glass of wine and drifted off to the kitchen, where Rupert joined her, saying to me, "I won't be long."

Five minutes later Rupert called me to the table, where we had a delicious omelette, a salad, and more of that good bread I'd enjoyed before. The radio was playing soft pop in the background, and no one made any attempt at conversation. I guessed that this was their usual practice at the dinner table and wondered why on earth I'd been invited. Their silence seemed to me to be carrying eccentricity to an extreme, but far be it from me to break the spell.

Suddenly Zora looked at me and said, "What did you think of Osborne House?"

Startled, I said I thought it rather charming.

She frowned, glancing at Rupert and back to me. "You hadn't been there before?"

"No."

Rupert still appeared to be absorbed in his own thoughts and made no remark.

This was certainly no time to bring out my little discoveries of the afternoon. I'd wait till they were both tuned in, if that ever happened.

Suddenly Rupert swallowed his last bite and stood up. "I must be off if I'm to catch the next ferry."

Stunned, I stared at him. "You're leaving?"

"Yes. They're taping the next show tomorrow and I must go back tonight."

"Why didn't you tell me? I'd have gone with you."

He looked puzzled. "Sorry, didn't think of it. Stay here and finish your meal. Zora will see you home."

He walked swiftly out the door and was getting into his car when I caught up with him.

Sizzling, I shook his arm. "Rupert, are you crazy?"

He glared at me, and his voice was filled with rage. "Don't ever say that, do you understand? Never!"

The car leaped forward and he was gone.

Bewildered, I went back to the dining table and sat down. May as well finish the meal, I thought. There was nothing but milk and bread at the cottage. I'd intended to shop for food but hadn't bothered, knowing I would be out for dinner.

Presently, Zora laid a plate of chocolates between us on the table. At my first bite, I said, "Mmm, delicious."

"They're from Brussels."

"Oh, my favorites."

I smiled at her. After all, it wasn't her fault if her brother was totally weird.

She gave me a rather dreamy look, saying softly, "It's odd to see you here."

I raised an eyebrow. "Rupert said you invited me."

"Yes, of course I did. But I didn't know if you would come."

I didn't follow this, but never mind. We ate chocolates for a while—just what I needed to calm my anger at Rupert—and then I said it was time for me to go, if she would be kind enough to drive me to Yarmouth.

"You're in the same place as before?" she asked.

"No, on my last visit I was at the Farringford Hotel."

She shook her head, as if I had made a mistake that she would kindly overlook.

I stood up and carried my plates to the kitchen. "May I help with the washing up?" I asked.

"No," she said, "Rupert takes care of that."

"But he's gone."

"So he has. Then, yes, if you please."

What does she do during term time when dear Rupert is in London? Oh, well.

I ran the tap till the water came on hot, made a suds with Fairy Liquid, rinsed each dish under the tap, and put it in the drying rack, while Zora put the food away and took up the mats from the table. I dried my hands and applied some lotion from a bottle on the drain-board.

Okay, I thought, I've earned my ride home. "I'm ready, now," I said, in my best professorial tone, friendly but firm.

This didn't seem to have the desired effect. She gave me one of her vague looks and started toward the stairs, saying, "Come along."

I already had my handbag over my shoulder, and I stood my ground. "No, thank you. I really must go."

Ignoring this, she went steadily up the stairs, turn-ing to say, "If you please."

Evidently she had something to show me. I may as well humor her, I thought. It might even be something interesting. If she didn't take me home after this, I'd simply call a taxi.

I plodded up the stairs after her, all the way to the top floor. She led the way to the attic room we had visited before, where she had shown me the place the letters were found. Now what?

Picking her way through the clutter, she reached the far corner of the room where an old armchair stood a foot or so from the wall.

"Sit there, please."

I sat.

Now she bent over me, lifting my hair and dropping it, as she had done the last time we were there.

"Very pretty. So fair. But I wasn't deceived. I knew from the first it was you."

"What do you mean, Zora?"

"Did you think I would forget?"

Out of a carton beside her she lifted a dark brunette wig, styled in a short cut. Stepping behind me, she smoothed my hair back on my forehead and, in one deft motion, pulled the wig over my head, tucking loose strands of my hair under it.

She came back to face me, sitting on a chair opposite and nodding at me with satisfaction. "There, now, you look more like yourself."

I shook my head. "I don't know who you think I am—"

"Come off it, Iris. No good pretending."

Iris!

Stunned, I stared at her. "Do you mean Iris *Franklin?*"

"You know your own name."

"But, Zora, *Iris Franklin is dead!*"

She smiled. "Of course you are. Don't you think I know that? It doesn't mean you can't come back."

I started to protest, but a look at her eyes stopped me. I felt a rush of intense pity. Poor creature, she was mad as a hatter.

Gently, I said, "But Zora, Iris Franklin's eyes were dark. Don't you see that mine are blue?"

She waved this away. "I know all about colored lenses. You can buy them at Boots."

No good trying to reason with her, I thought. Better to agree with whatever she says, and then make my way downstairs.

Now she gave me an earnest look. "You ought not to have asked about the letters, you know. Why should you want to see the originals? Only Rupert has seen them. I keep them hidden away where no one will find them."

It was one thing for me to absorb the fact that Iris had been acquainted with Rupert and his sister. Now, it appeared that she knew about the letters.

Feeling my way, I hazarded a question. "Why should no one else see the letters?"

Anger flashed from her eyes. "Because they're *mine.* You asked Rupert if they were authentic, and you see, you were punished for it."

What *did* she mean by 'punished'? Horrified, I had a vision of Zora ringing the bell at my flat on the day Iris was murdered. Too absurd, I thought, but I lowered my eyes so she would not see the fear that for the first time crept into my body.

I longed to stand up and say it was time for me to go, but I was afraid to confront her. Zora was a head taller than I and looked pretty muscular, to boot. I wasn't about to take her on physically.

Now, her anger seemed to subside, giving way to a tone of contempt. "I expect you believe that Rupert loves you. Don't flatter yourself. He never stays long with anyone."

I almost laughed. Who would put up with Rupert for very long?

Quietly, I said, "I have no designs on your brother, Zora."

"You said that before, but I knew you were not telling the truth. You were caught in a bad marriage, Iris, but you would never have had Rupert. His wife will not divorce him. He will never be free."

His *wife?* That was a new one.

Who was this long-suffering lady, and why would she hold on to Rupert? Religious belief? Money?

Hoping to distract her, I asked softly, "Do you and Rupert have other siblings?"

"No, no. Only ourselves."

"Is he the elder?"

A look of satisfaction crossed her face. "No, I am, by five minutes."

"Then you are twins?"

"Yes."

"Are your parents still living?"

"No. Mama died nine years ago, and Papa soon after."

That's when they came to the island, I remembered.

"Did you live in London before you came here?"

The quick anger flashed again. "Never you mind where I lived."

Oops! I ignored this and went on in what I hoped was a soothing tone. "Rupert seems fond of the island."

This went over well. Her eyes lighted. "Yes. It's his home now."

Seizing the moment, I stood up, leaving the wig in place so as not to distress her. "Well, Zora, I believe it's time for me to go now."

"No, Iris," she said calmly. "You must stay here. I can't have you upsetting things."

"I promise you—"

At that, her fist shot out and she pushed me hard in the chest so that I fell back into the chair. "You'll stay here, I tell you."

She walked swiftly across the room and closed the door behind her. I got up to follow her when I heard the sound of a key turning in the lock.

"Zora!" I called out, running to the door and pounding on it. "This is ridiculous. Please unlock the door."

No answer. Then I heard her footsteps receding down the uncarpeted stairs.

17

WHEN I FIRST FOUND MYSELF LOCKED IN THE attic room, I was sure Zora would come back in an hour or so, if only to check on her captive, and I made a plan for escape. When I heard her footsteps, I'd crouch behind an old bureau that stood against the wall by the door. When she came into the room, looking for me, I'd dart out and run down the stairs.

It was a great plan. The problem was, she didn't come.

At first, I wandered around the room, catching a glimpse of myself in a cracked mirror, with the bizarre black wig on my head. I pulled it off, shuddering at the thought of how seriously disturbed Zora must be to believe I was Iris Franklin. But she couldn't be homicidal, could she? Wouldn't this have shown up earlier in her life? And wouldn't Rupert know?

In the corner where Zora had ordered me to sit, a small chest stood against the wall, its marble top cracked and chipped. In the center on a cloth stood a basin, a pitcher, and a water glass. Peering into the pitcher, I saw that it was filled with water.

Farther along the same wall stood a cot, and now I saw that it had been made up and turned back at the top, where a pillow lay, ready for use. With so many empty bedrooms, why use this for a guest room?

The answer to that was plain enough. *The whole thing had been prepared for me.*

Zora had known that Rupert was leaving for the mainland, although nobody had bothered to tell me about it. Or was that why Rupert didn't tell me? Was he a party to this charade?

I could believe almost anything about Rupert, but one thing I knew. He certainly didn't think I was Iris. What would he have to gain by this absurd plot?

Now I made a careful circuit of the room, looking for any means of escape. I checked out the cupboard where Zora had found the letters, feeling along the adjoining walls for a door but finding nothing. The only hope was the windows, one on each side of the room, under the steeply sloping ceiling. The room I occupied was above the front of the house, the one window looking out toward a wilderness of trees and shrubbery that crowded up close to the house, the other overlooking the drive and the cleared space at the front. It was here that the scaffolding stood, and my heart gave a leap as I saw that it was within reach of the window. A closer look, however, revealed that its metal bars were dark with rust, and there were no planks across the struts. It must have been there for ages, abandoned, only the bare framework remaining.

There was no way out. I may as well settle in and make the best of it.

Easier said than done. I wandered restlessly around the room again, idly looking through boxes of discarded clothing, wondering if there might be old letters like the ones in Mrs. Ward's place. Nothing.

Not far from the door of the storage cupboard stood a battered desk. I pulled down the hinged flap and saw only a stack of writing paper, a bottle of ink, a pen, and a supply of steel nibs. No wonder these were consigned to the attic. Nobody had used steel nibs for decades, certainly not since fountain pens and ball-points came in.

Then it all came together. Iris had been here. She had seen this desk. She had asked to see the originals of the letters. She had asked Rupert if they had been authenticated.

Why?

She suspected that Zora had written the letters herself!

I picked up a sheet of the pale blue writing paper. Yes, it could be the same as the one in Iris's office, the mate to the one she had sent off for analysis.

I found a rickety chair and sat down, put a nib into the pen, and opened the ink bottle. On a sheet of the paper I wrote my name a few times, noting how difficult it was to write smoothly. I thought of the volumes of letters written by people in earlier times with these unhandy implements, impressed again with their incredible energy.

When the ink had dried, I folded the sheet on which I had written and walked over to the corner, where my handbag lay on the floor by the armchair. I put the folded paper away and sank into the chair, mulling over the possibilities.

Iris had been here and seen the desk? Yes, that was easy enough. She and Rupert were not only acquainted but perhaps had been lovers. Zora thought so, anyhow. Iris came to the island, stayed in Marjorie's cottage, came to dinner here at Thornbury. Zora took her up here to the attic to show her the place where the letters were found. The desk is standing nearby, the flap open. Iris sees it and begins to wonder.

Then what? She comes here with Rupert one day

when Zora is out and dashes upstairs to take a sample of paper and ink.

But why would Zora leave the desk open?

Because she had no idea anyone would suspect. It was only afterward that Iris asked those significant questions.

Next problem: what happens to the "governess theory"? There *was* a governess who evidently went through the woods at night to the summerhouse. Had Zora heard the rumors dating from that long-ago time and invented love letters to suit the case? Involving Tennyson himself as the suspected lover would certainly make them intensely interesting to scholars, and probably valuable on the market, as well. The problem there was that if the letters went to an auction house, they would be subjected to severe scrutiny. Would they pass such a test?

I got up and wandered to the tree-covered window. How did I feel about Iris and Rupert having perhaps been lovers? Oddly enough, I rather hoped it was true. It made me feel close to Iris, an experience we had shared. I was sure she would have found Rupert alternately amusing and exasperating, as I did. I was equally sure she would have found him an exciting lover but not someone she would want around for the long term.

With a shrug, I turned back to my chair, pulling out from my handbag the paperback I always carried with me. A new mystery novel by an English woman writer I hadn't read before, it held my interest until the light began to fade. I looked at my watch. Half past ten o'clock. The long summer day was at last coming to a close.

I stood by the window again, seeing a faint light on the greenery far below. Zora was still awake. Surely, she would come up to me before retiring for the night.

Suddenly the light downstairs went out. This was my chance. I sprinted over to the door, standing beyond the bureau, listening for footsteps. None came.

In a few minutes I heard what might have been a door closing down below. Then silence.

I pressed a light switch by the door and was pleased to see a small, unshaded bulb come to life in the center of the room. I wasn't keen on spending the night in total darkness. May as well go to bed, I thought. I'd spotted an old commode in another corner and gratefully made use of it before taking off my shoes and stretching out on the cot.

Getting to sleep was another matter. A replay of the weird events of the day ran relentlessly through my head, raising troubling questions. If Zora believed I was Iris, why did she bring me upstairs on my first visit here to show me where she'd found the letters? Presumbly, she had already shown Iris the place.

Maybe because Rupert didn't know about her fantasy that I was someone else. It was only when we were alone that evening that she touched my hair and said I had "lightened it."

Running like a leitmotiv through the puzzle was a thought that jerked me awake each time I started to drift into sleep: *If Zora believes I'm Iris, I'm already dead. Killing me now would not be murder in her eyes.*

Would her twisted logic work that way? Who could say?

I must finally have slept, because it was daylight when I opened my eyes.

My first thought was to wake up Zora and insist she let me go. The despair of the night before was gone, and I felt ready for anything. Why had I been so frightened?

I certainly didn't intend to wait around here till

Rupert came back. He might stay in London for days, and would he notice I wasn't around? I wouldn't bet on it.

I put my shoes on, rummaged in my handbag for a comb, and ran it through my tangled hair, not for appearance but for comfort. I poured water in the basin and washed my face and hands, drying on the towel Zora had thoughtfully provided. At least, she believed her ghost had corporeal form.

Now I picked up a heavy bronze paperweight from a collection of discards and used it to pound on the door of the attic, pausing only to listen for footsteps. The paperweight wouldn't be a bad weapon, for that matter, if things got to that point.

I kept up the pounding for what seemed a fair amount of time, calling out her name at the top of my voice now and then.

Silence.

At last I gave up and went back to the window where the branches of a huge chestnut brushed against the glass.

With no warning, I heard the key turn in the lock. Frozen with surprise, I stared across the room as the door opened.

Zora stood in the doorway in stockinged feet, looking at me with disapproval. "Really, Iris, you must stop making this racket. You are not leaving here, do you understand?"

Now I moved toward her. "Zora, please, I have no wish to tell anyone anything—"

She looked at me quite calmly, pulling her arm from behind her back. In her hand was a large kitchen knife. "Don't be tiresome, Iris. I don't want any unpleasantness unless it is necessary."

She stepped back, closing the door, and the key turned in the lock.

All the fear of the night before rushed back in full

force. I shook for a while. It's strange how that kind of fear can make your mind go blank. I felt utterly helpless, and I sank down in the chair, staring into space. Then I did something that sounds weird to me now but was involuntary at the time. I lay down on the cot and curled up under the covers. Some kind of fetal instinct, I guess, according to psychologists. I only knew that I felt safer that way.

How long I lay there, I don't remember. I know that I was pulled out of my trance by the sound of a car down below.

Leaping to the far window, I looked down in time to see Zora backing a small gray car and heading down the drive.

Now, my adrenaline surged up. Through the glass I saw the rusty scaffold. I released the catch on the window and pulled up on the sash. It probably hadn't been opened for years, and it wasn't ready to give up now, but I kept at it until I felt a slight give. I pounded along the sides of the sash with the paperweight to loosen it, pulled again, and up it went.

Heady with joy, I reached out and grasped the vertical bar of the scaffold at the end next to the window. The remainder of the structure stretched away to my right, beyond my reach. As I pulled, the scaffold leaned in toward me, then swayed away. Not very promising, but I'd try anything to get away.

Holding firmly to the window frame, I put one leg over the sill and stepped onto the bar that crossed a foot or so below. Tentatively, I shifted my weight onto the bar and felt the sickening tilt of the whole structure. It had obviously stood too long in the soil, and without support, it would never hold my weight. I looked down at the hard, bare ground on which I would fall. No way.

I rushed back to the other window and managed to get it open after the same fashion as the first. I studied the old chestnut tree in front of me, and hope rose again.

As a child, I'd never been much of an athlete, except for swimming, which I loved. But I had one physical talent: I was a champion tree-climber. I often beat the boys in the neighborhood, getting to the topmost branches in record time.

In any proper household, I thought, this grand old tree would have been trimmed back away from the house, but Rupert and Zora probably didn't even notice it was there.

Thank heaven I'd suited my dress to Rupert's casual style the evening before and come in jeans, a light pullover, and my trusty Reeboks. I looked down, noting that the drop was not so severe as that at Mrs. Ward's house. The Beeches was on a grand scale, while this house was considerably smaller, the ceilings not so high, and only one floor between the ground and the attic. It was still a formidable drop, but it also meant that the tree branches at this level were still substantial. Above me, at the top of the tree, they would not have been strong enough to hold me.

Quickly, I picked up my handbag and dropped it out of the window. Then I studied the configuration of the tree. The branches did not grow out horizontally like outstretched arms but rose sharply upward from the main trunk like arms upraised. This meant there were no convenient parallel branches on which I could place my feet. Still, it was my only shot and I decided to go for it.

I got both feet onto the sill and stretched as far forward as I could to get a grip on the branch at the thickest spot I could reach. Then I swung out into space.

The branch wasn't as sturdy as I'd hoped for, and it swung down with a sickening swoop. Fortunately, it dragged against the side of the house, and its movement slowed. I waited till it had swung back up and settled, then I started working my way hand over hand toward the center of the tree. Little cross branches, thick with leaves, made it slow going, but eventually I came to a fork where I could swing myself up and get my feet secured on a solid branch.

The big central trunk was still far below me, and I remembered the sacred rule of childhood: Don't look down. I kept my eyes strictly on my work, moving slowly down and inward.

Once, my foot slipped, and I clung with my arms around the swaying limb. Thick leaves caught in my hair, and I released one hand to pull them away, almost losing my grip. My heart pounding, I hung there by one hand for a few timeless seconds before my other hand came back and grasped the branch again. Slowly, I went on working my way along to another fork, where I finally got a foothold again.

My hands were slippery and oozing specks of blood, but I felt no pain. I was wholly concentrated on moving steadily down toward the center of the tree.

When at last I reached the big trunk, I remembered that on a tree this size, the lowest branch was still a considerable drop from the ground. For the first time, I allowed myself a good look at the ground below and rejoiced to see a green carpet of fern over the whole terrain.

I inched my way around the rough trunk and picked the best spot I could find. I hung for a minute, looking down, and finally let go. The landing wasn't what I would call easy. I fell sprawling but cushioned by the ferns; I was bruised but not really hurt.

Now all I could think of was getting away before Zora came back. I snatched up my handbag, sprinted around the front of the house, and started down the drive. Halfway down the hill, I heard the sound of a motor. If only it would be a stranger, a visitor, a workman, a delivery van.

Taking no chances, I shot off the drive and threw myself into the ferny undergrowth several feet away and totally out of sight. When the car had passed, I cautiously raised my head.

It was Zora, all right. She wouldn't be looking for me here, but how long would it be before she discovered I was gone?

I ran down the rest of the drive and out into a residential street, pounding along the pavement, hoping to see someone who could help. The morning was cloudy, and no cars passed me as I hurtled along. I would simply have to knock on a door, I decided, when I rounded a curve and saw an elderly man bent over a flower bed.

Panting and breathless, I managed to choke out a few words, asking if I might use his telephone.

He stood up and looked at me curiously. My hair standing on end, my clothes stained, and my hands scratched and bleeding, I must have been a sorry picture.

He studied me for a moment. "Met with an accident, have you?"

I heard the sound of a car coming, and in a flash, I darted up the walk and stepped behind a rhododendron bush, from where I could see the car as it passed on down the hill.

It wasn't Zora.

If the thought of calling the police had crossed my mind, it didn't linger there for long. I could hear myself telling this totally bizarre story of the madwoman in the attic. No way. I would certainly tell Rupert, if I ever saw him again, and let him deal with it. Zora wasn't likely to be a threat to anyone else. For the moment, my only goal was to get away, and fast.

Now the old gentleman gave a chuckle. "Had a row with the mister, have you?"

I liked the sound of that. "Yes! Please, may I ring for a taxi?"

Slowly, he shuffled his way to the door and asked me to come in.

I rang Directory Assistance and got the number of a taxi service, asking my host for his address.

The driver came within minutes. Thanking the old gentleman, I scanned the street for any sign of Zora before getting into the cab.

At Meredith's house in Yarmouth I asked the driver to wait and dashed inside. After a quick wash, I threw my things into the flight bag, which was my only luggage, ran next door with the key, and was driven to the ferry terminal, where I mingled with the crowd of foot passengers waiting for the next crossing.

I didn't see how Zora could very well attack me in these circumstances, but as a precaution, I had tied my head in a dark scarf and put on a windbreaker she had never seen. I stationed myself where I could see every foot passenger who came into the waiting area, and when at last we boarded, I began to breathe again.

Hours later, back in my flat, I asked Meredith to come and share a meal with me. I hoped that telling her my bizarre story would restore me to the real world again.

18

For days after I got back to London, I looked over my shoulder whenever I ventured out of the flat. I even got out my pepper spray, which I usually carried only if I had to be out late at night, and kept it handy in the daytime as well.

I thought a good deal about Zora, wondering if I ought to have reported the whole episode to the police on the island. Her animosity was so clearly directed at me as the phantom Iris, that I was sure she posed no threat to other people. It was obvious that she was seriously disturbed. I was reluctant to become involved in giving evidence against her, and I hated the thought of the skeptical looks I would get from the police with my bizarre story. On the other hand, I wasn't all that confident that Zora might not come after me in London.

Talking it over that first night with Meredith had helped me deal with it. I had told her about working with Rupert on the research, leaving out any reference to romantic associations. With her commonsense approach, she agreed that my first step was to find Rupert and tell him, so that he would know about his sister's condition and could act accordingly, but finding Rupert was easier said than done. Of course, there was no London number listed for him. I tried Kings College and got nowhere. Knowing Zora would recognize my voice, Meredith phoned the number of Thornbury on the island and was told by Zora that Rupert was not there and was not expected. Asked for a London phone number, she was referred to the college. I knew it was no good trying to get his number from the BBC. I'd been told they were so secretive you virtually had to be cleared by MI5 to go to the loo.

In the end, we agreed I'd have to wait till I heard from Rupert. Meanwhile, I settled down and worked like a beaver on my manuscript. The text itself was substantially finished, and only odds and ends remained to be done. Angus MacFinn already had a good part of the final draft, and by Thursday I was able to deliver another batch to his office, leaving only fragments for winding up. The bibliography was ready, and a professional would do the index. It was now early July, leaving me plenty of time to make whatever revisions Angus might want before I went back to California.

By Friday afternoon I still had heard nothing from Rupert, and I was working away on some endnotes when I heard the doorbell.

There he is at last, I thought, but it wasn't Rupert. A child's voice. "Miss Camden? It's Penny."

"Hello, Penny. Have you come to meet your mum?"

"No. May I talk to you?"

"Yes, of course. Come up one flight."

I buzzed her in and met her at my door. One look at that solemn little face and I knew it was trouble.

I said simply, "Has it happened again?"

She nodded, looking up at me with an expression of such despair that pain closed my throat. Then her face crumpled. I held out my arms, and she clung to me, her head against my chest, great gulping sobs shaking her body.

I waited till she was ready. Groping in her pocket for a tissue, she blew her nose, rubbing the tears away with her hand. I led her to the sofa and took a chair nearby, remembering her pride, not wanting to crowd her.

"Was it today?" I asked.

"Yes, this morning." She had control of her voice now, and I avoided any expression of sympathy, letting her tell it her own way.

"I was dressing for school when I heard him shouting and Mum trying to calm him down. Then Mum came in to me and gave me some money and told me to go straight on to school, only to stop for something to eat on the way. So I did."

She swallowed hard and went on. "It's the last day of term and we had only a half day. When I came home, Mum was in her dressing gown, and she turned her face away so I couldn't see, and she said she'd rung up the office to say she was ill and couldn't come in to work. Then she said she was going to lie down for a bit, and I said I'd make the tea, and she said very good. But when she stood up and started to walk, I could see she was limping, and I went straight to her and looked at her face, and it was all—"

I nodded. "I understand."

She flashed me a grateful look. Then her face clouded. "I *hate* him. *I wish he was dead!*"

She stole a glance to see if that shocked me. It didn't.

I asked, "Will he be at home this evening?"

"No, he'll be away until late tomorrow. He was to go on a long haul up into Scotland and all."

"I see. Do you think your mother might let me come to see her?"

A pause. "Mum said you're very busy. She doesn't want to be a bother."

So Joyce did want me to come. "No bother," I said.

I picked up my backup disks and put them in the car for safekeeping. With Penny directing, we drove along Theobald's Road, up Rosebery Avenue, and onto a narrow street that angled off and up the hill. I parked the car and followed the child into a dismal building like a dozen others in the area, where the tentacles of gentrification had not reached.

As we climbed two flights of stairs, I thought of Iris making this same journey, hoping, as I did now, that she might be able to help a woman in trouble.

I found Joyce Hansen lying on the sofa, and at the sight of her face, I fought to control my impulse to cry out. It was much worse than I had imagined. Her face was a mass of cuts and bruises, one eye was discolored and swollen shut, and her lips were puffed and distorted where cuts had bled.

When she put out a hand to greet me, it was obvious her whole body was in pain. She spoke in a hoarse whisper. "It's good of you to come, Miss Camden."

Penny was now transformed from the weeping child to the caregiver. She picked up a bottle of tablets from a table and shook one out onto her hand, saying, "It's time for the next one, Mum."

Holding a glass of water to her mother's swollen lips, she helped her swallow the pill.

"It's for the pain," Penny said to me. "We had them from the dentist last year."

Now Penny announced she was off to the shops. "She'll be able to take bits of toast in milk," she said to me like a mother speaking of her sick child, "and I'll do a custard."

I was sure she was leaving the field clear for me,

knowing her mother would speak more freely without her, and she was right.

The moment the door closed behind Penny, Joyce whispered, "I know I ought to do something to end this, Miss Camden. Your friend Miss Franklin told me that, but I still blamed myself each time it happened. This time, though, I knew I was not at fault. This was the worst he's ever been. He was like a madman."

Gently, I said, "What happened to set him off?"

"At first, I had no idea what was wrong. It all began yesterday evening. He came home early and was obviously upset, but when I asked him what was the trouble, he wouldn't say. He has been in such good spirits lately that I was surprised. I could see he was obviously trying very hard to control his temper. He hadn't stopped at the pub, and that was a good sign. Later in the evening, he watched the telly and seemed calmer. When we went to bed, he was—"

She paused, her throat showing the flush that splotched the reddened face.

"Amorous?" I suggested.

She nodded. "Yes, but more—that is, more sort of violent, not loving."

I could see how difficult it was for her to speak of such matters, and it was a measure of her desperation that she would do so.

Now she took some sips of water, and her voice seemed stronger. The pill was no doubt starting to help the pain.

"This morning he woke early, and I heard him banging about in the kitchen. I looked in and saw he was drinking from a bottle of whiskey. His eyes were wild, and he glared at me with such hatred that I recoiled. Then he shouted, calling me a bitch and a whore.

"I was so astonished that I said, 'Whatever do you mean?' Now, this was something he couldn't tolerate. If I 'talked back' to him, as he put it, it always made him angry, but this time, I didn't care. I asked him again what he meant, and he said he had seen me the afternoon before, with one of the solicitors in my office. It seems he left work early and came along to see me home, and one of the gentlemen had walked out at the same time I did. I remember he made some light remark, we both laughed, and I went along to my bus.

"Kurt said he walked the other way and tried to put it out of his mind, but he kept seeing the way we had looked at each other, and he knew something was going on. He shouted, 'You're having it off with him, aren't you?'

"Penny was dressing for school, and I quickly gave her some money and told her to go on and have her breakfast along the way. Then I went back and faced Kurt, and for the first time, I told him I was fed up with his tempers and his suspicions. I said I'd never looked at another man from the day we met, that I'd tried to be a good and loving wife, and then I broke into tears. That set him off, and he went absolutely round the bend. He hit me with his fists, and when I fell, he kicked me. I truly believed he would kill me, and I was terrified. Then suddenly he stopped and went out, banging the door."

We sat in silence for a few moments. Then I said, "You told me that Kurt's father was an alcoholic. Did he also abuse his wife?"

Joyce nodded. "Yes. Kurt said he grew up believing a husband had the right to 'chastise' his wife, as he put it. His dad always said a man had to keep a woman in line. His mum wept a lot and talked about leaving him, but she never did."

Another pause. Then I said quietly, "Joyce, I believe you are ready to break away from Kurt now, aren't you?"

She looked down at her lap, and I saw tears moving over the hideously swollen face. "I know I ought to leave, but, you see, Kurt truly loves me, and he is such a fine person when he is—that is, most of the time. If I desert him, he will never get better. If I stay, I may be able to help him overcome his problems. I know he *wants* to be good."

Reading about cases like this one in the news, I thought again how easy it was to say, "Why doesn't she just walk out? How could anyone put up with such abuse?" The reality was more difficult and certainly not made easier by the traditional role of the woman to keep the home together, whatever the odds.

There was one shot that might help, and I tried it now. "I wonder if you have thought about what all this does to Penny?"

"Oh, yes, I know it is terrible for her. But if Kurt improved—"

"I'm afraid that's not very likely, Joyce. You can see for yourself that his spells of violence have been progressively more severe. What I mean about Penny is this—in a few short years, she will be a young woman, and you are giving her an image of a woman who submits to abuse. Just as Kurt followed his own father's pattern, Penny may grow up believing such abuse is acceptable. She loves you dearly. It's not too late to show her a different picture."

Joyce had been slumped over in a corner of the sofa. Now her back straightened and her one open eye came alive.

"Yes," she whispered. "Yes. Only I must be very careful. Kurt has threatened to kill us, as you know, if I leave him."

Before she could waver again, I stood up. "We must

find a temporary place where he can't find you. Then will you consider going to your family in Canada?"

She nodded. "I've never told them about Kurt. They think we have a marriage made in heaven, but I'm willing to tell them now. Yes, that's what we must do."

"I'd take you to my flat, but I'm afraid it's the first place Kurt would look."

When Penny came back, Joyce told her our plan, and the joy on that little face must have been all the impetus Joyce needed. Penny brought out the suitcases, and together we packed up everything we could cram in, supplementing with shopping bags. With Joyce dressed in slacks and a pullover, a hat down over her eyes, and a scarf high around her neck, we loaded everything into my car and drove to one of the many bed-and-breakfast hotels in my neighborhood, giving a false name.

Penny and I went out for take-away food, and I left them settled for the night.

It was nearly seven o'clock when I parked in the square and walked along toward the flat just as my gorgeous neighbor, Deirdre Kemp, stepped out of a taxi. No luggage, this time, only a bag labeled "Harvey Nichols." We went up the steps together, and I asked, "Have you time for a drink?"

"Oh, Lord, yes. Just what I want."

The flat was warm at the end of a sunny day, and I opened the windows to a light breeze.

I fixed our drinks and sat down, admiring Deirdre's stunning linen suit and the low-heeled pumps I'd seen in a Bruno Magli window.

I smiled. "Shopping?"

"Yes. I'm a totally useless creature. I'm like the woman in the opera—Violetta. She lived entirely for pleasure—and then what's-his-name fell in love with her—"

"Alfredo?"

"Right, Alfredo." She raised her glass. "To love. It can be a bloody nuisance at times."

I said, "I'll drink to that. I've just encountered a grim example."

With no names, no places, I gave her a brief outline of Joyce's predicament.

Deirdre said, "She's so right to leave, but I know it's not easy. When I was young, before my first marriage, I lived with a bloke who looked like Mr. Wholesome. It was my first real love, and I thought we'd be together forever. Then one day he flew into a rage and slapped me across the face. I was so shocked I had no reaction at all, just stared at him. He apologized and said he'd never do it again, but a few weeks later, he hit me with his fist. My eye turned blue, and I ran home to my parents, sobbing. My father threatened all sorts of revenge, but my mother just said, 'You must leave him, dear. Such men only grow worse with time.'"

"Did you leave?"

"Yes, but it was made easy for me. Mummy took me off to the Continent, and by the time we came back, I had met several charming young men and was on the road to recovery. I realize that most women don't have such options. Besides, my chap hadn't reached the point of threatening to kill me. That kind of obsessive love can be the very devil."

Deirdre stared into her glass. "Sometimes I think my early disenchantment cured me of sentimentality. I've married twice, and I've had assorted lovers. Both of my husbands were very well off—I'd never marry without money. But love—it takes all forms."

She looked up at me, and I saw the steel in her beautiful eyes. "When push comes to shove, one has to do what's needful."

This didn't seem to require an answer, so I got up

and refilled our drinks. We chatted pleasantly for a while about the progress of my book, about her travel plans.

She thought Switzerland next. "Lucerne is enchanting in the summer. Have you been there?"

The name touched me like the sharp point of a knife. "Yes," I said. "It's lovely."

When Deirdre had gone upstairs to her flat to get ready for an evening engagement, I sat on the window seat, looking dreamily out at the square, haunted by visions of a weekend with Neil, sitting on a steamer on Lake Lucerne. Neil had taken an honors degree in literature before becoming a policeman, and one of the things we had going for us was our endless chat about poetry and fiction. On that magic weekend at Lucerne, we had looked up at the ring of dramatic mountain peaks around the lake, talking about their effect on the English poets, arguing, laughing.

Damn Rupert, anyway. When he behaved, he'd been a wonderful distraction. Now all the pain of wanting Neil was back in full force.

Deirdre was right. Love could be a bloody nuisance.

19

SHAKING OFF MY GLOOMY THOUGHTS, I RANG up Meredith to report the news about Joyce and Penny.

"I'll pay for their hotel for a few days," I told her. "Joyce is sending to her parents in Canada for money."

Meredith said, "They could stay at the house in Yarmouth. Mother isn't going over till August, and I suspect you're not eager to go back at the moment?"

I laughed. "Too true."

It was an ideal solution. We agreed they would be safer there than in London, and Meredith offered to take them down herself the next day, Saturday, as she was free.

"I'll stay the first night with them. I haven't been to the island for some time. I'll look up some old friends there."

I rang up Joyce at the hotel, and she was tearfully pleased. "It will be lovely for Penny!" And so it was arranged.

At last I got around to food. I put a steak on the grill, tossed up a little salad, and turned the TV to face the table as I ate. I caught the end of a crime show, tried a comedy that wasn't funny, switched to an old film that was dull, and finally gave up.

Restless, I wandered back to my computer, pulling up the notes I'd been working on when I dashed off with Penny, making sure I'd saved the file. With no intention of working, I put in a few words here and there, entered the citation, and was soon hooked. I'd filled in some missing data, tidied up some notes, and suddenly realized more than an hour had passed and I was cross-eyed with fatigue.

Reaching for the backup, I remembered taking the disks to my car. Ever since the crisis with Iris's manuscript, I'd been faithful about taking them out of the flat when I left. Picking up my keys, I walked down the stairs and out the front door, surprised to see it was already dark. My Volvo was parked on the inner side of the square, next to the railing that enclosed the planted area, with its towering trees, black now against the darkling sky.

I unlocked the passenger side of the car, and as I bent over to open the glove compartment, I heard footsteps behind me. I wasn't alarmed, as I still thought of it as too early for muggings, and as for Kurt Hansen, he wouldn't be back from his run to Scotland till the next day.

I was wrong.

Strong arms pulled me up, a hand reached out and slammed the car door, and as I twisted, trying to get free, I came face to face with Kurt.

He pushed me hard against the side of the car, pressing his body against mine and pinning my arms down to my sides.

"Where are they?"

I struggled, helpless against him, but it didn't take me long to realize I wasn't going to get anywhere against a man whose steel arms hoisted heavy objects every day in his work.

I simply stopped trying to resist him. The effect was dramatic. He dropped his grip on me and spoke quietly.

"You know where they are. Tell me."

I tried denial. "I don't know what you mean, Kurt."

His eyes took on a look I didn't like much. "The neighbor said they went away with a good-looking blond lady, driving a green Volvo."

He had me there, at least the Volvo part. I tried sweet reason. "Look, Kurt, you must realize your wife can't go on with things as they are."

The nasty expression didn't improve. "What happens between me and my wife is none of your bloody business. You stick to your books and your la-di-da friends, like I told the dark-haired bitch."

"Joyce *asked* me to help her. I didn't force myself on her."

"So you say."

I tried to sound casual. "By the way, I see you came back early from Scotland."

"Ha! She bought that story, all right. I didn't go to bloody Scotland. I did my haul here in London. Then I hung about to see if her fancy man came to call. When I went up to the flat, I saw she and the brat had done a flit. That's when the neighbor told me they'd gone off with you. I've been walking up and down the bloody square here, watching your car, to see if you'd come out. If you didn't, I'd be back in the morning."

Now I tried denial. "Okay, I did take them away from the flat, but I don't know where they are now. I dropped them at the Holborn tube station. Your wife said they would go to a friend."

"You know what I think about that? It's bloody shit, that's what. I know your type. You'd get them all tucked up safe and sound somewhere and get her bloody solicitor to rally round."

At least he was talking rationally. I tried another ploy. "Look, Kurt, even if you do find them somewhere, Joyce will call the police and they'll charge you."

"Joyce won't call the bloody police. I know how to handle Joyce." His scowl smoothed to a grotesque semblance of the conciliatory face he would show to his wife. "She knows I love her, and she understands me."

Now was my chance. "I'm sure you do love her, Kurt. Don't you see that if you get help with your problem, you might be able to work things out some day?"

His anger flashed. "Get bloody help? The only help I need is to find my wife. *Now, where is she?*"

"I really don't know—"

His arm swung out, and he slapped me hard across the face. My head snapped back against the frame of the car.

"You know, all right, and you're going to tell me."

He gripped my shoulders and shook me so that my head struck the car again with a blow so severe that I felt my vision blur. Twice more he banged my head, repeating, "Tell me, tell me where she is!"

He doubled his fist and hit the side of my face. My knees bent under me, and as I started to slip down, I heard a voice shouting, "Hoy, there!"

I don't remember reaching the pavement. It was like one of those dreams in which you're falling, and you wake up before you hit the ground. Only I didn't wake up. At least, not then.

Anybody who's ever come to consciousness in a hospital, not remembering how they got there, will recognize my confusion when I opened my eyes and saw that I was in a white world, in a strange bed, among a row of similar beds.

At first, I felt dreamy and relaxed, not really caring where I was. Then I heard low voices, and I raised my head to look around.

Not a good idea. Pain shot through my head, and I let it fall gently back on the pillow. Exploring with my fingers, I learned that the back of my head bulged out oddly and painfully.

Something on the left side of my face invited more investigation, and I found it swollen and an agony to touch.

I blinked, puzzled. Then, quite suddenly, it came back. Kurt, of course. But how did I get here? No memory of that at all.

Somehow, it didn't seem to matter. I closed my eyes and drifted.

After a time, a familiar presence loomed up, and I saw Chief Inspector Dietrich, accompanied by a constable.

"How are you feeling?"

I tried a smile and found it hurt the left side of my face. "Fine," I said, idiotically.

Dietrich grinned. "Relatively speaking, I'd say. Do you feel able to answer some questions?"

"I'll try."

"Good."

He sat in the chair beside the bed, and the constable disappeared and came back with another.

"I'm very glad you asked for me when you were brought in," Dietrich began.

"I did? I don't remember."

"That's not uncommon. You have concussion, and you did not remember much in the beginning except that it was Kurt Hansen who attacked you. That's why I'm here. Are things a bit clearer now?"

"I think so." I clearly recalled Kurt's actions:

pulling me out of the car, demanding to know where his wife was, causing my head to strike the car, and battering me with his hand and fist.

"What I don't remember," I said at last, "is why I was in the car in the first place."

The chief inspector nodded. "That baffled us, too. You see, you had no handbag nor identification with you. When you were brought in to the hospital, you were unconscious. The passerby who rescued you saw a man attacking you and assumed it was a mugging. When he called out, the mugger ran off, but the witness was certain the man was not carrying anything as he ran. It seemed more important to get help for you than to chase the perpetrator. He flagged a motorist, who went to a call box and rang 999.

"The constable who answered the call was told where you were standing when the attack occurred. He found your keys lying in the gutter. One fit the door of the car, so he reported your number plate and learned the name of the owner of the car. When you first awoke, you were asked your name and didn't respond, but when you were asked if you were Claire Camden, you said yes. Later on, you came up with Kurt's name and mine."

"I see."

"Now, what can you tell me about our friend Hansen? We have his address, of course, but he's been canny enough not to make an appearance there."

I found that as I talked, memory began to flood back. I recalled the sequence of events with Penny and Joyce and Kurt's demands to know where they were. Then at last I remembered popping out to my car to retrieve the backup disks.

"I ought not to have gone out, Chief Inspector, but it seemed so early to me. I was quite surprised to see that darkness had fallen. And, of course, I believed that Kurt Hansen was in Scotland."

"Yes, I understand. And where are Mrs. Hansen and her daughter now?"

I named their hotel, adding, "Mrs. Evans, whom you've met, will take them down tomorrow to her place in Yarmouth in the Isle of Wight."

"Very good. We'll bring Hansen in sooner or later. He will turn up eventually either at home or at work. When he does, we'll also question him about the murder of your friend, Miss Franklin. I don't know how far we'll get, but we'll have a go at him."

When they at last rose to leave, Dietrich handed me my ring of keys and told me they would have a statement drawn up for me to sign. "We'll bring it to you tomorrow, if you like, so that you needn't come into the station. If you think of anything you wish to add, please let me know."

I thanked him, and he wished me a speedy recovery.

When the officers had gone, I realized I had a murderous headache and was glad when the medicine nurse arrived and gave me a pill. I had been told I must spend the night in the hospital, and I made no protest. Lying still was fine with me.

I slept soundly, awakened by noise and clatter and a voice at the foot of my bed. "Ready for the pan?"

Without waiting for my answer, a young woman in white raised my covers and inserted a cold object under my hips.

"We'll just raise you up a bit," she cried out cheerfully, turning a crank. As my head rose, it also hurt like the dickens.

When she stopped, I said, "Can't I get up and go to the loo?"

Briskly, she picked up the chart hanging at the foot of my bed and glanced at it. "Sorry, luv, not yet."

And so it went, the morning routine of hospitals everywhere. Brush your teeth, wash your face, then wait. Only here, you got a little pot of morning tea before breakfast. Nothing had ever tasted so marvelous. I ate my breakfast when it came and drifted off to sleep again.

Eventually, a young doctor came along and said I might go home. I dressed, went through the paperwork, was wheeled to the entrance, and went home in a taxi.

20

WHEN I TOTTERED UP THE STAIRS TO MY FLAT, I was annoyed at how wobbly I felt, and I wished the blood would stop thumping in my head. Nevertheless, I felt much better than the night before, and I knew I was on the mend.

I found several messages on my machine.

Sally: "Mums, sorry I missed you. Ring when you can."

Rupert, sounding testy: "Claire, where on earth are you? I've rung twice!"

David Franklin: "Claire, good news on Mother's manuscript. It's all back on the disk, and I've spent days running a printout!"

There was a pause, and David added, "I'd like to talk with you when you're free. I'm in Brighton." And he left his number.

I took one of the tablets I'd been given and settled on the sofa with cushions under my head and the telephone at my side, pulling an afghan over my legs. I had a good chat with Sally, giving her a modified version of my visit to the hospital, assuring her I was absolutely fine.

Then I pressed out David's number in Brighton.

If Rupert phoned, he could jolly well wait. He hadn't sounded much like a candidate for tea and sympathy.

David said he was coming up to London in the afternoon.

"Good," I said. "Come along here when you're ready. I'm looking rather banged up, so don't be alarmed. I'll explain when I see you."

It was close on to four o'clock when David arrived. One look at my face stirred his affectionate concern. I told him the whole story of Kurt and his possible connection with Iris's murder, including my theory that Kurt might have sweet-talked his way into the flat.

David looked thoughtful. "Yes, Mother might have hoped that he was truly repentant."

We tossed that and other theories around for a while before David got down to what was troubling him. I wasn't surprised that it had to do with Fiona.

The essence of it was that he was having doubts about his lady love, although he didn't say that at first in so many words.

"When the insurance money is paid up, she wants me to buy a place in Brighton for my last year at university. I admit our tiny flat is fairly dismal, but I don't know where I'll be afterward. I'm applying for graduate study, and it could be anywhere. I don't mind living modestly, as we've been doing. Her mother gives her money, unbeknownst to her father, and I thought we were comfortable enough."

"What does she have in mind for you to buy, David?"

"That's just it. She's been all over Brighton, looking at luxury flats and dragging me off to give my approval. I've told her we can't make a commitment until the money is actually there, but even then, I'm not sure that's what I want to do.

"Also, she's talking about our wedding. Where will it be? What will she wear? Who will be the bridesmaids?"

"You *are* planning to marry, then?"

His dark eyes were troubled. "It was never explicit. More as if some day it might happen. Frankly, Claire, I wasn't at all sure Fiona would want to marry me. It would be a long wait through graduate school until I'd have a position and an income. I was afraid she might not last out the course. Now, I ought to be overjoyed that she wants to marry, only I'm uneasy about it."

I wondered how frank I dared to be. Tentatively, I said, "She seems very pleased that you will have the money from the insurance."

"Yes, of course, and Fiona is accustomed to living well. I know that if we married now, she would want to live on the scale of her parents, and the money wouldn't last long at that rate. You see, Claire, it may be the only large sum I'll ever have, and I'd like to have some security for the future. That's what Mother would want, I'm sure."

No problem agreeing with that. I sensed that David was working his way toward something definite, and at last it came out.

His voice shaky, he said, "We've been together for more than a year, and I've loved Fiona very much. She's a bit of a spoilt brat, but I'm not perfect either, and we got on very well, on the whole. Our only real quarrels were about Mother. Fiona was convinced that Mother disliked her and wanted me to break off with her. I've told her a thousand times that Mother never even hinted at such a thing to me, but it became an obsession with Fiona. In the end, we avoided any meetings between them. I saw Mother on my own."

I reflected that from what Iris had told Meredith, it

was true Fiona was not her choice for Daughter-in-Law of the Year, but I knew Iris was far too fond of David to actively interfere in his life. Her guess had been that Fiona would drift away in the course of time, just as David himself had come to believe.

That was before the money came into the picture.

Now David got down to the nitty-gritty. "There were times when I felt Fiona actually hated Mother. She has always made cutting remarks about clever women, saying she was glad she was not a bluestocking herself. She has slipped through school and university with average marks, too lazy to make a real effort, but at the same time she resents other women who excel.

"You see, Claire, it's been bad for me since—since my mother's death. It's almost as if Fiona's glad about what happened. She doesn't try to feel what I'm going through. Frankly, I've never cared much for Fiona's father. He's a pompous, stiff-necked ass, in my opinion, and he detests the very sight of me. But, good God, Claire, Fiona's fond of him, and if he died, I'd give her all my love and comfort."

This was such a burst of indignation for gentle David that it told me how deeply hurt he was.

I made inarticulate sounds of concern. David's awakening to Fiona didn't need any help from me. He was getting there on his own, but I felt his pain. Easy enough to say he'd be better off in the end without her. That didn't make it better for him now.

While we talked, a constable came with the statement summarizing Kurt Hansen's attack on me the evening before. As I signed, I didn't like the feeling in the pit of my stomach. Kurt wasn't going to like this.

David, having promised to take all of *The Court Wits* material to Duncan Dimchurch, set off, getting my assurance that I was absolutely fine.

In fact, I was surprised at how much better I felt.

The pain was still there but subsiding nicely. Some dizziness made me reluctant to move, but there was nothing wrong with my appetite. I was on my way to the kitchen when the doorbell sounded.

Rupert, of course. "Where on earth have you been?"

I buzzed him in and opened my door. He took one look, and the irritable tone evaporated. He put his arms around me very gently. "What happened?"

"I was attacked out there in the square."

He led me to the sofa, tucked the afghan around me, and sat, holding my hand, while I told him the story, Rupert murmuring "the rotten bastard" and other epithets.

With a delicate touch, he examined my head and cheek and asked what medicine I'd been given. Then he kissed me ever so lightly. "Are you hungry?"

I nodded, smiling.

Half an hour later, he called me to the table, where he had laid an enticing meal. "One glass only," he announced, pouring my wine.

This was no time to launch into the tale of Zora and the attic. It could wait.

Over our supper, he talked about how lovely Scotland was in the summer, and I wondered if that was where he had been all week, but being Rupert, he didn't say.

Now, at last, I told him about my discovery when I visited the site of the old grammar school in Freshwater.

"In one of the letters at Mrs. Ward's place, there was mention of gossip about John Hendrick, the local schoolmaster, and his wife. As I recall, it was written some time after the death of the governess. The story was that the wife had taken the children and gone to live on the mainland.

"Now, in the newspaper accounts of the coroner's

hearing, you remember the schoolmaster's wife came to call on the day the governess died, but she was not present at the hearing because she had gone with her children to her family in Hampshire. Putting these facts together, it occurred to me that if the separation were permanent, the schoolmaster would probably have given up a dwelling large enough for a family and taken lodgings somewhere. The town was very small at that date. There might have been only a few permanent residents who took in year-round lodgers, as opposed to summer visitors,

"With that in mind, I examined the old records of the school—the only one of its kind in the area—and guess what? Some six months after his wife departed, John Hendrick's address was changed to Thornbury, Freshwater!

"Now, here is poor Tennyson, in possession of letters from his lady love. He can't bring himself to destroy them, nor can he risk having them discovered. What more likely than that he's on friendly terms with the schoolmaster—an intelligent, educated man. He puts his treasures into a locked metal box, telling his acquaintance they are documents of some sort, asking him to put them in a secure place until he calls for them. So, what do you think?"

I paused dramatically.

Rupert's eyes had begun to shoot flashes during my recital. Now he fairly sizzled. "By God, Claire, I think you're onto something. I've found it difficult to see our poet handing over his hallowed hoard to just anyone. This could explain how the letters got to Thornbury. But why did they remain there?"

"I've pondered that one. After the Tennysons built their new place in Sussex, they spent much less time at Farringford. I suppose Alfred intended to retrieve them some day and simply put it off."

Rupert frowned. "Would he take the chance that

they would be found and their secret revealed? What about this? The schoolmaster dies. Now, what does Tennyson do?"

"He could tell the widow he left some documents with the schoolmaster and ask her to look for the box."

"Exactly. And she doesn't find it. Who would think of looking among the bricks of the chimney in the attic?"

"Yes. Even if he came and searched the place himself, he would never have found the box!"

When we had finished our meal, Rupert put me back on the sofa and brought our coffee there.

I could delay no longer. "I have something very serious to tell you, Rupert."

His look of mild surprise turned to a deep scowl as I gave him the story of what Zora had done on the Sunday evening after Rupert left for London, and how I had managed to escape the next day.

When I had finished, he sat in rigid silence, staring at me with eyes like ice. At last, he said, "What did you say that provoked her?"

So much for kind, compassionate Rupert. My voice edged with anger, I said, *"I* did absolutely nothing. Zora thought I was Iris."

"Yes," he said, "she was perturbed over questions about the authenticity of the letters."

I looked at him curiously. "You never told me you knew Iris well."

He dismissed this as a matter of no interest. "Didn't *she* tell you?"

"No. We had no chance to talk. Zora seemed to think you were lovers."

"We dallied a bit, yes."

I sat up and looked into his eyes. "Rupert, didn't you *care* when Iris died?"

He blinked, as if this had not occurred to him

before. "Yes, I expect I did. Certainly, it was a shocking thing. Most regrettable. But what you tell me of my sister—"

Obviously, Zora's condition was more important than Iris's death. "Zora has had emotional problems for many years," he went on, "but she has never been known to be violent or to threaten violence. You are certain it was a *knife* in her hand?"

I stood up, went into the kitchen, and returned, holding a ten-inch knife by its black handle. "Very much like this one."

Then I walked to the entry and handed him his coat.

"Good-bye, Rupert."

He gave me that odd look I'd seen before that said he wasn't quite sure who I was.

"Yes, thank you," he said. "I must go back to the island at once."

21

THE FOLLOWING MORNING I DAWDLED OVER the Sunday paper, still fuming about Rupert's behavior the evening before. I'd thought I'd seen it all with Rupert, but when he doubted my word about the whole ghastly episode with Zora, I was nearly as astonished as I was angry. Family loyalty is all very well, but did he really think I would invent a *knife?*

I'd been tolerant before, had even found him amusing, but this was too much. Exit Rupert.

When I switched on the telly, I remembered this was the day for *Arts Chat,* the BBC show he had taped on the preceding Monday. May as well watch.

The host introduced his guests, announcing the topic as "Unsolved mysteries in literary research." There was Rupert, looking arrogant and sexy. I felt a fleeting regret, tempered with relief that I'd stepped off the roller coaster of his mood swings. The other guests were a fiftyish Thomas Hardy scholar and a young literary critic, evidently intended to play the role of gadfly.

The discussion began with an account of the controversy that arose in the 1960s with the publication of claims that that eminent Victorian, Thomas Hardy, had fathered an illegitimate child by his cousin, Tryphena Sparks. Much of the "evidence" rested on rather dubious recollections by aged family members.

The Hardy scholar said, "There is little doubt that Hardy was extremely fond of his cousin Tryphena, but there's not a shred of evidence that she felt more than a cousinly regard for him. He was an extremely shy young man, and references to his cousin reflect admiration from a distance rather than the triumph of a successful lover."

The young critic smirked. "What is this reluctance to acknowledge that famous writers may have been as promiscuous as anyone else, then or now?"

His opponent smiled. "In Hardy's case, I simply find the accusation, if one may call it that, unconvincing."

The host played straight man, asking, "Why unconvincing?"

"I believe we have the answer in Hardy's own words. In *Jude the Obscure,* surely the most autobiographical of his novels, young Jude is deceived by Arabella into believing she is pregnant. What does he do? We must remember that Hardy was a product of rural Dorset, not a hardened sophisticate, and I believe his character Jude did precisely what young Hardy himself would have done. He *married* her. If Hardy was the prospective father of his cousin's child, I have no doubt that he would have done precisely what Jude did."

They tossed that one around for a while before the host turned to Rupert. "I believe Mr. Mortmain can tell us something about another unsolved mystery."

Rupert gave a brief summary of what had become known as the Tennyson letters. Now I wondered if he would mention our joint discoveries.

He did.

"With the aid of another scholar," he began, "I have begun to uncover evidence of the identity of the young woman who wrote the letters."

No name for the "other scholar," I noticed.

"From the evidence of contemporary letters, the young woman appears to have been a governess, living in Freshwater, not far from Farringford." He described the photograph of her by Julia Cameron, and the references to her "lovely red tresses," mentioned in both sets of letters. Finally, he stated that she had been observed entering Tennyson's summerhouse late at night.

Now he read from a letter not previously disclosed.

" 'My dearest: It has been two days since our last meeting. I shall leave this letter in the niche, when I have the opportunity to slip away. I am desolate that there was none from you yesterday, but I understand how difficult it is for you to manage. I did not wish to cast a shadow upon the felicity of our last time together, so I said nothing then. Now, I can tell you that I was followed that evening. The young cousin of my eldest charge has been with us since the beginning of the month. He is a good boy, but he rather follows me about, making sheep's eyes, until I speak firmly to him. He must have seen me as I left the house, for I heard footsteps behind me when I reached the path leading to the summerhouse. I stepped aside and waited. He stopped also, and then, as he turned back, I saw clearly that it was he. I have no fear that he will tell, however, as he would be punished for coming out, and fortunately, he leaves for home tomorrow.

" 'I have read with interest the book you gave me. How stimulating it is to read Mr. Huxley's account of the theories of Mr. Darwin, which he elucidates so clearly. I, too, wish that we might go together to the Dorset coast to examine the beds of fossils so prevalent there.

" 'Of course, I deplore, as you do, the secrecy we must employ, but please believe me when I say that nothing in the universe matters to me except my love for you. I can scarcely believe that it has been only two weeks since that night that has become a sacred memory to me, when my true life began.

" 'I was deeply moved when you quoted the lines from *Maud* that describe our first meeting:

> She came to the village church,
> And sat by a pillar alone;
> An angel watching an urn
> Wept over her, carved in stone;
> And once, but once, she lifted her eyes
> And suddenly, sweetly, strangely blush'd
> To find they were met by my own . . .' "

Rupert paused, with a supercilious smile. "The remainder of the letter contains more protestations of endless devotion."

Then Rupert was asked a number of questions about his discovery of the letters pertaining to the governess, to which he doled out bits of information but deftly avoided naming Mrs. Ward, or for that matter, the "other scholar" who had led him to the source.

I wasn't going to let him get by with that, but all in good time. If necessary, I'd tell Angus MacFinn, and with his backing, I'd have a little chat with the press.

The program ended with an exchange of humorous quips among the participants. I switched it off, resolving that that was my last sight of Rupert Mortmain.

For several days, I was reluctant to exhibit my bruised countenance to the world. In the enforced seclusion, I finished the last pages of my book and sent them by messenger to Angus, who rang up, ecstatic. "Darling! Everything so far has been lovely. Just bits and pieces to tidy up. I'm clearing Friday morning for our conference, if that's agreeable?"

I told him it was, and after another exclamation of "Splendid work!" he rang off.

Time to relax and celebrate. I phoned Meredith, offering to take her to the restaurant of her choice, and she said to come to her place at seven o'clock and we'd go from there.

What other self-indulgence could I engage in? What would Deirdre Kemp do? Of course. Shopping. I'd go to Bond Street to look for a pair of shoes, then have a light lunch somewhere.

Wearing my favorite summer dress, I studied my face in the mirror. My left cheek had progressed from purple to green, and the swelling was subsiding. I had liberally applied liquid base and decided it looked exactly like a massive bruise covered with makeup.

Oh, well. This was my day for pleasure.

Or so I thought.

It turned out to be the beginning of a nightmare.

At the sound of the doorbell, I pressed the intercom and heard a gruff male voice. "Mrs. Claire Camden?"

"Yes."

"Police here. We should like to speak with you, if you please."

It sounded a lot more like a command than a request.

I released the catch but left the door to my flat on the chain until I saw who was there. Two uniformed officers, a sergeant, and a constable.

I let them in and was about to ask them to sit down when the sergeant gave me a severe look and informed me that I was to accompany them to the police station to answer inquiries concerning the death of Mrs. Iris Franklin.

Astonished, I tried to protest and was met with a

stern look. The constable accompanied me as I went to pick up my handbag and a jacket. Then I was escorted to a waiting police car and taken to the local station.

I said nothing along the way. These two were merely the messengers. No use complaining to them.

I was taken up some stairs and placed in a room with a plastic table and matching chairs. There I waited. And waited.

If this was intended to soften me up, it didn't work. I simply took out my current paperback and read until the door opened and two officers came in, one in uniform.

The thin one in a gray suit looked at me with extreme distaste in his little gray eyes. "Mrs. Claire Camden?"

"Yes."

"I am Detective Chief Inspector Garvey. This is Sergeant O'Brien. I shall ask you some questions."

He switched on a tape machine, giving the time, date, and the names of those present. Then he went on, "You are not obliged to say anything, but anything you do say may be taken down and used in evidence. Do you understand?"

"Yes. I understand I have just been given the legal caution. Of what am I accused, please?"

The chief inspector's lips pressed tightly together, then opened to a narrow slit. "You are not as yet charged with a crime, madam. Do you wish to answer my questions?"

I shrugged. "Obviously, there is some mistake. I'll answer whatever you want."

The look in his eyes gave me a chill. "Let us begin with the evening of Tuesday, the fourteenth of June last. You received a telephone call from a Mrs. Iris Franklin?"

"Yes. She asked if she might spend the night in my guest room."

With a sneer, he repeated my words. "In your *guest* room."

"Yes."

"And were you expecting that she would come to stay with you?"

"No."

"But you were pleased that she came?"

"Yes, certainly. She was a close friend and we hadn't seen each other since last year at the Christmas holiday."

Now we went over in detail the whole story, from Iris's arrival at about seven o'clock until my discovery of her body the next day. When we had gone through the same details again, I finally said, "I've told all of this to Detective Chief Inspector Dietrich. Why is it necessary to repeat it now?"

Garvey's voice dripped icicles. "Chief Inspector Dietrich is no longer in charge of this case. I am."

That was the first time my heart did a blip. "Is he ill?" I asked.

"No, indeed, madam. His health is excellent."

I saw the sergeant put up his hand to hide a grin.

Now I remembered Dietrich's words about my being a suspect in the eyes of some of his fellow officers.

Garvey gave me a salacious look. "How would you describe your relationship with Miss Franklin?"

"We were good friends. I've already told you that."

"Very good friends, I believe?"

"Yes, certainly."

"Please think carefully before you answer this question. Have you and Miss Franklin been lovers in the physical sense of the word?"

I shook my head. "No, never."

His voice was gruff. "I put it to you that you had conceived an unnatural attachment to Miss Franklin and that you quarreled with her concerning this when she came to spend the night at your flat."

I'd had enough of this. I gave him a cool stare. "If you expect an angry denial, you've come to the wrong place. If I had been inclined in the way you suggest, I can think of no better partner than Iris. It happens, however, that for better or for worse, our genes dictated otherwise. I can only say that what you have suggested is totally untrue. I have answered all of your questions, Chief Inspector. Unless you have some specific evidence—"

As if I had pressed a magic button, Garvey opened the folder that lay in front of him, picked up the top sheet, and pushed it across the table to me.

At the top was Iris Franklin's letterhead, with the college address, and the date, 6 June. As I began to read, I felt as if I'd moved into a twilight zone, out of touch with reality.

Dear Claire,

I scarcely know how to reply to your recent letter. You know that I am reluctant to hurt you. It is true that we have shared wonderful moments together. You have a beautiful body, my dear, but I have never intended for our relationship to go beyond those occasional nights of pleasure. Yes, it is true that my marriage is a shambles, but I am not ready to make the commitment to you that you have asked for. In the months you have been away, other persons have come into my life. For the present, I have found that my needs and desires are best fulfilled by a variety of partners. I hope you will understand this. When you return to London, we will talk further. Someone's here. I shall finish this later—

I stared at the chief inspector. "Iris Franklin could not have written this letter. Where did it come from?"

He looked positively gleeful. "It came from Miss Franklin's word processor."

"I'm no computer expert, Chief Inspector, but common sense tells me you can't make that kind of identification. It's not like the old typewriters of crime fiction, with the chipped letters or what have you."

He gave a twisted smile. "Perhaps not, but it can be shown to be compatible with her system. It is written on her letterhead, and the contents are clear."

He stood up, and for the first time, when I saw the hatred in his face, I felt a surge of fear.

Unbelieving, I heard his words: *"Claire Camden, I charge you with the murder of Iris Franklin . . ."*

22

Immediately after charging me with Iris's murder, Chief Inspector Garvey gave me again the official caution, beginning, "You are not obliged to say anything . . ."

I said, "I am absolutely innocent of the charge. I have nothing further to say except that I wish to make a telephone call."

I needed a solicitor, but who? The Camden family solicitors were fuddy-duddies who dealt with wills and deeds and would no doubt faint at the mention of murder. For that matter, I knew that most British lawyers didn't handle criminal cases.

When I was at last permitted to use the phone, I rang up the firm that occupied the ground floor of my building in Bedford Square, asking to be referred to an appropriate person.

Two hours later, to my enormous relief, a young woman with a mass of brown curls and a sprinkle of freckles over her nose came in. Holding out her hand, she said, "Hello. I'm Joanna Reeve," and handed me her card with the name of a firm of solicitors.

I thanked her for coming and asked if she knew the charge against me.

"Yes, I've spoken with the chief inspector in charge of the case. Now I should like to hear what you can tell me about it."

I gave her a summary of events, ending with the assurance that I was absolutely innocent of the charge.

She nodded, as if she was accustomed to hearing that. "Our first concern is the matter of bail. On a serious charge like this one, the magistrate may refuse bail, or he may set a very high figure. People generally believe that bail is not granted when the charge is murder, but this is not correct. If we can show that the accused is not a danger to the community and is not likely to bolt, it may be granted."

Thank heaven for the Camden money. In the divorce settlement Sally was provided for separately, and I had been given a large sum which I had never touched, wanting to make it on my own and keeping the account only for a time of need.

This looked like the time, if ever there was one.

That afternoon I was taken to the magistrate's court, where, to the disgust of Chief Inspector Garvey, who argued vigorously against it, the magistrate granted bail. It was set at a high figure, all right, but one I could meet. Since I was an American, the court would hold my passport, preventing me from fleeing the country.

Joanna Reeve proved a model of competence, guiding us briskly through the proceedings. A date was set for trial three months away, and I was cautioned to inform the police if I wished to leave the greater London area.

As we left the court, my young woman looked at her watch. "You'll have questions. I have an hour. Shall we have a coffee?"

She led the way down the road to a coffee bar. When we were settled, I began, "Miss Reeve—"

She smiled, "Joanna, if you like."

I smiled back. "Thanks. I'm Claire. Now, my first question is this—I'm scheduled to return to the university in September. Will I be allowed to go if I return for the trial?"

She frowned. "Probably not. I'd suggest you make other arrangements if you can."

That wasn't as easy as it sounded, but I'd worry about that later. I moved on to what I saw as the crucial question.

"As you know, the evidence the police are relying upon for my so-called motive is a letter presumed to have been written by Iris Franklin. If we can find out who actually wrote the letter, will that in itself secure my release from the charge?"

Joanna pondered. "It would certainly knock the props from their case. We might get a dismissal from the magistrate, but nothing is certain. I was told only the principal facts of the letter, but I did not see it. Was it dated and signed?"

"Dated, yes. The sixth of June, as I recall. But it wasn't signed. It broke off, saying she would finish it later."

"Handwritten?"

"No, word processor. Garvey told me it was compatible with her system."

"Was there an envelope?"

"No. At least, I wasn't shown one. Iris knew I was coming to England on the tenth, going directly down to Devon for my daughter's graduation at Exeter. It would have been too late to send it to the States, but whoever wrote it may not have known that. I suppose they could say she planned to post it to my London address."

"Yes. It's very much in our favor that there is no

signature or other handwriting on the letter and that it was not posted."

"How on earth did the police get hold of it, anyhow?"

"That is one of the first questions we shall ask. They are obliged to disclose to us what evidence they have, but it often takes time to obtain it."

I told her that DCI Deitrich had been pulled from the case. "He had heard hints from other officers that I was a suspect, but he was working on another lead." And I gave her the whole story of Kurt Hansen.

"Kurt did this," I said, pointing to my cheek. "He is in custody now for his attack on me."

Joanna's eyes shot sparks. "That bloody Garvey knows about another suspect and chooses to charge you anyway. I've dealt with his type when I was with the Crown Prosecution service. I'll have a chat with Dietrich and find out what I can about Kurt Hansen."

She looked at her watch again. "Before I go, I should explain to you that we must brief a barrister before we go to trial."

I nodded. "I know something of the British justice system. My husband was in the Home Office, and since we parted, I've had a long relationship with Neil Padgett, a CID officer. He's in Australia now for several months."

She smiled. "I remember Padgett. An intelligent officer. He went down to the west country, I believe?"

"Yes, to Devon."

"Excellent man. A pity he's not here for you now."

I left it at that. No point in going weepy over Neil.

She answered a few more questions for me, and I told her how fortunate I felt to have her on my case. "You've heard what the letter implied, and you haven't treated me like a leper."

"You're right. A few years ago, I might have been

less open, but my husband and I lost a very dear friend to AIDS last year, and it has given us a better perspective. I happen to believe you when you say the letter is false, but it wouldn't matter if I didn't."

As we walked out together, she said, "You're taking this very well, Claire."

I felt bitterness all the way to my throat. "Actually, I'm not taking it well. I didn't kill my friend, and I can't believe any of this is real. But more than that, I'm angry. I'm going to find out who wrote that letter, and when I do, I'll make sure the whole world knows it!"

My first thought on getting back to the flat was relief that I didn't have to tell Sally I was charged with murder. She had left the day before with a girlfriend for a ten-day tour of Greece and Turkey, and it certainly wouldn't make the news there.

By the time I was ready to meet Meredith at seven, I had changed and had just stepped out into the square when a flash nearly blinded me. The press hadn't wasted time tracking me down. The photographer stepped aside, and a reporter dogged my footsteps as I walked to my car.

Mercifully, the contents of the letter had not been disclosed at the hearing, only that there was "evidence of a quarrel."

The reporter spoke in my ear. "What was the quarrel about, Miz Camden?"

I had often wondered why people answered at all, and now I understood. If I said nothing, it felt as if I'd confessed something.

I hurried on. "There was no quarrel. It's all a mistake."

He hurled a few more questions, but these I ignored, driving off as calmly as I could.

Meredith was a major consolation. I'd been dumping my problems in her lap ever since I got to London, and this was the worst yet.

Her first question when she heard the news was, "What have you eaten today?"

Startled, I realized I'd missed lunch and had had only a coffee.

"Right. I'm bare bones here. We'll go to Mario's. It's all nonsense that people who've had a shock are unable to eat."

We went to a small Italian restaurant only a few doors from her place, where we started with two whiskeys and a selection from the antipasto trolley.

She was right. I was ravenous.

I gave her the details of the putative letter from Iris, adding, "Since Garvey and his cohorts had already tagged me as the killer, I suppose it's only fair to see that the arrival of the letter—wherever it came from—would seem to justify their suspicions. No excuse for their nasty attitude, of course."

Meredith said, "Fortunate you were able to make bail. The courts tend to be sticky about it on serious charges, I understand."

I told her about the Camden money and the magistrate's decision that I wasn't a risk to the community nor a risk to run off before my trial.

She nodded. "Now, as I understand it, the time of death seems to be fairly pinpointed between nine o'clock and half past nine. The police theory is that you committed the murder and then went on to Ealing. You arrived at your interview at close to ten o'clock. Even if your dotty old gentleman could confirm the time, it wouldn't help much, would it?"

"Exactly. The postmortem shows that Iris ate something within half an hour of her death, but they have only *my* word about the time. Normally, she would have been up earlier, but she slept late because she had taken a sleeping tablet the night before."

"Yes. Now, let's think about the letter. You were told that the type was 'consistent' with Iris's system. That must refer to the printer. Whatever software program is used, the only variations in a sample of this type would occur in the printing. Iris's printer was a popular model, three or four years old, as I recall. I bought mine at about the same time. Theoretically, the letter could have been done by anyone in the United Kingdom, but isn't it more likely that whoever did this used Iris's own system or one like it, not taking the risk of detection?"

I agreed. "If I were doing something like this, I'd hesitate to use my own printer, in case it might be identifiable."

"In any case, it's likely to be someone who had access to her office and her letterhead paper—someone who knew of her friendship with you, and who knew that you were coming to London this summer."

"If the letter was intended to damage Iris's reputation, why wasn't it sent to Professor Griswold, who would no doubt be pleased as punch?"

Meredith looked grim. "Unless he wrote it himself, of course, and was planning to use it when the time was right."

"It's dated the sixth of June. Why wasn't it used earlier? Why now, when it can no longer matter to Iris?"

Meredith's brown eyes bored into mine. "The date may be as false as the letter itself. If I'm inventing a spurious letter, I can surely invent the date as well. It gives *you* a motive for murder, Claire. It may have been written *after* her death!"

23

AFTER A MISERABLE NIGHT OF BROKEN SLEEP, I staggered up the next morning, made a pot of coffee, and set out a plate of croissants and Danish. I'd rung up Duncan Dimchurch the evening before to say I desperately needed to talk with him, and he'd agreed to come to the flat first thing in the morning. I wanted to stay in as long as possible, to avoid the press hounds.

I let the machine answer my phone. I'd even changed my message to say that I had no statement to make and please don't ring again. Fat lot of good that did.

Duncan arrived, looking flustered. "My dear, there are two chaps from the press on your doorstep. They saw me ring your bell and were all over me!"

"Did you tell them anything?"

"No, of course not. What could I tell? Of course, I know you've been charged with—with—"

"Killing Iris."

"Yes. It's so absurd. I *did* say that there must be a dreadful mistake. Then you pressed the release and I popped in the door. I thought one of them was about to follow me, but I gave him a severe look and he stepped back."

I almost giggled at the vision of Duncan looking severe.

When we were settled, I fixed him, like the ancient mariner, with my glittering eye. "Duncan, dear, I am going to tell you in confidence what's really going on, and I want your help."

I gave him the details of the letter, getting his round-eyed look of shock and disbelief.

"I don't understand. I mean to say—I'd always rather thought it obvious that you and Iris—"

"Preferred men to women?"

Duncan's face was pink. "Well, yes, rather."

I spelled it out for him. "That's correct. You see, someone *invented* this letter."

"Oh, dear. How very shocking. But how can *I* help?"

"I want you to think very carefully about your colleagues in the department. Was there anyone who disliked Iris, who perhaps resented her accomplishments?"

Duncan blinked. "I'm sure no one disliked Iris. Certainly, I've heard nothing of that sort."

I sighed. Maybe Duncan, the original see-no-evil, wasn't my best source for this problem.

Thinking of my own department with its petty squabbles, I said, "No controversies among you over one thing or another?"

"Oh, I see. Yes, some time ago, there was much agitation over changing the requirements for the honors English degree, but it all rather died down and I've heard nothing recently. You see, each of us lives rather in his or her own world."

That rang a bell, all right. Academia, like other occupations, was the same the world over.

I tried again. "Is there someone who might have regarded Iris as a rival for promotion?"

"Mmm. Of course, there's Harris, the elder of the two Renaissance men. He has little on his publication list, but he's rather a favorite with the head. I believe their wives are great friends, and the four take holidays together. Actually, Harris's wife asked me on one occasion for my opinion of Iris's work, as we are in the same field, you see, and of course, I said it was perfectly splendid. But one can scarcely see a chap like Harris writing such a letter."

Patiently, I said, "Had a scandal erupted involving Iris, might it not have given Professor Griswold a sort of justification for excluding her and sponsoring the promotion of his favorite?"

"I expect it might do."

"Then, isn't it possible Professor Griswold invented the letter himself?"

Duncan gasped. "The *head?*"

I may as well have accused the Queen.

"I'm just considering all the options, Duncan."

"Oh, I see."

Casually, I said, "I know it's the long holiday, but does Professor Griswold sometimes come into the office to sign letters or whatnot?"

"Oh, I should think it very likely."

"Good. Perhaps I can catch him."

As I started for the phone, Duncan gave me a woebegone look. "Claire, you won't accuse him of—that is—"

"No, absolutely not. Nor will I mention your name."

I reached the secretary, Mrs. Hester, who told me the professor was there now but would be leaving shortly.

"Will you ask if I may have a brief interview with him? I can be there in ten minutes."

She sounded doubtful but came back on the line to say the professor would see me.

Duncan agreed to find a taxi for me. "If there's none in the square, there's sure to be one in the Tottenham Court Road," I told him.

We went down together, and I waited inside until I saw the taxi draw up and Duncan step out. Ignoring the newsmen, I waved thanks to Duncan and leaped in, arriving at the college in minutes.

Breathless from running up the stairs, I found Griswold sitting majestically behind a fine old desk. He rose to greet me, his face bland, and gestured me to a chair. "Good morning, Mrs. Camden. Sherry?"

"Thank you, no."

Now Griswold's eyes glinted with curiosity. "To what do I owe this pleasure?"

I needn't have hurried. I could see that he'd never have passed up a visit from an accused murderess.

I said, "I believe you know that Ms. Franklin's manuscript was retrieved from the disks?"

"Yes. Splendid news, indeed."

"Now, the police have a letter purporting to have been written by Ms. Franklin on her word processor here in her office. The letter contains material which, to *some persons,* would be of an unflattering, even scandalous, nature. I have come to you to ask if you can suggest anyone here at the college who might write such a letter, even perhaps in jest."

Now the bland countenance was coated with ice. "It may be that such pranks are common in American universities, Mrs. Camden. You would know that better than I. Here, I assure you, it is not our practice."

There was only one way to deal with that one. I stood up and, without a glance in his direction, walked out of the office.

In the corridor I paused, then walked along to the common room, where I waited till I stopped seething.

I hadn't for a moment expected that he would break down and confess to writing the letter. My goal had been to let him know that he was on the list of suspects. His nasty remark merely confirmed my opinion of his pettiness.

I stalled around, combing my hair and refreshing my lipstick, hoping Griswold would be gone when I emerged.

And he was.

I gave Mrs. Hester a radiant smile. We had always got on well. As Iris's friend, I was high on her list.

She told me how shocked she was that I had been accused of the murder. "You couldn't have done such a thing, Mrs. Camden. What are the police thinking of these days? They arrest anyone in order to make themselves look clever."

I thanked her, and we chatted for a while about our grown-up children, then got back to Iris. She said, "It was marvelous that her manuscript was saved."

"There must have been a good many people going into her office through all that time."

"Her son, David, came, of course, and Mr. Dimchurch had a key. You were all there together once, were you not?"

"Yes. It was a sad occasion, sorting through her things."

She paused. "Then, Miss Ward-Jones asked for the key one day. Oh, no, that was *before*—"

"Before Iris died?"

"Yes."

"Do you remember what day it was?"

"Yes, it was the Monday after end of term. That was just two days before—before the murder." She managed to say it that time.

I decided to pretend to knowledge I didn't have. "I

believe Miss Ward-Jones mentioned coming to collect a book for Iris."

"That must have been so. She took the key and returned it almost at once."

I nodded and went on to another topic, before bidding her a cordial good-bye.

As I walked back toward the flat, I thought hard about Fiona Ward-Jones. What had she been doing in Iris's office on the first day of the summer holidays? Iris had certainly never sent her to fetch a book. She returned the key to Mrs. Hester "almost at once," but she could easily have unlocked the door, returned the key, and gone back to the office. With the door closed, she could have stayed for hours and no one the wiser.

Would Mrs. Hester have seen her leave? Not necessarily. The stairs were not visible from where she sat at her desk, and there was also an alternate staircase at the other end of the passage.

So, was our Fiona busily erasing the disks and the backups containing Iris's manuscript? It wouldn't have occurred to me before, until David told me about Fiona's resentment toward her future mother-in-law.

And, more exciting to contemplate: Did she also compose a letter that she hoped would shatter David's image of his mother? If the purpose of the letter writer was to imply Iris's relationship with me, that alone might not have sufficed, the younger generation being generally more tolerant than their elders. However, the added declaration of Iris's purported desire for a variety of lovers might have given David a more distressing picture.

If Fiona did write the letter, why didn't she send it to Professor Griswold? It was only a guess, but Fiona may have cared less about Iris's promotion than about David's opinion. If so, she wouldn't want the whole thing to be exposed and subject to denial. What she may have planned was to place the unfinished letter where David would run across it as if by chance, knowing that he would never mention it to anyone. The poison would enter his soul, but only he would know.

By the time I got back to the flat, I was determined to have a chat with Fiona.

I was relieved to see that the hounds of the press had gone off to bay at some other quarry. They must have concluded that I had nothing to tell them, and, the fleeting nature of news being what it is, my case wasn't important enough to engage their attention for long.

I rang up the Ward-Jones residence and was put through to Fiona, who said in a sulky tone, "David isn't here. He's in Brighton."

"Actually, it's you I want to see, Fiona. Are you free for luncheon?"

"No, sorry."

"Tea, then? Something's come up, and I need to talk to you. Can you meet me at the Savoy at four o'clock?"

"I thought you were charged with murder," she said nastily.

I said, "I'm quite free," hoping she would misunderstand.

She did. "Oh, I see. All right, then, I'll come at four."

I arrived a few minutes before the hour and was shown to a cozy sofa and adjoining chair. Soft music from the piano floated like an *obbligato* among the muted castanets of china cups and saucers.

I was sure Fiona would be late and was pulling out my trusty paperback when she arrived, looking both haughty and curious, as if she couldn't make up her mind which line to take.

I cut to the chase. "No point in making small talk, Fiona. I asked you to come because I had a chat with Mrs. Hester at University College today. I believe you went to the English department on the Monday after end of term and asked for the key to Iris's office. I have a pretty good idea what you did there, but I'd like to hear it from you."

Some people are expert liars, who play it cool without a second's hesitation. Fiona was not one of those. Her eyes widened, her hands made little fluttering movements, and her voice came out a tone higher than usual. "I don't know what you mean."

"You must have known Iris wouldn't be in that day. She told Meredith she was taking a few days' rest before getting back to her project, and she may also have said the same to David. I suggest that you sat down at her word processor and systematically deleted the files and the backups of her work on the court wits."

She gave me a look of such intense loathing that it bolstered my theory more than all the denial in the world could have done. "Why should I do that?"

"Because you hated her, just as you hate me now."

"What if I did hate her? She wanted David to break off with me. But that's not to say I did—what you said."

At this auspicious moment the waiter arrived to take our order. Fiona said, "Nothing for me, thank you. I shall be leaving."

But she stayed in her seat, staring at me as if I had hypnotized her.

I said to the waiter, "I'll have the set tea for one, please."

I settled back on the little sofa. "Was it that day or later that you wrote the letter?"

"What letter?"

"The letter the police now have in their possession. The letter that caused me to be charged with murder."

Denial again, but with a gleam of triumph she couldn't conceal.

When she spoke, her tone was venomous. "You needn't blame me for that, Claire. Meredith told David the police suspected you all along. You and Iris were there alone in your flat, and no one else knew she was there but you."

I sat back and waited. Fiona was stunning to look at but far from swift. She didn't seem to realize how much she had given away. Time to try a little pressure.

"Fiona, destroying Iris's work constitutes malicious mischief, but I doubt if one could be successfully prosecuted for it. However, the letter is another matter. Whoever sent such a message to the police could be in very big trouble, and the police have ingenious ways of tracing such things."

Now, fear got the better of her, and she stood up. "I've told you, I know nothing about any of this."

She slung her bag over her shoulder and walked quickly away.

My heart was still giving delicious little thumps when my tea came. The moment I got home I'd call Joanna Reeve, my solicitor, but meanwhile I'd have my tea. I hadn't bothered with lunch, and I looked with pleasure at the tiered plate of goodies.

I took out my book, poured a cup of tea, and picked up a cucumber sandwich.

24

THAT EVENING I REACHED JOANNA REEVE WITH a full report of my chat with Fiona Ward-Jones. Joanna cautioned me not to be too hopeful. She would tell Chief Inspector Garvey and let him take it from there. My guess was that, while Garvey was hardly a member of the Claire Camden fan club, he would be madder than hops to find out he had been duped by a fake letter. If Fiona didn't do a better job of concealment with Garvey than she had with me, he would have her head on a platter in no time.

Maybe it was false optimism, but I slept soundly, and promptly at nine o'clock the next morning, I arrived at Angus MacFinn's office for our editorial conference.

He greeted me, as I expected, with exclamations of horror. "Darling! It's too dreadful! Surely, the police have gone mad! Do tell!"

"It's all a misunderstanding, Angus. I have an excellent solicitor who's taking care of everything for me, but I've been told not to talk about the case."

Once he saw that I wasn't about to give him the

217

juicy details, he squeezed my hand, assured me of his undying loyalty, and got down to the business at hand.

Angus was the ideal editor, making perceptive and helpful suggestions that I welcomed. Except for a short coffee break, we worked steadily through the morning, finishing up at shortly after one o'clock.

Angus stood up and stretched. "A fine piece of work, darling! Bussola's for luncheon?"

"Yes, lovely."

We strolled along the Strand, cut over to Trafalgar Square and up St. Martin's Lane, through warm sunshine tempered by an artful little breeze.

Over lunch he tried to pump me about Rupert Mortmain, his nostrils quivering for gossip. "I believe you saw something of him on your visit to Freshwater?"

He must have got that from Duncan, I thought. Except for Meredith, I hadn't mentioned Rupert to anyone else.

"Actually," I said, "we did some research together on the island."

"Regarding his Tennyson letters, no doubt? On *Art Chats* on Sunday, he mentioned 'another scholar.' Is that *you?*" Angus's eyes gleamed with pleasure.

"It is. I'd like you to know that. If you should publish Rupert's letters, just be sure he names his source."

"I shall, darling, I promise you."

I asked how things were with Duncan and Iris's manuscript.

Angus smiled. "He's already signed a contract with us and is soldiering on."

Later, over our coffee, we talked about Iris for a while. Angus had been fond of her and remarked that it must have been dreadful for her son. I longed to tell him about Fiona but prudently refrained.

"My greatest regret," I told him, "has been that Iris and I never had the chance to talk. When I went to your Grainger and Jones event the evening before her death, she had come to stay the night at my flat. I couldn't persuade her to come along to the party, and when I got back, she was already asleep."

"Yes, I knew she was at your place that night."

"I don't remember mentioning it to you. How did you know?"

"I rang her up to ask her to change her mind and come along. One of the VIPs wanted to chat with her about the court wits. I went to the telephone and found that Iris had put a message on her machine saying she could be reached at your flat."

I stared. "Angus, think carefully. What did her message say?"

"Oh, I believe it was directed to her son. Something like, 'David, if you ring, I'll be at Claire's place tonight,' or words to that effect."

"Did you ring my number then?"

"No, it wasn't necessary. When my celebrity saw that I hadn't reached Iris, he drifted off, saying not to bother."

"At what time was this, Angus?"

"Oh, quite early on. Shortly after seven, I should say. The guests were only beginning to arrive."

The significance of this news was sending bubbles up my spine, but I said nothing more to Angus.

When we parted, I walked over to the Charing Cross Road and plodded slowly homeward, scarcely looking into the windows of the bookshops where normally I would browse.

We had always assumed that no one knew Iris was at my flat that night. It wasn't likely that anyone looking for her would have rung my number, since I had just come back to London that afternoon. But that message on her machine changed everything.

Now, a magic phrase shone like a neon sign in my vision: *Anyone could have known where she was.*

What about Owen? He might have rung her to make peace, but it didn't sound like it. He was out drinking with his friend Josh. Chief Inspector Dietrich had verified their visits to various pubs, at some of which they had met up with friends. Then Owen had spent the night with Josh to avoid seeing Iris. That much I believed.

But what about the next day? He certainly hadn't phoned my number before I left. But when he did ring home later in the day and got my message about Iris, wouldn't he also have heard *her* message? If so, he must have erased it, because when I phoned their number, only his voice was on the machine.

The only problem with all this was that Iris was already dead hours before that call was made.

Okay, then, what about Zora? Until now, it had seemed impossible that she could have known where Iris was. But what if she did ring and heard that message? Would she know who "Claire" was and where I lived? Certainly possible. Iris might have spoken of me when she was there on the island. Rupert had had my card, with my address, in his possession for months. If I knew Zora, she probably kept tabs on everyone he knew.

I had had a vision once of Zora coming to the flat looking for Iris. What if it was more than a vision?

If she had rung the doorbell, Iris would certainly have let her in, surprised perhaps, but not frightened. The old myth that women don't strangle their victims wouldn't apply to Zora, in my view. She was physically strong, and in a psychotic state, the usual inhibitions wouldn't prevail.

There was still Kurt Hansen on the list of suspects. This new development would add nothing in his case, since he already knew from his wife's phone call where Iris was. Dietrich had told me they couldn't confirm Kurt's whereabouts at nine o'clock on the morning of the murder. By ten o'clock, he was on the road, leaving the possibility of his guilt still open.

Now I remembered what Kurt had said to me that night in the square. In his fury, he had told me to stay out of his affairs, and he had added, "That's what I told the dark-haired bitch." This could only mean Iris. But when did he see her to tell her anything? So far as we knew, they had never met.

Had he come to the flat that morning, after I had gone? Had his rage got the better of him?

Then there was Fiona. If she wrote the letter in which I pleaded with Iris to be my exclusive lover, she may have had a more vital goal than upsetting David. What if Fiona had phoned that evening and learned where Iris was? What if she had come to the flat, fortunately found Iris alone, and felt all her hatred culminate in a flash of fury so intense that she took her by the throat? Now she could use the letter to give *me* an apparent motive for killing Iris.

I liked this scenario, except for my uneasy feeling that Fiona wouldn't actually have murdered Iris out of sheer resentment.

Come on, Claire, an inner voice said. You've forgotten something. *What about the money?*

That made more sense. Married to David, with a tidy sum of money to spend, she wouldn't have had to while away her days in Daddy's office or in some other dreary place. When the money was gone, she might move on to greener pastures.

Back at the flat, I found a message from Joanna Reeve. When I pressed out the office number, the receptionist said Ms. Reeve was in court and would ring me back.

I changed into sweats, stretched out on the sofa, and opened the mail that had come that day. One letter, postmarked Brighton, contained a note from David. "The enclosed letter to mother was sent on to me here. I'm not sure what it's all about, but I thought you might like to see it."

The letter was headed "Autographs, Ltd.," signed "F. B. Smith," and was sent in reply to Iris's request for an analysis of an enclosed sheet of paper. I picked up the pale blue sheet and studied it. There was little doubt that this was the paper she had taken from the desk in the attic at Thornbury, and now I saw that she had written her name across the sheet, evidently using the steel nib and the ink from the desk, just as I had done.

Reading through some technical details of the process used for the dating of paper, I came to the essence of Mr. Smith's findings. It appeared that the year 1861 is a pivotal one. Papers before that date were almost exclusively composed of rag content, either of linen, cotton, flax, or hemp. After that date, papers often contained esparto grass, and in the 1880s, sulphite pulp came to be widely used. The sample in question was of rag content and was "laid," with a watermark used by a popular manufacturer, dating from the early nineteenth century.

Mr. Smith then gave the example of a famous poem first published in 1842. Fifty years later, a volume appeared on the market purporting to be a first edition, but the paper on which it was printed was proved to contain sulphite pulp, not used at that date.

As for the ink, Mr. Smith explained that in the sample enclosed, the ink consisted of iron gall with the addition of natural indigo. After the year 1861, synthetic indigo began to be used, becoming common by 1880.

His conclusion was that the enclosed paper and ink were in existence before 1861. That was not to say the document itself was *written* before that date. Indeed, anyone with access to such paper and ink might use these materials at anytime up to the present.

His letter concluded by suggesting that if forgery were in question, he would need further information and would be happy to render an opinion.

So, what did all this tell me? Nothing definite. Since nobody, so far as I knew, had seen the actual letters from the governess except Zora and Rupert, we didn't know if they matched the paper and ink from the attic. If they did, it would look highly suspicious, but at least we had learned that the attic paper and ink were genuinely old. If Zora *had* written the letters, it would be pretty hard to prove they were false.

Actually, I didn't care if they were. That was Rupert's problem. I had promised to go down to Yarmouth the next day to take some papers to Joyce Hansen and to visit Mrs. Ward. Now that I knew about Iris's phone message saying she would be at my place the night before the murder, I regretted that I couldn't sound out Rupert about Zora's whereabouts that day, but it wouldn't be worth it. I'd had enough of him.

Of course, the phone rang. "Claire? Rupert here."

"Yes?"

"My dear girl, I've just learned that you've been charged with murder! Surely, there's some dreadful mistake. What can I do to help?"

About to make a rude reply, I realized this was the very chance I'd been wishing for. Why not give it a whirl?

"Are you on the island?"

"Yes."

"As it happens, I'm coming down to Yarmouth

tomorrow to visit friends. If you care to meet me in the square at three o'clock, I can see you *very* briefly then."

"It's beastly hot here. Wear something cool, darling!" And he put down the phone.

Being Rupert, he hadn't noticed my freezing tone. Never mind. He'd get the message when we met.

Presently, the phone rang again. "Claire, it's Joanna. Interesting developments. I saw Chief Inspector Dietrich in court this afternoon. He's still fairly pissed off at being supplanted by Garvey on the Franklin case, so he's keeping tabs on what's going on. He learned that this morning, Garvey had your Fiona Ward-Jones brought into the station for questioning. Evidently she was horrified at finding herself in such a nasty place and burbled out that she *did* write the letter."

"Marvelous! Will this get me off the hook?"

"Not yet, I'm afraid. It seems that our Fiona swore that she 'knew' it was all true about you and Iris, so she wasn't actually saying anything false. Garvey longs to believe that and won't give up on you.

"However, he's not happy that the letter isn't genuine, and it occurred to him, without prompting, that our young lady might have done the murder herself and invented the letter to throw suspicion on you. At this point, the story goes, she became hysterical and claimed she was having breakfast with Mummy that morning. Of course, Mummy will confirm that, I'm sure."

"So, now he has two suspects."

"Yes, and he may have a third. The police finally caught up with your Kurt Hansen. He's being held on the charge of his assault on you, and Dietrich is making sure he's also questioned about the murder of your friend."

We agreed we were shedding no tears over DCI Garvey.

Now I told Joanna about the message on Iris's machine the evening before the murder. "This may help, as I'm sure Fiona swore she didn't know Iris was here."

"Yes, very good! I'll get the message through tomorrow."

I said, "One more thing. I need to go to the Isle of Wight tomorrow. Must I obtain permission?"

She told me she would take care of it for me, and we rang off.

25

BEFORE GOING TO BED THAT EVENING, I GATHered up some books to be returned to the library, including three biographies of Tennyson and two of Julia Cameron. As I set them down on the table in the entry, something clicked on my internal radar screen.

Last Sunday on *Arts Chat,* Rupert had read a letter in which the young woman had referred to the "two weeks" since the day when "her life began," or in more mundane terms, the day when the two lovers had first consummated their affair.

I thought back to the letter about the nephew who came to visit and who followed the governess one night as she slipped away to the summerhouse at Farringford. Dated 21 August 1865, the day after the death of the governess, the news of which must have spread all over the island within hours, the sister of Mrs. James referred to her son Robert's visit to his cousins "this month," that is, in August, from which he had evidently just returned before the tragedy took place.

I looked down at the volumes on Tennyson. Picking

up the one on top, I turned to the chapter covering the events of the poet's life in that year.

There it was: "In July, Alfred and Emily set off with their sons for a journey to the Continent, returning in September, in time for the boys to return to their school."

I checked the other volumes. One mentioned a summer trip to the Continent without giving specific dates. The other gave pretty much the same information as the first. I stood transfixed, as the truth struck me.

It wasn't Tennyson to whom the letters were written, because he wasn't there!

Why hadn't Rupert—or Zora, for that matter—noticed this before?

The answer to that was quite simply that the letters in their possession had no dates! All the available dates came from the court records of the death of the governess, from the newspaper accounts, and from the letters found at the Beeches.

Without the last letter's reference to their affair as having begun only two weeks earlier, and with no time reference for those weeks, one could assume that the affair had begun at any time when Tennyson *was* still at Farringford.

I went back to the study and pulled out my notes, reading over all the jottings I had made from the beginning.

How much did we really know?

We knew there *was* a governess named May at the Beeches. We had her photograph, taken by Julia Cameron, and many references to her in letters. We knew that she had lovely red hair and that she visited the summerhouse at night in August in the year 1865. We knew that she had met her death on the twentieth day of August of that year when she fell from the cupola room of the house where she was employed.

Unless there were two red-haired young women visiting the summerhouse at that date, we must conclude that May was the writer of love letters to someone whom she met there.

So, if Alfred Lord Tennyson was innocently dashing about the Continent with his wife and sons, to whom were the letters written?

The answer could be any middle-aged man who lived in the neighborhood and suggested meeting in the summerhouse when the poet was gone. Everybody in the area would know when their local celebrity was at home and when he was away.

When her lover quoted passages of Tennyson's poetry to his lady, what could be more natural, if he were an educated man? If people everywhere were prone to declaim favorite Tennysonian passages at the drop of a hat, what more likely from a man who lived in close proximity to the poet, perhaps had met him?

I thought I knew the answer.

John Hendrick, the local schoolmaster, had gone to live at Thornbury after his shrewish wife left him.

Why did she leave him? Because she learned that he was having an affair with the governess at the Beeches?

She called at the Beeches, knowing the family was away, and asked to speak to May. Did the governess confess the truth? Whatever happened, there was only one candidate now for the lover.

It was John Hendrick who kept the letters in a metal box in the attic at Thornbury. It was John Hendrick who treasured the letters as the testimony to the great love of his life.

In the last letter Rupert had read on the BBC, the young woman had referred to their meeting in church. The Tennysons rarely attended services, but the schoolmaster would certainly have done so. She also mentioned understanding that it was difficult for her lover to come to their meetings. Tennyson could have popped out to the summerhouse at almost any hour of the day or night, and often did, but the schoolmaster's chances would have been limited.

Now I faced the question of whether to tell Rupert that we could rule out Tennyson as the lover or let him stumble across the fact himself, as he inevitably would if he went on with the project. He was too good a scholar to miss it.

I'd see how things went tomorrow when we met.

When I arrived on the island, I went first to the Beeches to see Mrs. Ward, who was making a slow but steady recovery from her stroke, her speech somewhat impeded but quite comprehensible. We sat in the garden again while I told her the story of the letters and my conclusions about the schoolmaster as the lover.

She gave me a mischievous look. "I confess I'm a bit disappointed that it wasn't Tennyson after all, only because one would like to dispel his image of stiff propriety. According to people who knew him here, he was rather bluff but open-hearted and unpretentious."

Our talk turned to the tragedy of the governess, and Mrs. Ward said, "It's puzzling that the young lady's letters, so far as we know, give no indication of anything but happiness, yet there were rumors that she had taken her own life."

Sitting here at the house where I had had the terrifying fall, I felt something hovering at the edge of my mind. If the governess had merely slipped, as I had done, why didn't the gutter stop her?

Mrs. Ward had heard through the village grapevine of my near disaster. Now, I asked, "Was there always a gutter on the roof where I fell?"

"Oh, yes, my dear. They have been replaced many

times over the years, but not very recently, I'm afraid."

"Then May would have had to throw herself beyond the gentle slope of the gable."

"It would seem so."

Now my vague suspicions crystallized. *"But what if she were pushed?"*

A puzzled look, followed by a flash. "The schoolmaster's wife? I do see."

We looked at each other while the possibilities swirled in our minds.

I said, "We'll never know, but it's possible, isn't it? When May heard who had come to call, she snatched up the schoolmaster's letters and burned them in the grate so that nothing in his handwriting could be found."

Mrs. Ward nodded. "Somehow, Mrs. Hendrick lured her up to the round room . . ."

"Yes. Perhaps she gave no sign of suspicion at first, acting as if it were merely a social call. She may have asked to see the famous view from the cupola . . ."

"The window is open because it is a very warm day in August . . ."

"They stand by the window, talking. Does Mrs. Hendrick accuse her now . . . ?"

"Do they quarrel . . . ?"

I said, "I believe the wife would pour out her accusations. She is angry enough to kill, and suddenly the opportunity is there. In a blind rage she pushes with all her might and sees her rival pitch forward and roll helplessly over the edge."

Mrs. Ward sighed. "What must she have felt when she heard the sickening sound of the body as it struck the ground?"

"She must have been terrified that she would be found out. Imagine her relief when no one shouted for help, no one stirred in the house or the grounds. She must have crept down the stairs, waiting, and finally walked away unnoticed."

Mrs. Ward nodded eagerly. "Then she went home, packed as if for a visit, and took her children straight-away to her parents in Hampshire."

"And never returned!"

"Exactly. Does her husband suspect?"

"I think he does, but he has no proof. He will never live with his wife again, but he cannot accuse her without revealing the whole story."

Of course, we agreed, it was all speculation, but somehow it made sense of the facts as we knew them.

Eventually, we went on to talk of other things. When she asked about the "charming gentleman" who had come with me to the hospital, I managed to give a vague reply, and moved on to other topics.

When I rose to go, she said this had been quite the most delightful time and asked if I would include the story of the schoolmaster's wife in my biography of Mary Louise Talbot, and I told her I would put in as much as my editor would allow. With best wishes for her continued recovery, I took my leave, reflecting with pleasure that neither advancing age nor a physical ailment had quenched the fun-loving spirit of this delightful lady.

I reached the little house in Yarmouth by one o'clock, in time to take Joyce and Penny to lunch in the village. With Kurt locked up, Joyce had pointed out that they could have gone back to London, but it took little persuasion for her to stay on the island. I brought papers for her to sign from the solicitor who was handling her divorce petition, and in the following week, she and Penny would go up to Heathrow to catch their plane for Toronto, then on by train to Alberta to her parents.

As we sat at an outdoor table, shaded from the hot

sun, laughing and chatting, I saw the transformation in Joyce. Timidity gone, she sparkled with confidence, while Penny glowed.

After lunch we strolled through the shops, buying little gifts for each other, and selecting one for me to deliver to Meredith for them.

I knew there would be no quick happy ending to their situation. When Kurt was free again, he would probably move heaven and earth to find them. It would be a long time before Joyce could stop wondering if he would catch up with them some day, and what he would do if he succeeded. What she had going for her, however, was the hope for a new life and the escape from the emotional bondage she had endured.

Joyce said nothing of this to me until Penny was safely browsing in another part of a shop. Then she expressed her fear about Kurt. I didn't pretend it couldn't happen. We agreed instead to hope Kurt would simply give up, probably finding another woman to whom he would repeat his pattern of abuse.

"I'm not going to let it stop me," Joyce said, her eyes clear and alert. "I'll never be a victim again."

Back at the house, I told them I was meeting a friend in the village and would go on to the ferry from there, giving Penny a special hug, again catching a reminder of Sally at that age in that piquant, almost twelve-year-old face.

I wasn't at all sure Rupert would turn up, but he did, looking fetching in shorts and a cotton shirt. I was wearing a California sundress and sandals, and he looked at me with approval. "Good. We'll go to Colwell Bay. It's not far."

After a short drive, he parked the car, picked up a couple of large towels, and led the way down to a little sandy beach. We sat in the warm sun, among the crowds of holiday-makers, children splashing in the water or building sand castles, sunbathers stretched full length in the welcome heat.

Rupert bent over and took my hand. "Now, tell me."

I retrieved my hand and gave him a brief summary of the charge against me.

He snorted. "You and *Iris?* They must be mad."

"Rupert, I asked you to meet me today because I want to talk to you about your sister. Have you spoken to her about what she did to me?"

A look of pain twisted his features. "Yes. She says she has no recollection of it."

"Does that mean you don't believe me?"

"Oh, God, what can I say? No, I do believe you. I did from the beginning, but I hoped somehow it was not true. You see, Claire, Zora has been ill since her teens. After our parents died, I've done my best to look after her. When she takes her medicine, she does well, but sometimes she either forgets or refuses to take it.

"She wanted to come here to the island. We bought Thornbury, and she has been stable a good deal of the time. I was permanently separated from my wife, and it's been a home for both of us."

Kind, compassionate Rupert was back, and I felt my antagonism melting. "Is Zora here on the island now?"

"No, she's in hospital in Dorset. I've been there looking after her, so to speak. She has been extremely perturbed by the problems with my wife. I'd gone up to Scotland to settle some questions of money. She lives up there with a bloke who likes his bottle."

Feeling myself drawn in, I said softly, "Can't you divorce?"

"No, it's better this way. Neither of us wants to marry."

"I see. Rupert, it's difficult to ask you this, but I must. You remember that Zora was distressed when Iris seemed to question the authenticity of the letters in the attic. Until now, we have assumed that no one could know that Iris was staying at my place when she was killed. Now we have learned that she had put a message on her machine the evening before to let her son, David, know where she was. Obviously anyone who rang her number would have heard this.

"We know that Zora identified me with Iris, seeing me as a wraith come back from the dead. Isn't it possible that she heard that message, came up to London the next morning, and came to my flat—"

I stopped, but he said it for me. "And killed Iris?"

"Yes. Is there any way to know where she was on that morning?"

He looked out at the sea for a time, then spoke softly. "It was just after end of term, was it not? I had come down on the weekend and gone back to my flat in Islington. I don't believe there is anyone who would know where she was."

He hadn't denied the possibility. I said, "Rupert, when doubt was cast on the letters, did you wonder if Zora had written them herself?"

Now his answer was unequivocal. "No, not a chance. She becomes obsessive over things, and finding the letters was, as you saw, a dramatic event for her, but she could never have *invented* them."

"Are the originals on pale blue paper?"

"No, rather a cream shade, I would say."

Then he was probably right. Zora was not angry at Iris's suspicion because she herself had written them, only that someone would question the authenticity of her sacred discovery.

Now was the time, I decided, while Rupert was in a receptive mood. "I have made some discoveries concerning the letters. Do you want to know about them?"

"Yes, of course. I haven't given them a thought for the past week."

The hot sun was getting to me, and I looked at the inviting water. Slipping off my sandals, I walked in, standing up to my knees in the gentle surf. Rupert kicked off his shoes and joined me, and we stood facing each other, the water sloshing around our legs.

I gave him the bad news first. "I'm afraid the letters were not written to Tennyson."

He greeted this with a raised brow, and I went on, giving him a quick summary of facts and dates, ending with my theory that it was the schoolmaster who was the lover.

"I'm sure you would have seen this for yourself sooner or later. I'm so sorry, Rupert."

He reached out and took both of my hands in his, swinging them back and forth as children do. "Claire, you *are* a dear!"

Now it was my turn for the raised eyebrow.

"You were afraid this news would distress me?"

"Doesn't it?"

"Not really. It's never been important to me, only to Zora. But, my dear, it is so kind of you to be concerned. You might easily have been triumphant."

Now, for the first time that day, his eyes shot their lightning bolts. "Have you told anyone else about this?"

"Only Mrs. Ward."

"The old lady at the Beeches?"

"Yes."

He nodded, then pulled me close to him and gave me a casual kiss. "We'll go to my place. It's cool there."

He started off, expecting me to follow, but I stood

where I was, picturing the empty house with Zora away, attraction and repugnance pulling me backward and forward like the tide that pulled at my feet.

He looked back and called, "Come along," and in that moment I knew I wouldn't go with him.

I shook my head. "No, thank you. Please take me to the ferry."

And he did.

26

THAT NIGHT, FOR THE FIRST TIME, I BEGAN TO feel real fear. In the initial shock of being charged with murder, it had all seemed too absurd, like one of those nightmares when you know you are dreaming and that somehow you'll wake up and it will be over. Now I was haunted by specters of a trial, of a jury pronouncing me guilty, of prison bars enclosing me.

I thought back over the day on the island: my visit with Mrs. Ward, seeing Joyce and Penny, and then the talk with Rupert. Although I had come to expect the unpredictable with Rupert, I was still astonished at how well he had taken the revelation that the governess's letters were not written to Tennyson but to someone else, possibly the local schoolmaster.

It had never mattered to him, he had said, only to Zora. Certainly, it was clear that a big mark on the plus side for Rupert was his sincere devotion to his troubled sister. Self-centered and inconsiderate as he usually appeared to be, at any sign of distress, he switched instantly to sympathy and concern. There was the night he came to the Tennyson library, when I was in tears over Mrs. Ward's illness. There was his tenderness the evening here at the flat when he found me battered and bruised.

Today on the island, he had tried to show the same concern over the police accusation that I had killed Iris. He had spoken movingly of his sister and his care of her. I had begun to soften toward him when something stopped me. When he asked me to go to the house with him, I longed to have him as my lover again, yet a stronger impulse held me back.

Was it merely that I was fed up with his vacillations? Since I had no desire for a permanent, or even lengthy, relationship with him, why did his moodiness matter?

Or was there a deeper source for my reluctance?

Why did he ask me if I had told anyone else about the letters? What if he had, in fact, cared deeply about the whole matter? He could certainly use the money they might bring. Furthermore, he had clearly enjoyed the minor celebrity of his appearances on the BBC. It would be a bitter pill to have to acknowledge he had been mistaken.

Was Rupert merely eccentric, or did he share, in a lesser degree, the instability of his twin? I remembered the occasion when his bizarre behavior had caused me to say, "Are you crazy?" and he had cried out in fury, "Don't ever say that—never!"

Could *he* have written the letters and planted them for Zora to find?

I thought back to my suspicion that Zora might have committed the murder of Iris. Now I realized that everything that applied to Zora would apply equally to Rupert.

He might have rung Iris's number the evening before and heard the message that she was at my place. He had my card with my address and phone. He might then have rung my number and talked with

Iris there, learning that I was leaving at nine o'clock the next morning for an appointment. He might even have waited along the square until he saw me leave.

Finally, I wondered if he had come on to me in the beginning in order to find out if Iris had told me anything that might have been damaging to him.

But if all this were true, how would we ever prove it?

The next day was Sunday, and in the afternoon, Meredith called for me in her sports car. We drove up to Kenwood at the northwest corner of Hampstead Heath, to the beautiful eighteenth-century house and park given to the nation by Lord Iveagh.

In perfect weather, we strolled down to the lake, over lawns green from the summer rains, and sat on a bench with a view of the charming little bridge.

When I told Meredith about my discovery that the Mortmain love letters could not have been written to Tennyson, she grinned wryly. "That certainly knocks in the head their potential value, I'd say. Even my bookshop wouldn't touch them now."

"Yes. I was surprised Rupert took the news so well."

"He's an odd duck all around, isn't he?"

That was the understatement of the week, I thought.

Then I told her my theory about Rupert and the murder.

Her brown eyes did their flash and bore. "It makes good sense to me, Claire, but can it be proved?"

"That's the problem."

We chewed it over for a while, finally going on to other topics.

We talked books, theater, anything to avoid the subject of the murder, but inevitably, we were drawn by its magnetic force. At some reference to Owen

Babcock, I asked her if she had seen him when she went with her friend to sort out Iris's belongings.

"Yes, he finally arrived with the key, late as usual. He'd been out somewhere and agreed to meet us at three o'clock, but knowing Owen, I wasn't surprised when he turned up at half past the hour, panting and full of apologies. Iris had given up hope that he would ever mend his ways and watch the time. He gave us a drink, played the grief-stricken spouse for my benefit, and made off again, leaving us to cope."

"That's Owen to the life."

Meredith was vocal about Fiona having admitted to writing the letter that caused me to be charged with killing Iris but was less inclined to cast Fiona as First Murderer. "Frankly, I don't think she'd have the nerve to do it. As for the letter, it may be painful for David to hear of it, but it's better for him to know the truth about her now than to marry her and find it out later on. What I don't understand is why this doesn't release you from suspicion."

"Joanna, my solicitor, says that Fiona insists the information was true, and that beast Garvey won't let me go."

We sat in silence for a while. Then Meredith asked, tentatively, about Neil Padgett, whom she had met once or twice in the past. I felt comfortable enough with her by now to give her the basic facts of our breakup.

I said, "I'm still hurting, but I didn't expect a quick recovery."

I asked if she was dating anyone at the moment, and she shook her head. Meredith's husband had died some ten years earlier, and, according to Iris, she had known some interesting men but had shown no desire to marry again.

Now, her voice husky, she said, "I know about hurting. Six months ago I was involved with a man who for the first time engaged my whole being. I was as madly in love as a girl of twenty. While it lasted, it was the most intense experience of my life."

She gazed out over the water of the lake, while I absorbed my surprise that matter-of-fact Meredith was capable of such passionate feeling.

"Then he left me for someone else."

I wondered if I would be saying this about Neil one day. Would he come back from Australia with an attractive bride?

Eventually, we walked back up the hill and had a pot of tea in the garden beside the old carriage house, thronged with visitors taking advantage of the warm sun.

Afterward, we went through the house itself, savoring the fine collection of paintings, sharing old favorites from former visits. It was an altogether pleasant afternoon, and good therapy for me.

Around seven o'clock that evening, my restlessness returned, and I went out for a walk, finding myself heading for Covent Garden as I'd often done in the past. Although it was a Sunday evening, some of the shops were still open, and a few street stalls remained to catch the late strollers.

I wandered at random, looking at merchandise without really seeing it, standing with a crowd listening to a band without noticing what they were playing. I strolled on, coming to a restaurant with outdoor tables, enclosed with rows of potted plants. I'd had only a slice of cake with my tea, and at a whiff of pasta, I knew I was hungry. I waited in a short queue, and in five minutes I was shown to a table.

More potted plants stood here and there among the tables, giving an illusion of privacy. I ordered a glass of wine, studied the menu, and taking out my paperback, I read until the waiter came back.

When I'd given my order, I looked to my left, and through the fronds of a tired-looking palm, I noticed a shoe that seemed familiar. A Bruno Magli belonging to an extremely shapely leg.

Of course! My neighbor, Deirdre Kemp.

About to rise and speak to her, I looked at her companion and sank back behind the palm tree.

It was Owen Babcock.

Their table was far enough away so that, what with the general noise, I could hear nothing of their conversation, but I could see them from the side as they faced each other. They had evidently finished a meal and were having their coffee.

I was struck at once by Owen's demeanor. He was bent forward, gazing intently into Deirdre's luminous eyes, while she leaned back in her chair, frowning slightly. In contrast to his usual arrogance, Owen was clearly beseeching her and getting no response.

Deirdre shook her head, and holding out her hand, evidently asked him for something.

At this, Owen looked so stricken that I thought he might burst into tears. Then he reached into his pocket and brought out a key, which he laid on the table between them.

Deirdre quietly picked it up and put it in her bag. Then she stood up, putting out her hand in a gesture that said, "Don't get up," and moved gracefully away, threading a path between the tables to the exit, getting a few admiring glances as she went.

I looked back at Owen, astonished to see him bent over, his hands covering his face, his body shaking with dry sobs. That Owen could feel so deeply about anything that he would forget his social aplomb to this extent in a public place signaled an emotional upheaval of no ordinary dimension.

It was evident that Deirdre was breaking off their affair and that Owen knew her decision was final. This was not a tiff between lovers. I remembered Deirdre's remark to me, her deep blue eyes as hard as sapphires, that sometimes one must do what was needful.

When Owen raised his head at last, his face haggard, he laid some pound notes on the table and walked slowly away, his body sagging as if weights were attached to his limbs.

Did I feel pity for him, as for any suffering human being? Not on your life. Owen was a big boy. He could look after himself.

When the waiter brought my pasta, I went back to my book, putting Owen out of my mind.

It was after nine o'clock, the sun still above the horizon, when I walked along to my flat, where I stood looking out the window at the shadows cast by the massive trees in the square.

I was tempted to ring up Deirdre, but I couldn't very well say I had watched the little melodrama from behind a potted palm. Some day, when I had the chance, I'd sound her out.

Thinking back over the whole series of events since Iris's death, I reflected upon the handful of persons who might have derived some benefit from her death, but none had the powerful motive that I now knew Owen possessed. A desperate love, a desperate desire for money, for Deirdre wouldn't stay long with a lover who didn't have plenty.

Then I recalled something Meredith had said that very afternoon as we sat by the lake, something I ought to have remembered before.

The answer was there, if only I had seen it before!

But there were some things I needed to do first, before I told the world.

27

AT FIVE MINUTES TO NINE THE NEXT MORNING, dressed in sweats and running shoes, I stood outside the door of the office of Morgan Associates in the Tottenham Court Road. A man in a dark suit stepped out of the lift and came toward me but went on down the passage, where he unlocked the door of another office.

My watch said two minutes after nine o'clock when a young woman with blond, spiral curls appeared.

"Good morning," she said. "Sorry to keep you waiting."

She opened the door, heard the phone ringing, hurried through to the inner office, and picked up the phone.

I found myself in a small waiting room, sparsely furnished with a few chairs and a central table piled with tattered magazines. Along the wall to my right stood an armchair, and beyond that the glass window behind which the young woman could be heard on the telephone.

When she had finished, I went to the window.

She slid back a panel and gave me a friendly smile. "How may I help you?"

I said, "Sorry I have no appointment, but I'd like to see Mr. Morgan. I've done programming in the States, and I'm looking for a contract while I'm here in London."

She took my name, saying, "Yes, very good, Mrs. Camden. Mr. Morgan will be in shortly, if you'll have a seat."

I picked up a magazine and took the chair against the inner wall, where I noted that she couldn't see me unless she leaned out of the window and looked my way.

I waited a few minutes, then went to the window again. "I'm afraid I need to run to the ladies'—that time of the month, you know."

She gave me a sympathetic nod. "Up one flight and at the end of the corridor."

I thanked her and went out the door as the phone rang again.

Then I took out a stopwatch. At exactly nine minutes past the hour, I pressed the Start button.

Ignoring the lift, I ran down the stairs, turned right for twenty yards, and turned right again on Bayley Street, a short dash to Bedford Square. At my flat, the third building from the corner, I inserted my key in the outer door, sprinted up the stairs, and pretended to press the buzzer.

I counted the seconds, seeing Iris walk toward the door, take a quick look through the peephole, confirm who it was, and open the door.

I counted again, shuddering. No time to think. As she turns to walk toward the sitting room, take her by the throat, press till she falls, lifeless, to the floor. Pick up her slight body and drop her on the sofa.

Now I ran down the stairs, back along Bayley

Street, around the corner, up one flight to Morgan's office, and sank into the chair against the wall.

Exactly ten minutes.

Pray that Morgan hadn't come in. Pray that the receptionist hasn't noticed how long I had been gone.

When I'd caught my breath, I stepped casually to the table, glancing toward the glass partition.

She wasn't there!

I waited, holding the magazine, until she came back from an inner office with an apologetic smile. "I'm afraid he's a bit late this morning."

I smiled back. "It's quite all right."

And it was. Telling her I'd come back later in the day, I went back to the flat, walking this time.

I went straight to the phone and rang up Deirdre Kemp, who didn't impress me as an early-rising type. She was there, and when I told her it was a matter of great importance, she said, "I'm still in my dressing gown, but do come up."

She handed me a cup of coffee, and I told her I had by chance seen her the evening before with Owen Babcock.

In her forthright way, she needed no prompting. "Yes. Actually, I broke off our relationship. He had become tiresome, I'm afraid."

"This may seem an odd question, Deirdre, but was Owen reliable about keeping appointments on time?"

She rolled her eyes upward. "No, he was chronically late. It drove me mad."

So, he hadn't reformed, I thought, even for his lady love.

"How did you and Owen meet, Deirdre?"

She shrugged. "Actually, it was here in the building, last year at the Christmas holidays. I was putting my key into the outer door when Owen came dashing up, saying he was late meeting friends at your flat. We went up the first pair of stairs together, and he said he hoped we might meet again. A few days later, he rang me and said he'd heard my name at your place, and so it all began."

"I can see why neither of you mentioned your acquaintance to me, Deirdre, but when I first told you of Iris Franklin's death, you didn't tell me then that you knew Owen."

She gave me a lazy smile. "No. I was startled, of course, but I didn't want to be involved if it wasn't necessary."

"Yes, I see. What did Owen tell you about it?"

"He said the police had questioned him and that he was absolutely cleared. Since nothing further happened, I saw no reason to doubt him. When you and I chatted the other day, there was no point in speaking of him, especially since I was ready to banish him from my life."

"Are you aware that I have been charged with the murder?"

"No! I'm afraid I don't follow the news as faithfully as one ought to do."

"It hasn't made the headlines." I told her the story and was gratified that she thought the police were out of their minds.

Now I laid it on the line. "Deirdre, I believe Owen did kill his wife, and I want your help."

She skipped the protests and said simply, "What can I do?"

I described the series of events from the time I found Iris's body and Owen's account of where he had been.

"I was chatting with a friend yesterday and was reminded that Owen was habitually late for appointments. So, why did he turn up at Morgan's office promptly at nine o'clock that morning? Not only was Owen always late himself, he knew that Morgan always kept *him* waiting."

"Yes, I see. It's most unlike him."

"He could have known where Iris was. I've told you about learning that she had left a message on their machine at home telling her son she was at my place. If Owen heard that message in the evening, not the next afternoon, as he told the chief inspector, he might have phoned Iris at my place, and in the course of their conversation, she mentioned that I was going out for an appointment in the morning at nine o'clock. Then, it occurred to him that he could set up an alibi with the receptionist at Morgan's office."

"But would he have had time to do this?"

"Yes!" I described my trial run and the fact that the receptionist hadn't noticed my absence.

"Even if she had noticed," I added, "she would have assumed I was in the loo."

Deirdre gave me a long, solemn look. "Yes, I'm beginning to see how it could have happened."

"There was another puzzling fact," I went on. "When Owen first got my message that Iris was dead, he came to my place, walked in, said something like, 'What happened?' and marched directly into the sitting room. From the entry, you couldn't see that Iris was there, yet he didn't hesitate or wait to be shown where she was."

I asked Deirdre what Owen had said about Iris during the time she had known him.

She leaned back in her chair. "In the beginning, he told me he and his wife lived separate lives. Of course, I've heard that often enough from married men, but I found him attractive and good company, and I saw no reason to doubt his word.

"Unfortunately, Owen developed what I can only call an obsessive attachment to me. He talked about marriage, and I rather flippantly said I never married unless there was money. Then, quite recently, he told me his wife was talking seriously about divorce. She was reluctant because it might affect her career, but she disliked living in such a false relationship as their marriage had become.

"What surprised me was that, with all his talk of marriage, he seemed distressed at the idea of divorce. I'd have thought he might welcome it, although I had made it quite clear I had no intention of marrying him."

"Has he ever told you about the insurance he would collect from Iris?"

"Insurance? No."

I told her the amount.

"Oh, my God. Poor Owen, did he think I would change my mind if he had this money? I wouldn't have married him if he'd had millions!"

We looked at each other again, aware of the powerful motive Owen had believed he had for killing Iris.

"Deirdre," I asked, "did Owen have a key to this building?"

"Yes. I asked him to return it to me last evening. I had told him for some time that we must end our affair. Not only had he become possessive, he had also been extremely nervous and jumpy in the past month, and I no longer enjoyed his company. He begged me repeatedly not to break off with him, saying he could not go on without me. I knew I had to be firm, for his good as well as my own. I agreed last evening to a sort of farewell meal together, and we got through nearly to the end without his usual pleading, but when I asked for the key, he began again. My only recourse was to take the key and leave."

Without mentioning what I had seen in the restaurant, I said, "His having the key would have made it easier for him to come into the building that morning without having to ring the buzzer and risk having the solicitors' receptionist hear the buzzer release and perhaps look up to see him."

Deirdre frowned. "It *is* rather a shock to think that Owen did this, Claire, but I'm afraid it's possible."

"If only we had more evidence."

"Yes. When he told me Iris was murdered at a quarter past nine that morning, while he was at an appointment, of course I believed him."

I stared. "He told you *what?*"

She repeated her statement.

"You are quite sure of that?"

"Of course. He said it more than once."

"And you will tell the police that?"

"Certainly."

"Because you see, *the police never told Owen the time of her death!*"

28

IN THE NEXT FEW DAYS AFTER MY CONVERSATION with Deirdre Kemp, she had made her statement to the police, and my solicitor, Joanna Reeve, had reported that Chief Inspector Dietrich was back on the case, along with the detestable DCI Garvey. They were all agreed that the charges against me would be dropped, once they had sorted out all the red tape.

Owen Babcock had been questioned and had denied everything. His high-powered solicitor had instructed him to say nothing further, and Owen had taken his advice.

I'd heard from David, who said it was definitely over with Fiona. When he learned she had tried to destroy his mother's work, he was shaken but half inclined to weaken when she claimed she did it because she loved him. But when he heard about the letter she invented concerning Iris and me, that did it. She had collected her things from the flat in Brighton and gone home to Mummy and Daddy.

I had felt my life swinging back to normal when, on Thursday evening, Neil phoned from Australia. "I'm coming into Heathrow tomorrow, Claire. Can you meet me?"

"Of course."

I expected a lot of stiffness when we met, some circling around who was to blame, or what would happen now.

It was nothing like that at all.

We took one look and our arms were around each other. A lot of laughing and kissing, and somehow it was as if nothing had happened. We both burbled a lot about being stupid, but it was only the froth. I knew that whatever it was we had between us, it was solid enough to be worth working for.

When we finally got around to sensible talk, he explained that he'd managed to get someone to take over the remainder of his tour of duty. "I want the rest of the summer with you, if you'll have me."

I said I would.

Driving back into London, he asked for the story of Iris's death and my being charged with her murder.

"You knew about it?"

"Not until it was nearly over. I had a phone call from a DCI named Dietrich who used to be in my unit. He didn't tell me much but enough that I knew he had been pulled from the case and believed you were innocent. I was packing to leave when I heard from Dietrich again that you were going to be cleared."

On the Saturday evening, Neil and I went to a party hosted by Angus MacFinn at his charming house in Highgate. Angus had told me how shocked he had been when he heard that Rupert Mortmain's letters were not written to Tennyson at all, but Rupert had laughed and convinced Angus to publish a little account of the whole episode as a "literary curiosity," taking the tone of the last *Arts Chat* program on unsolved mysteries.

"And he's giving you full credit for your part in it, darling," Angus had burbled. "Of course, it's not truly a scholarly work, but it promises to be good fun and may sell like hotcakes!"

I noticed Rupert hadn't offered to share the profits with me, but after all, the first batch of letters were his discovery. He was welcome to it.

Meredith Evans was at the party, looking attractive in black silk. She and Neil had a long chat about Australia.

Halfway through the evening, I saw a familiar figure across the crowded room. The long, bony face was turned my way, and I saw Rupert's eyes take in the handsome presence of Neil Padgett. When Neil had been absorbed by a group to one side, Rupert made his way slowly through the press of people toward me.

"I see your friend is back."

"Yes."

He gave me one of his charged-up looks. "You are positively glowing, my dear. I hope he realizes his good luck."

Meredith was standing beyond Neil, and I saw her face flush painfully as Rupert approached. Then she turned away. Oh, dear, was Rupert the faithless lover she still mourned? I hoped not.

Some time later, caught in another press of bibulous types in a corner, I heard Rupert's voice, purring softly. "Are you married?"

I looked in time to see him standing inches away from Fiona Ward-Jones. She looked at him and murmured, "No," and Rupert put a hand on her arm. "Not that it would matter," he said, and turned away.

Repressing a giggle, I decided that line must have served him well for years. I caught a glimpse of Fiona's face, flattered, mesmerized. Someone had brought Fiona to the party, but I'd be willing to bet it was Rupert who would take her home. I couldn't think of two people who deserved each other more.

Duncan Dimchurch was there, giving me mournful looks but assuring me he was happy that my friend was back. Dear Duncan. When I asked how the book was going, he cheered up at once and told me that Angus was extremely pleased with what he had done so far. They expected to have it ready for next year's fall list.

The party was winding down when Neil and I decided it was time to go. We had said our good-byes to Angus and were standing in the hall when I heard what sounded like someone sobbing. I stepped over to the dark corner under the stairwell and saw a huddled figure in black silk.

"Meredith?"

Her swollen face turned up to me, a trail of mascara on one cheek. "Claire, you won't believe this. He wouldn't speak to me. Just sort of nodded."

She was very drunk, her speech slurred. Iris had told me that Meredith occasionally did this, but I'd never seen it. I said, "Meredith, did you come in your car?"

Her eyes rolled a bit. Then she shook her head. "Taxi."

"Good. Now, give me your hand. We'll take you home."

"I'm fine. I like it here."

I called Neil, and between us we got her out of the house, down the steps, and into my car, still talking.

"He was everything to me, Claire, my whole life, and now he won't speak. Bloody cruel. And who did he leave me for? None other than Iris! Perfect bloody Iris! She didn't know, I never told her who it was. Wasn't her fault really but I hated her anyway. Always had everything, had bloody Iris. Her family paid her school fees. I had to sit exams to get a place. She's a senior lecturer and I work in a bloody bookshop."

Meredith stopped, her head fell against her chest, and I hoped she had passed out, but no luck. The slurred voice began again.

"So I borrowed money from her. First time, a thousand pounds. I was in debt, and I promised to save up and pay it back, but it was bloody impossible. Then I took it out of the bookshop accounts, and I thought I was safe until they said they were sending round the auditor. That time, Iris gave me another thousand and I was clear. But it was so easy to manage the bookshop accounts, I sort of went on taking more than I had before."

"So that was why Iris withdrew the cash amounts from her bank account?"

"Right."

"You told me you didn't know about them, Meredith."

The bleary eyes rolled toward me. "'Course I didn't tell you. But I told Iris. And this time, when I told her I was in trouble, she wouldn't help me again. She said it would never stop if she gave in once more. 'You can borrow from the bank, Meredith,' she says. The bank. What a laugh. They wouldn't give me a fiver. It's always been 'sensible Meredith,' 'down-to-earth Meredith,' be content with your lot, never want what others have.

"I knew she was at your flat that morning, Claire. I begged her. I told her I was desperate, I told her the auditor was coming to the shop again, and I could go to prison. Then, the irony. They put off the audit for another six months."

Now huge sobs shook her body. "I didn't mean to do it, it was an accident. Iris turned away from me, and I was in a fury. I took hold of her throat and told her I wouldn't let go till she promised to help me once again."

Looking at Meredith, I said, "How could you behave so normally since that time? I've seen you often and you gave no sign."

She straightened in the seat beside me, her voice suddenly more controlled. "I've always hidden my thoughts, never let anyone know what I was feeling. Jealous of Iris? No, I loved Iris, was happy for all her achievements. Envy people their wealth? No, I'm content tilling my corner of the field."

Then she gave me a look of indescribable despair. "But I *did* love Iris. I hated her and I loved her."

This time her head fell forward and she slept.

29

NEIL WAS CONCERNED THAT MEREDITH WOULD retract what she had told us in her alcoholic state, but she didn't. On the contrary, she seemed relieved to have it out at last. She assured me she would never have permitted me to go to trial, if it had come to that. I believed her, mainly because she seemed so desperate to confess and get it off her conscience. In the end, she pleaded guilty to manslaughter and was sentenced to a span of years in prison.

Much as I disliked him, I was relieved that Owen Babcock had never been charged with the murder. Even so, he raised all kinds of hell about being questioned. When asked how he knew that the time of Iris's death had been estimated at a quarter past nine that morning, he waffled about but finally admitted that a friend knew someone who knew a police officer at the local station who had given out the information. Neil said the officer in question would be back to walking his beat for a long time to come.

And why did Owen arrive so early at Morgan's office that morning? He'd phoned for a minicab, he explained, and instead of the usual delay, the driver came almost at once. Then they slipped through the traffic with astonishing ease and arrived at their destination at least twenty minutes earlier than he had expected.

A week later, while Neil was in Devon sorting out the rest of his leave time, Sally stopped in London on her way back to the States and we had several glorious days together.

When she heard the story of my being charged and then cleared, she had said, "Honestly, Mums, how do you get yourself into these scrapes?" But I noticed she was particularly affectionate with me during the days of her visit.

When Neil came back to London, we spent hours working out ingenious plans that would give us a satisfactory life together. I agreed to take a leave without pay in the spring, spending the time from January until September with him in Devon. After that, we would play it by ear, confident that somehow things would work out for us.

With tongue in cheek, but with real commitment underneath, Neil was wont to quote from Tennyson's great lyric:

> Ask me no more: thy fate and mine are seal'd;
> I strove against the stream and all in vain;
> Let the great river take me to the main.
> No more, dear love, for at a touch I yield;
> Ask me no more.